BREAKPOINT

ALSO BY RICHARD A. CLARKE

Against All Enemies: Inside America's War on Terror

Defeating the Jihadists: A Blueprint for Action

The Scorpion's Gate

The Forgotten Homeland

G. P. Putnam's Sons

New York

RICHARD A. CLARKE

G. P. PUTNAM'S SONS
Publishers Since 1838
Published by the Penguin Group

Penguin Group (USA) Inc., 375 Hudson Street, New York, New York 10014, USA ·
Penguin Group (Canada), 90 Eglinton Avenue East, Suite 700, Toronto, Ontario M4P 2Y3, Canada
(a division of Pearson Penguin Canada Inc.) · Penguin Books Ltd, 80 Strand,
London WC2R 0RL, England · Penguin Ireland, 25 St Stephen's Green, Dublin 2, Ireland
(a division of Penguin Books Ltd Penguin) · Penguin Group (Australia), 250 Camberwell Road,
Camberwell, Victoria 3124, Australia (a division of Pearson Australia Group Pty Ltd) ·
Penguin Books India Pvt Ltd, 11 Community Centre, Panchsheel Park, New Delhi–
110 017, India · Penguin Group (NZ), Cnr Airborne and Rosedale Roads, Albany,
Auckland 1310, New Zealand (a division of Pearson New Zealand Ltd) · Penguin Books
(South Africa) (Pty) Ltd, 24 Sturdee Avenue, Rosebank, Johannesburg 2196, South Africa

Penguin Books Ltd, Registered Offices: 80 Strand, London WC2R 0RL, England

Library of Congress Cataloging-in-Publication Data

Clarke, Richard A.
Breakpoint / Richard A. Clarke.
p.   cm.
ISBN-13: 978-0-399-15378-5
ISBN-10: 0-399-15378-0
1. Terrorism—Fiction.   2. Terrorism—Prevention—Fiction.   3. Political fiction.
I. Title.
PS3603.L377B74   2007   2006027009
813'.6—dc22

Printed in the United States of America
1   3   5   7   9   10   8   6   4   2

BOOK DESIGN BY NICOLE LAROCHE

To those who seek truth through science,
even when the powerful try to suppress it

ACKNOWLEDGMENTS

Writing a novel is a solitary experience, but publishing a book is a team effort. The team behind *Breakpoint* are all-stars: Neil Nyren at Editor, Len Sherman at Agent Plus, Beverly Roundtree-Jones playing Executive Assistant, and Rob Knake as Sounding Board and Researcher. I am also deeply indebted to Mudge, my friend and guide through cyberspace. Many helped me understand technologies and trends, most notably the brilliant futurist and scientist Ray Kurzweil. Others assisted me in exploring the locations that appear in *Breakpoint,* from Elbow Cay to Hong Kong, from Rappahannock to Russian River. To them all, my sincere and very appreciative thanks.

Many readers of *The Scorpion's Gate* thought they saw real people slightly disguised as fictional characters. Some may think that about the characters in *Breakpoint.* Both books are works of fiction and, therefore, all the characters are fictional.

RAC

1 | *Sunday, March 8*

0730 Eastern Standard Time

Off the New Jersey Coast

The yellow flame leaped into the air where the ocean hit the land. It was followed by a boiling, churning blue-black cloud, climbing up around the now orange-red fireball. The cloud kept growing, forming into a pedestal shape above the water's edge.

"Atlantic City, Atlantic City," the pilot said calmly into his chin microphone, "Coast Guard forty-one ten. We see what looks like a gas pipeline explosion at our ten o'clock position about fifteen miles ahead. Estimate position of flare as Pine Harbor. Over."

From the flight deck of USCG 4110, an old twin-engine Casa 212 maritime patrol aircraft flying over the New Jersey coast, the plume had stood out against the dull-gray Sunday-morning sky. "Roger, forty-one ten. Proceed Pine Harbor for a visual and report," the radio cackled. "We'll check with Ops at headquarters to see if they know what happened."

Lt. Anne Brucelli had been out of the Academy for five years and loved flying, loved being part of the Coast Guard and the Department of Homeland Security.

She was looking forward to her new assignment in the vertical liftoff Osprey aircraft, but for now she was happy just to be in command of an old Casa. It got her up in the air, over the sea, and looking at things from a perspective that most people never had the chance to enjoy. Her copilot today was an Academy classmate, Lt. Chuck Appleton. He flipped down her visor and tapped it for telescopic mode. "Jesus, Anne, there's another flare way out there at our two o'clock," Appleton called. "That's over by Banning Beach." From the low cruising altitude of five thousand feet above the coast, the visual horizon was almost eighty miles. The second flame seemed to be coming from somewhere on western Long Island.

Before they could report the second flare, they heard a crackling and then: "Coast Guard forty-one ten, this is Atlantic City, cancel that. Proceed south instead to Miller's Hook and perform low-level surveillance on white blockhouse at the end of point. Copy that? And, Anne, this one came to us from Department Ops, Homeland Security."

Brucelli pulled the bright red striped aircraft into a tight bank to reverse its direction of motion, reaching the waters off Miller's Hook in four minutes. Appleton looked again through the visor that showed him the image from the aircraft's nose-mounted cameras. He zoomed in on the end of the point of land in front of them. "Got a visual on a small white building, no windows. Got a fence around it. White truck next to it." He moved his head slowly to the right and examined the road on the Hook. "Two bikers driving inland pretty fast; otherwise it's pretty empty out there." The aircraft continued its rapid descent toward the narrow promontory.

The pilot flicked the toggle to report in. "Atlantic City, Coast Guard forty . . . Holy shit! Hang on, Chuck." A yellow-red tongue filled the cockpit windshield with flame, as she pulled the plane into a steep left bank. A klaxon sounded loudly and then a recorded female voice replaced it over the speaker, saying calmly, "Left engine fire. Fire in the left engine requires your attention."

Brucelli hit the big red fire-suppression button above her head and struggled to right the spinning aircraft. As she did so, Lt. Appleton spoke clearly into his chin mike, "Mayday, Mayday. Coast Guard forty-one ten. Going down half mile off Miller's Hook, request SAR support." The problem, he knew, was that the unmanned aerial vehicle that would normally have been on patrol over the Jersey shore was down for maintenance. They were the search-and-rescue patrol that morning and they were going to crash.

0745 EST

Horizon Communications Network Operations Center (NOC)

New Creighton, New Jersey

Less than fifty miles to the northwest, under a rolling hill of manicured grass, Constance Murphy was getting the handover brief from the midnight shift director at the Horizon Communications Network Operations Center. From the command balcony, Constance looked out at a two-story-high map of the United States, criss-crossed in yellow lines, connecting blinking green dots. They called it the Big Board. Below, on the floor of the NOC, the night-shift engineers were handing over their seats to their daytime replacements. The blinking lights represented twenty percent of the world's internet traffic, which was routinely carried on the fiber-optic cables of Horizon Communications. Running in pipes and conduits under wheat fields, along rail beds, over bridges, and up city streets, twenty-three thousand miles of Horizon Communications' specialized glass fiber carried the photons that routers would convert into electrons and then into billions of Internet Protocol packets of ones and zeroes: e-mail and web browsers, buy and sell orders, travel reservations, pornography, and inventory updates.

As she stood sipping her coffee, Murphy scanned the teams on the floor below and half listened to Joshua Schwartz, the midnight watch director, say five or six ways that everything was routine. Then something in her peripheral vision caught her attention and she looked up to see a light just south of New York City switch from green to red. Then another light, east of the city this time, blinked red. She put her hand on Schwartz's arm to stop him from talking and nodded toward the upper right of the Big Board.

"What . . . ?" Schwartz said, furrowing his brow and squinting, "That's all three of our Atlantic cables. Why?" He quickly sat down at his computer console, his fingers flying across the keyboard.

"New Creighton is getting no reading from the Pine Harbor, Pleasant Bay, or Banning Beach routers. Syn-Ack messages are being black holed. Nada. How could all three go down at once? There are two rollover, backup routers at every landing."

Constance Murphy stood over Schwartz and looked at his screen, "That says we got nothing going to or from Europe."

"That's because we don't, Connie. We just had all nine routers at our beachheads simultaneously decide to shit the bed. Horizon Communications is cut off from Europe!" Schwartz shook his head. "We'll have to go hat in hand to Infotel and ETT and ask if we can redirect our load onto their fiber until we figure out what the fuck is going on."

Murphy picked up a green phone on top of which a big light was blinking furiously. "Horizon Communications, Murphy." As she listened to the voice at the other end, she stared at Schwartz and her eyes grew. "Hang on one second," she said into the phone and then leaned forward. She grabbed a long, flexible microphone that was connected to speakers on the floor below. "This is Murphy. Night shift, do not depart. Repeat, do not depart. Day shift, activate the Emergency Engineering Notification Plan." Then she looked back at Schwartz. "I got ETT on the green phone. We ain't switching load to them. All *their* beachhead routers are deader than a doornail, too."

They looked at each other, their expressions changing from dumbfounded to horrified. Finally, Schwartz stood up. "You call a VP. I'll get onto the National Communications System."

0805 EST

Aboard the MV *Atlantic Star,* Two Miles Off Squirrel Island,

Booth Bay Harbor, Maine

"It's too cold to be diving, no?" the captain asked in Russian.

"Not with these," the diver replied, slapping his side. "New suit. Latest technology from Russian Navy labs. Never feel the cold. Besides, I'm just there to guide the drone. It does all the work, hauls the cargo down to the bottom, sends us back the pictures."

The MV *Atlantic Star* was registered in Panama and flying its flag. In smaller letters under the ship's name on the stern, it said "Colón." The captain and crew were Lithuanian, and paid by the company that owned the ship, in Antigua. For this trip, they were also being paid by someone else who had also hired the six Ukrainians who had boarded in Newark. The ship's instructions were to stop in a few places off the coast and let the divers place their experiments on the ocean floor, using the drones that had been in a container on-loaded in Hamburg. For this odd business and for total secrecy about it, each crewman got $50,000 and the captain got a million in cash. So maybe they were really the Russian Navy, the captain thought, as he watched the divers readying themselves. Maybe it was placing listening devices on the ocean floor again to find the American submarines. It was smart to use Ukrainians, in case they were caught. Moscow could deny. Moscow was good at denying.

The diver went over the side. Despite the new Russian gear, he felt the cold right away, piercing to his bones. He tried to think of how heated his body had been two nights ago, with the American hooker. She was not like the women he had hired in Europe. She was athletic, muscular. And yet she had beautiful fruit aromas, one in her hair, one around her full breasts. . . . His daydream was terminated by the voice in his ear. "Do you see the sled, Gregor? Is it stable?" He looked through the new underwater binoculars and saw shades of green and black on the ocean floor beneath him.

"I see it fine. It's sitting right next to the cable. Sitting flat. The big rock next to it will protect it from shifting in deep swells. Nothing fell off the sled on the way down. I can even see the little light blinking."

His whole body involuntarily shivered. Then he heard the voice from the surface again in his ear. "Good. Then come up. We need to deal with the crew."

0945 EST

Homeland Security Department, National Communications System

Arlington, Virginia

Two miles west of the Lincoln Memorial, in one of the many high-rises in the Ballston neighborhood of Arlington, Virginia, a quickly called meeting started in the Board Room of the National Communications System. The NCS had been established after the breakup of Ma Bell in the 1970s. It was a place where all the phone and internet companies could come together, without worrying about illegal-collusion charges, to share information necessary to keep America's communication systems running in support of the Pentagon and, of course, the consumers. It was one of the few places where federal bureaucrats cohabitated with competing vendor companies.

Around the table, both industry and government representatives were comparing notes, balancing coffee mugs, and trying to activate the flat screens that were discreetly placed into the mahogany-and-cherry conference table.

"Okay, okay, let's get going," Fred Calder, the director of NCS, said loudly and seated himself at the head of the high-tech table. Around the table, the talking stopped as people sat down behind signs that read "Defense Department," "Infotel," "FBI," "Pacific-Westel," "Homeland Security," "ETT," and a host of other three-letter agencies and corporations. "Jake Horowitz is the director of infrastructure protection at NCS. Jake, give us what we know."

"Here's what we have so far. Between 0730 and 0745 this morning explosions took place at seven of the ten Atlantic beachheads, the shacks near the beaches where the transoceanic fiber-optic cables come ashore from Europe and go into routers and switches. About the same time, three of the Pacific crossing beachheads in Washington State were hit by explosions and ceased to function." The room grew quieter.

"New Jersey State Police have preliminary reports that suggest at least one explosion was a truck bomb. No one was injured in any of the explosions, because these places are usually not staffed. A Coast Guard plane saw one of the explosions and then went missing.

"Although three of the ten Atlantic beachheads are still functioning, they are the older ones and together carry about ten percent of the load. State Police in Massachusetts and the Mounties in Nova Scotia are setting up defenses at the remaining three beachheads. Teams from Horizon Communications, Infotel, PacificWestel, and others have begun to shift the load to the Pacific fiber, to get to Europe the other way round, but we got serious capacity problems and we are dropping packets all over the place.

"Couple of the older Sytho routers at PacificWestel began flapping under the load, so we are coordinating flow control, but we have no way of knowing what traffic is priority and what is grandma writing to the kids at college. We're still at less than twenty-five percent of normal outbound traffic to European Internet Service Providers, and a lot of that is garbage because of dropped packets. Latest thing we heard is that traffic to the domain name root servers is way off. They act like the four-one-one of the internet, converting www addresses into numbers. Traffic to them is off because most of the world can't get to eight of the ten roots, which are all here in the States. Means a bunch of internet traffic doesn't know how to get where it's supposed to go."

"What about protecting the Pacific beachheads? Isn't it just about seven A.M. there now?" the FBI rep asked.

"That's being done," Fred Calder responded. "We placed calls to the state police in the three West Coast states."

"State is unable to get through to any U.S. Embassy in Europe, Africa, the Mideast, or South Asia, doesn't matter whether its classified or unclassified comms," the Department of State rep declared.

"You still have voice to the embassies, right?" the man from ETT asked.

"We can talk to them, but no data links," the State Department man complained.

John Peters from Treasury punched the button activating his microphone and announced in a high-pitched voice, "The New York, American, and NASDAQ exchanges are all reporting an inability to communicate test messages with London and the other European markets. Will we have this fixed by opening bells tomorrow?"

"No, we won't," Fred Calder said flatly, and turned to the three-star Air Force general sitting behind the Defense Department plaque. "General Richards, I assume the Pentagon still has connectivity abroad?"

The Air Force man frowned at being called on, but he pulled out a set of half-glasses and opened a loose-leaf notebook in front of him. He had been a fighter pilot most of his career, but he was now in charge of Pentagon cyberspace activities. The General read, "PACOM reports some degradation to the classified SIPRNET and unclassified NIPRNET, but high-priority traffic is moving without problem on SIPRNET. EUCOM and CENTCOM report serious outages in connectivity on both classified and unclassified networks. Defense Information Systems Agency has initiated an INFOCON ALPHA condition, switching some SIPRNET traffic to unutilized bandwidth on space-based national assets, but four of the seven war-fighting commands are reporting nonoperational mission-critical functions because of NIPRNET outages and, as Jake there just indicated, we cannot prioritize NIPRNET traffic." With that, the General removed his half-glasses and closed his book.

There was a moment of dead air as some in the room pondered the implications of what the General had just said and others tried to figure out exactly what it *was* that the General had just said.

"I'm sorry, General . . . is it Richardson? I'm not a military man or really very technical at all. I represent the Commerce Department. Could you or somebody explain what you just said in words I might, well, *understand*?" It was Undersecretary of Commerce Clyde Fetherwill, who had played an important role in the President's campaign in Florida.

Gordon Baxter, a seasoned CIA bureaucrat, leaned forward and activated the microphone in front of his seat. "NIPRNET is Defense's unclassified internet system. SIPRNET is their internet for classified information, Secret and higher. What he said was that more than half of our forces overseas could not fully carry out their wartime missions right now because they do not have unclassified internet connectivity to the U.S."

Harvey Tilden from the White House seemed surprised. "Is that right, General? Is that really the meaning of your report?"

"Hell, yes," General Richards replied. "That's exactly what I just finished saying."

Trying to regain control of the meeting, Fred Calder called upon the industry representatives from Sytho and SpruceNetworks to report on how quickly they could get replacement routers to the beachhead locations. The Sytho man grabbed his mike. "Well, of course, we do on-demand assembly and just-in-time delivery. It's not like we have inventory. If we got a valid purchase order now, we could have routers on location by the time the buildings to house them and the electrical and fiber were restored. Or a little while after that, at the latest."

Tilden, the White House man, looked upset. "Mr. Chairman, if I may, it seems to me the real issue is . . . Well, does the FBI have any claims of responsibility . . . I mean, who the hell did this?"

Without speaking, with a wave of his wrist, Fred Calder invited the FBI representative to speak. The man in the double-breasted suit adjusted his tie. "Special Agent Willard Mulvaine, sitting in for Deputy Assistant Director Murrow. We will be reporting through appropriate channels, but I must be frank—it will be on a need-to-know basis only, of course, in order to protect any potential prosecution and to preserve sources and methods. But, since I have the floor, I need to stress again, Mr. Chairman, that all agencies and the private-sector partners here must provide the Bureau with all information they acquire relevant to this criminal investigation and should not share that information with the media or other agencies of government, be that state and local, or federal. We are the lead agency on this, ah, incident. Sharing information with others could constitute obstruction of justice and make individuals involved liable themselves for prosecution under relevant federal statutes."

Fetherwill, from Commerce, leaned over to the CIA man who had been so helpful earlier and whispered, "What the hell did he just say? Is he going to arrest us?"

Gordon Baxter answered in a loud voice. "He said that if you give him the dots, he may connect some of them—but he won't tell anybody if the dots paint a picture. *Probably* because he wouldn't know."

"Mr. Chairman, I object to that lack of interagency comity . . ." the FBI special agent sputtered.

"Some comedy," CIA's Gordon Baxter muttered. "I thought CIA was screwed up. The Bureau is FUBAR." He spoke up louder. "Here's what our analysts conclude with high certainty: This attack was carried out by a nation-state, perhaps subcontracted to a witting or unwitting criminal enterprise. Now all we have to figure out is who."

Through the large plate-glass window in the Board Room wall, Fred Calder looked at the National Communications System's own Big Board, an integrated feed from all of the U.S. internet backbone providers. Washington, Philadelphia, New York, and Boston were now blinking red. And as he watched, thinking of the Wizards tickets he had finally managed to get for that afternoon, and how he would never get to use them, Chicago switched to red and it began blinking, too.

He leaned forward in the chair and let a moment of quiet pass in the room. Then he summarized: "So let me see if I got this right: Some group has crippled the international financial system and degraded our military command control by blowing up obscure, unprotected, little buildings on beaches? We don't really know who did it or why they did it? And it will take us weeks at best to repair the damage? And we don't know if the attacks are over yet? Is that about it?"

There were nods of agreement around the table. Harvey Tilden, the man from the White House, looked pained. "Oh, I can't tell the White House that. They won't like that at all."

1330 EST

Pentagon Officers' Athletic Center (POAC)

Arlington, Virginia

"I'm open!" Jimmy yelled across the court, then leaped to catch the ball thrown to him in response. He spun, dribbled, and went for the three-pointer. The ball rolled around the rim like a train on a rail, then just dropped in and through. As he raised his clenched fists over his head, Jimmy felt the vibration near his waist and pulled the Bluetooth earpiece out of his pocket. Walking to the side of the court, he pointed to the bench, to Darren, the tech-support guy who never got to play. "You're in."

"Yah get one decent basket and yah walk off! What the fuck, Jimmy?" he heard a teammate say.

"Detective Foley," said the voice in his ear, "this is Operations. The Director would like you to meet him at the British Embassy ASAP. Can I tell him your ETA?"

Jimmy Foley looked down at his sweat-drenched T-shirt and calculated how fast he could shower, change, and get on his Harley Fat Boy. "Where's the embassy?"

There was a pause, which at first he assumed was the duty officer on the other end looking up the address. Then, from the officer's tone, he realized it had been stunned silence at Jimmy's ignorance at what apparently everyone in Washington should have known. "On Embassy Row? Mass. Ave?"

"Thirty minutes from now," Jimmy guessed as he moved into the locker room. "Say, two o'clock." Turning the corner on the row of lockers, Jimmy's six-foot-two-inch frame almost collided with the frail, naked body of a man in his seventies or eighties. The skin seemed to hang off the old man's body. The POAC, as Jimmy's military buddies called their gym, always had retired colonels and generals doddering around trying to stay fit, trying to recall their younger, military lives. "Sorry, General," Jimmy mumbled as he deked around the open locker door. He looked at the old man and admired the fact that he was still keeping in some sort of shape. He thought of his father, locked up inside a jumbled mind, staring at a television in an assisted-living home on Long Island. Wouldn't it be great if he could take his dad to a gym and work out with him once in a while?

"That's Admiral, not General, asshole," Jimmy heard behind him as he threw his clothes on the floor and moved off toward the showers.

1335 EST

Northeast Women's Crisis Center

2nd Street NE, Washington, D.C.

"I gots to get out of D.C.," the woman on the other side of the desk said. "My man is gonna find me. Thought I saw his ass down the corner yesterday. Only so many battered shelters in this town. He gonna find me."

Susan Connor looked at the woman. It was possible they were about the same age, but the woman looked older, her eyes sunken, her nose broken. "You're afraid he'll hurt you again if he finds you?" Susan asked.

"He ain't bringin' me fuckin' flowers, sister. Wants his money back, but I done spent all that on the bus tickets, get the kids gone to my momma."

Susan felt unsure of what to do or say, which was unusual for her. This was really not her world. "I'm sure the people here at the center could get you a lawyer, get a judge to issue a restraining order to keep him away from you. . . ."

The woman's mouth dropped open and she stared at Susan, dumbfounded. "You talkin' 'bout me going to court? When I ain't been arrested? And Darnell gonna care what some guy in a robe say?"

"Look, we can help." Susan stopped as she heard the tone in her earpiece. She pressed the receive button. "Connor here." The woman shook her head and wandered off to sit with three others watching a television.

"Ms. Connor, this is Operations. The Director is at the U.K. Embassy and wants you there now."

"On my way," she said, getting up from the old metal desk. "ETA fourteen hundred. Out."

As she moved quickly out of the cafeteria, Susan heard the woman call after her, "No need you comin' back, with that kind of advice, bitch."

Susan sped up Massachusetts Avenue from the Women's Crisis Center on Third Street, through the underpass at Scott Circle, around the rotary at Dupont Circle, darting the new, Chinese Chery K522 through the Sunday-afternoon traffic. In her head she kept hearing lines from a twenty-year-old song by Tracy Chapman: "Last night I heard the screaming, loud voices through the wall." Every other Sunday, Susan tried to help out at the shelter. Was it her way of atoning for her own success, of trying to reach out to others of her own race? Whatever had motivated her to start, she had almost convinced herself that she was doing no real good and should find some other way of giving back.

The Chery, built in Shanghai, was powered entirely by ethanol from switch grass. Its engine kicked in as she accelerated on the open stretch approaching the British compound. She smiled at the statue of Churchill outside the fence line. Winston was one of Rusty MacIntyre's heroes. She wondered why Rusty was at the British Embassy on a Sunday afternoon and, more important, why he wanted her to join him. She had worked with MacIntyre for only two years now, but they had been through a lot together. When he'd become director of the Intelligence Analysis Center last year, one of his first acts had been to put her in charge of the new Special Projects Branch. It was a job that made it exciting to go to work every day. She never knew what off-the-wall tangent Rusty would dream up next, only to have it appear in the headlines a month later.

As she shifted the car into park at the first guard booth, a motorcycle shot past her and skidded to a halt by the gatehouse. Two Royal Marines appeared from behind the gate. Both lowered short, Fabrique National P90 light machine guns. "Ho, I'm a friendly," the biker yelled, peeling off his helmet.

Susan recognized Jimmy Foley, the NYPD detective who had just arrived on loan to the Intelligence Analysis Center. Her boss, Rusty, had assigned him to Susan's team at Special Projects a week ago, "to give you guys some street smarts," he said. Susan was still trying to figure out Foley. He was handsome, easygoing—everybody *else* had instantly taken to him.

"Foley," Susan yelled out of the car window, "don't get shot. It'll look bad on my record." Foley laughed, reluctantly handing over his .357 SIG-Sauer to the embassy security guard.

1350 EST

British Embassy

Washington, D.C.

As Susan and Jimmy walked into the grand foyer of the embassy, they seemed, amid the grandeur, out of place and an unlikely couple. Foley, tall, freckled, and in a polo shirt and jeans. Connor, short and black, was wearing a blouse and chinos. Neither was dressed for the British Embassy. The last of the departing luncheon guests were getting their coats from the staff. The luncheon had been in honor of the visit of Sir Dennis Penning-Smith of the Cabinet Office, where he served the U.K. as the intelligence coordinator. As the British Ambassador said good-byes at the door to the usual suspects he had invited to brunch with him and his honored London guest, Sir Dennis walked into the library with Sol Rubenstein. Sol had recently been promoted to the position of director of national intelligence. Behind the two Intellocrats walked Rusty MacIntyre, the head of the U.S. Intelligence Analysis Center, and Brian Douglas, newly installed as deputy director for Operations of the British MI6, or as it is officially known, the Secret Intelligence Service.

". . . no proof yet," Rubenstein was saying as he lit a cigar. "But it has to be China, of course. Some sort of shot across the bow over

Taiwan. They really wanted to scare the shit out of Taiwan to effect their election. What happens? The voters, in a show of defiance, elect the Independence Party in an upset instead, and we announce our support. Beijing said there would be consequences. Maybe this is the beginning of the consequences. A signal to us to stay away while they get ready to do something to Taiwan—or they will hurt us here in ways we had not even thought about."

"Perhaps. But still no claims of responsibility?" Sir Dennis said, pouring a snifter of Napoleon Cognac.

"Oh, there are plenty of claims of responsibility, Sir Dennis," Rusty injected. "Al Qaeda of North America, which does not exist, the Aryan Separatist Army, which barely exists, and the Merpeople for a Clean Ocean, which might as well not exist." Catching Susan and Jimmy in his peripheral vision, MacIntyre waved them into the library. "Sir Dennis, Brian, these are the SP Branch folks I mentioned." There was a round of handshakes.

"Now, James, as a policeman," Douglas asked Foley, "wouldn't you say that this took real skill? Ten truck bombs over five states and no one caught, no one killed? And the beachhead switches they left untouched—they were so old and decrepit they weren't worth bombing. They obviously knew that."

Catching a perplexed look on Foley's face, MacIntyre responded. "Susan and Jim are not read in yet, Bri. I just called them."

"Well, you have to admit, Rusty, this was a very well planned and sophisticated operation," Brian said, turning away from Foley. "Many players."

"Right. The explosive was a shitload of RDX, hard to get hereabouts and hard to get into America in large amounts without somebody in Customs noticing. And here's the latest I just got from the Watch—Navy now says that in addition to the beachhead attacks, there were undersea explosions. So even if they rebuild the beachheads, it won't be enough. The fiber has been cut underwater, and that's hard to repair."

"That says nation-state to me," Sir Dennis asserted. "I didn't think China was that capable."

"Could be they had help." Rubenstein exhaled a cloud of Cuban tobacco smoke. He plopped down in a large, green leather chair and looked up. "Well, SP Branch, that's your job, and you'd better find out fast. Because whoever's responsible, I can guarantee you this attack today is not the last."

"Us?" Susan asked, looking at Rusty and Jimmy. "But—there's a whole big bureaucracy out there set up to do exactly this."

"You mean the Keystone Kops?" Rubenstein said. "Oh, they'll be out there, don't worry about that. FBI, Homeland Security, the works. But while they're stumbling all over themselves as usual, we'll do our own . . . nonconventional exploration. I need someone smart, agile, quick, and that's you. We must find out who is doing this, because they obviously know how to hurt us, figured out where our weak spots are. And this is unlikely to be a one-off. What's your legendary instinct tell you, Russell?"

Sir Dennis, Brian Douglas, and Rusty shifted, forming a semicircle facing the seated Sol Rubenstein. "With this many people involved in the attack and the preparations—must be at least a hundred—its a nation-state or a large terrorist network, or both," said Rusty. "I agree, it's most likely China, but we can't rule out Iran and Hizbollah, getting back at us for the beating they got two years ago in Islamyah. It would probably take that long to put a strike like this together. Or the Iraqi Revenge Movement."

"Of course, we need to look at all possibilities," Rubenstein said from behind a cloud of smoke.

"Quite right, Solly," agreed Sir Dennis, producing a series of instruments to pack and light his Peterson pipe. "You have your people charge hard, and Brian and his boys will do the same, separately. We'll compare notes in a week or so. But we must be swift. Whoever they are, these people have done enormous damage to the global economic system already. And they seem to know our dirty little secret." He looked at all of them. "The Global Village is held together by a very few, very fragile strands. Cut them and the thin veneer of civilization disappears. Like a puff of Latakia." He exhaled, lifting smoke from the Turkish tobacco in his Petersen. A small gray cloud floated toward the fireplace and was gone.

In the parking lot outside the embassy, Jimmy Foley recovered his Harley Fat Boy and walked it over toward his new bosses. Susan ignored his presence. "Rusty, you don't have to tell me this is a big deal. I get that. What I don't like is that we aren't part of the big, formal investigation. We're outside the tent, picking up the dropped popcorn. That's bullshit."

She turned to acknowledge Foley. "I'm sure Jimmy here is a great detective, but you give me one guy, and the Bureau is putting thousands on this, and you expect me to compete?" Foley flashed an ingratiating smile that made him look like a teenager. And that somehow made Susan more mad.

"Look, both of you, you have an important part of this," Rusty said. "You are not supposed to be competing with the other agencies. You're doing it our way, small and smart, unconventional, iconoclastic and separate." He put one hand down to Susan's shoulder and one up to Jimmy's. "We've seen before what happens when there is groupthink: WMD in Iraq. Look, there's more to this than Sol wanted to say." Rusty scanned the embassy lot to make sure that no one was within earshot. "The President is ripshit that this happened. He doesn't understand how we can spend over eighty billion on intelligence and law enforcement, and then some outfit plans and executes a series of bombings like this, and we didn't catch it. For one thing, he doesn't understand why these internet nodes were unprotected."

"Good question," Susan agreed. "Why do we leave important places unguarded?"

"That's something we need to rethink," said Rusty. "Meanwhile our operating assumption is that this whole thing is China achieving escalation dominance."

"Excuse me, sir, but what's that?" Jimmy asked.

"It means they not only hurt us, they demonstrate that they can hurt us a lot more, they can escalate in ways that we don't expect. That way, we're deterred from doing anything against them," Susan explained.

"Right. In this case, deterred from helping Taiwan, if China's next move is to attack Taiwan and stop them from declaring independence. But this President is not going to *be* deterred." Rusty looked from Susan to Jimmy, making sure they understood his implication. "FBI and Homeland have the lead, they'll crash away investigating. But there are two large tasks that we don't trust them to get right. That's where you in Special Projects come in. There were not a bunch of Chinese agents running around the country preparing these bombings, we'd have known about it. They hired somebody. Your first task is find out who.

"Second, somebody figured out an Achilles' heel in our technology and national infrastructure, one we obviously hadn't recognized ourselves. They will probably do it again. Before they do, you must find out what their next target is likely to be. FBI and Homeland will probably focus on refineries and bridges and things like that. But this was an attack on our technology—that's where we've got to look."

Susan nodded and smiled. She knew he was right; they had to avoid groupthink again. It had been way too costly before. And they had to focus on protecting what mattered now, in an information age, not back in the twentieth century.

"Sounds good to me," Foley said. He turned to Susan. "See you in the office in about an hour, boss." He grinned and moved off with his Harley.

Rusty read Susan's irritation. "Foley is not what he seems, Susan. Forget that surface attitude. The Commissioner told me he's the best detective they've had in years. He only loaned him to me to give Foley some Washington experience. The skills you have will complement each other well." He could see that she wasn't convinced. "Just crack this case for me, Susan. Crack it fast. The Bureau, Homeland, they're looking for the keys where the streetlights shine. You go into the shadows."

2100 EST

Special Projects Office, Intelligence Analysis Center

Navy Hill, Foggy Bottom, Washington, D.C.

They had been reading reports for five hours when Jimmy Foley suggested he make them some snacks. From the little office kitchenette, he called out to Susan, "You know what I still don't get? I thought Taiwan was independent?"

Susan Connor looked up from an ATF report on her flat screen. "Yeah, well, it is, for all practical purposes. Has been for almost seventy years, since the Nationalist Party fled there from the mainland when the Communists took over. But they maintain the fiction that they are still a province of China. And so does China.

Beijing wants them back someday, like Hong Kong. Whenever Taiwan says they're going to formally declare that they are no longer part of China, Beijing goes nuts."

Foley did not reply, but there was a continued clanging of pots and pans from the kitchenette. Susan went back to her report and yelled in the direction of her new staffer, "Man, there is one shit-load of explosives stolen in this country every year. You know that, Jimmy?"

"Uh-huh," Foley responded from the break room. "Most of it gets sold back to construction firms on the black market. Come get your dinner."

"My what?" Susan laughed and got up to see what the NYPD detective had been up to. "Jesus, Jimmy, you trying out for *Iron Chef*?" she gasped as she surveyed the spread on the little table. "Pasta à la pesto. Where's some Mick learn Italiano?"

"You mean some Mick cop, don't you?" Jimmy smiled and pulled back a chair for his new boss. "Five boys in my family. I'm number two, and for some reason Dad tagged me as the cook."

"And Mom?"

"Died when I was ten. Dad worked 'til dinner every night. Lawyer. So I got the dinner ready. After a while, even a bunch a guys get sick of pizza or beans and franks. So . . ."

"Hmmm . . . nice pesto. Lots of garlic." Susan spoke while eating. "I hereby forgive you for not working harder researching the case."

"Who says I haven't been researching the case, boss?" Jimmy

said, putting down his knife and fork. "You want to know what I've found out so far? The Fibbies are all over the trucks, VIN numbers, tracks, witnesses, explosive residue. They have twelve hundred agents on it already in a little over twelve hours. They've given it a major-case name—Cybomb; catchy, right?—and put an assistant director in charge. And so far they got dead ends, bupkis. For their part, NSA is going back over all the calls originating near the beachheads around the time of the explosions. Nada there, too."

Susan was impressed, but assumed that Jimmy had a source in the FBI who had simply read him a summary written for the assistant director. That did not count as research, as far as she was concerned. She had been spending the hours since they'd received the new assignment trying to understand the importance of what had been destroyed. "Okay, good, but we have to get to the why before we can find the who. Why does somebody want to reduce communications to Europe and Asia? The internet is still working here. It's slow from all the messages wandering around cyberspace that can't be delivered, but it's working. So who and why? An attack like this must hurt China, too. We've got to figure out why they'd do it."

Foley shook his head, rejecting the question. "Look, I figured that's what the FBI and NSA were doing, going after China. Like Rusty said, the Chinese army isn't running around Jersey. Maybe they hired someone. Maybe misled them, a false-flag operation. So I'd look for that. Also think about the Unabomber in a way.

Kaczynski was a whacked-out professor who wanted to stop technological advance. So what does he do? He starts sending bombs to other professors at universities around the country . . . professors pushing technological advance." He shrugged. "Something to think about. Also the fact that the Fibbies never caught him until his own brother dropped a dime on him." He went back to his pasta.

"Okay, so . . . little mail bombs fifteen years ago on college campuses and ten really big truck bombs today at internet nodes—one guy then, dozens now." Susan cocked her head and squinted. "And the connection is . . . what?"

"Come on, boss. What's cyberspace? Technology. The Chinese are after our technology. Stealing it first. Now for some reason blowing it up. Here, don't forget your salad. Good balsamic," he said, passing a little bottle across the table. "I did a search on incidents at technology-related facilities over the last twenty-four months. There's been an interesting pattern over the last six months. A cyberspace company or biomed lab has gone up in a fire or explosion of some sort almost every month for the last six. That big fire at the data centers on the Columbia River last month? The Bio Fab in San Diego? A place at MIT just last Friday."

She stared at him, locked eyes. The dumb-cop routine was an act and she had fallen for it like some stereotypical Washington bureaucrat. Foley gave her a cherubic little smile that revealed two dimples. Then he winked. She tried hard not to be charmed like everybody else in the office. She was the supervisor, damn it.

"Okay, Detective. What have we got on those incidents? Has the Bureau opened a major case on them, too?" Susan realized her voice was too flat, too professional. She should be friendlier. Even if he had caught her up with his big-jock act, he had also cooked her a not bad dinner, and using the office kitchen.

"Nope. Six minor cases, and mainly it's the local PDs and fire marshals investigating. The FBI hadn't seen the pattern; still hasn't." He shook Parmesan flakes over the pasta on his plate.

Susan digested the new information, and the pasta. "If those other attacks are related and we can find out who did them . . . we might be able to answer both of Rusty's questions: who the Chinese have doing their dirty work and what kind of things they are likely to attack next."

Jimmy nodded vigorously while he chewed. "Got a statie up in Boston I know who's workin' the MIT explosion, says he'll walk us through it if we come up."

Susan smiled and shook her head admiringly. "So let's go."

"We're on the seven-thirty JetBlue shuttle in the morning, boss."

Although she was beginning to wonder exactly which of them was in charge, all she could say was "How do you happen to know the State Police detective on that case in Massachusetts?"

"Cousin. All us Mick cops are related."

Laughing, Susan almost choked on her last bite. "All right, if I have to be up at five-thirty, I'm going home." She picked up the empty plates and put them in the sink. Then, gathering up her coat and bag, she walked to the door. "See you at the shuttle. Nice work today, and on the food. But unless you want me to call you Jimmy Olsen instead of Jimmy Foley . . . I'm Susan. Don't call me boss."

As the door shut behind her and she walked to the elevator, Susan Connor could swear she heard Foley say, "Right, Chief." Walking to her car, she conceded to herself that it might be valuable to have a cop assisting her, since this project was clearly going to require fieldwork and in the U.S. Even if Foley didn't seem to be appropriately deferential. That was not a new problem. Susan looked so much younger than she was and Rusty had promoted her rapidly despite her lack of experience in government. Of course, she thought as she drove by the security guard house, some of it might be due to her own attitude. She'd always resented men who seemed to make things look easier than they were, who got ahead on a winning smile and a pleasing patter. Maybe she should give Foley a chance. He did cook well.

2245 Mountain Standard Time

22,300 Miles Above the Pacific Ocean

The twelve-thousand-pound New Galaxy satellite sat still relative to the Earth below. Its antennae were simultaneously sending and receiving gigabits of digital packets via radio and laser channels. When reassembled on the planet below, the packets would turn into e-mails, data streams, voice conversations, and television programs. Few of the packets were processed onboard, only those routed to the satellite's housekeeping computer. With that minor exception, the packets merely passed through New Galaxy, quickly, quietly, from Los Angeles to Tokyo, from San Francisco to Sydney. In the frozen near-vacuum of space, as billions of data packets soared through its large antennae, New Galaxy made no sound that could be heard. Even when its ion xeon gas thrusters fired bursts for a microsecond to keep the station in the geostationary orbit, there was only silence.

At 2248 mountain time, the satellite received an update message, a series of packets on the antenna and frequency used only by PacWestel, New Galaxy's owner. From the header information on the packets, they were routed to the satellite's onboard housekeeping computer, decrypted, and reassembled into a message. The message was longer than any of the satellite's normal instructions. It filled the format line in the station-keeping program and then dropped an executable code into the computer. The code was in the same format as the many maintenance messages that adjusted the antennae or ran diagnostics on an onboard system, but it wrote over the existing program, eliminating certain limitations. The code adjusted the ion xeon thrusters to the six o'clock position and performed a xeon gas release. The thrust time in the code was not the usual three seconds. It was 300.00 seconds.

Quietly, New Galaxy moved farther away from Earth, its speed accelerating as it did. Then the last instruction on the update message was executed: New Galaxy went into energy-conservation mode, shutting down all systems for 999 days. When the systems rebooted, New Galaxy's antennae would not be facing toward Earth. The satellite would be well on its way to escaping the solar system.

2310 MST

Space Tracking and Detection Center, U.S. Space Command

Cheyenne Mountain, Colorado Springs

". . . so I had to leave home with the Avalanche down by one," Captain Fred Yang complained to Master Chief Sergeant Brad Anderson.

"That's what TiVo is for, Captain. By the way, you missed the shift-change briefing." Anderson was fifteen years older than the captain, who was technically in charge of the center for the next eight hours.

"I know, I know. I'll read in by running the change software. Nothing ever happens here anyway. I don't know why we have to be inside a mountain. It's so twentieth century, so Cold War . . ." Captain Yang mumbled as he sat down at his console and started keying in. For several minutes, Yang stared quietly at the screen, and then he said, with a note of concern, "Sarge? The change-detection program says we have three fewer birds aloft. And the ones that are missing don't make any sense."

Sergeant Anderson had just picked up the ringing green phone, the drop line to the National Security Agency at Fort Meade,

Maryland. He placed a hand over the mouthpiece before answering it. "Captain, we get debris all the time, old birds flaming out in the upper atmosphere. It's no biggie." He turned to the phone while Yang pounded away on a touch screen. "Yes, sir, this is Spacetrac. No, we haven't seen anything unusual over the Pacific. Why?" Anderson wrote down what they told him. "Okay, we'll keep an eye open. Right." He hung the phone on a hook next to four other color-coded drop lines, then spun his chair toward the young captain.

Yang stood up from his console. "Sarge, New Galaxy 3, Netstar 5, and Pacific Wave 7 are not old birds with decaying orbits."

"No kidding. NG-3 just went up last month, right after Sinosat-12. " The sargeant got up and walked toward Yang's screen. "What are you talking about . . . sir?"

"They're gone. Not deorbited. Goneski." Yang pointed at the screen.

"What the . . . ," Sergeant Anderson said, sitting down at the captain's position.

As Anderson began typing in commands, the white phone rang. Yang answered as the sergeant worked the screen. "Spacetrac . . . yeah. We just noticed that, too. . . . Well, I thought there might be a problem with that bird . . . that one, too. . . . We're checking. Sure. Get right back to you."

Anderson looked up at the captain questioningly. "It was DISA in Virginia," Yang reported. "They said they lost connectivity with some commercial comm sats in the Pacific. I thought the Pentagon had its own satellites."

Anderson reached for a headset. The Defense Information Systems Agency was the phone company for the entire Defense Department, globally. "Yeah, they rent space on private satellites, a lot of it. They can't fight a war without them." As he spoke, he flipped through the Space Command directory, then hit the touch pad to connect. "Maui, this is Spacetrac, Colorado Springs. We need a visual on three geosyncs immediately. . . . We have the Commander's override priority and we need to look at these birds now!"

At the summit of Mount Haleakala, nine thousand feet above the waters of the Pacific, Space Command's Maui Space Surveillance Site turned its optical telescopes and laser-tracking devices to three parking orbits twenty-two thousand miles overhead. Fifteen minutes later, the results of their search were clear. "Spacetrac, Maui here. There are no satellites in those locations, turned on or stealthy. Nothing but cold, black emptiness," the civilian contractor from Raytheon reported back to Cheyenne Mountain. "We can broaden the search, use the Deep Space trackers if you got the juice to pull them off their current missions."

"Thanks. We may have to do that. Get back to you," Sergeant Anderson, said and took off the earpiece. "Captain Yang, I think you'd better do this yourself." Anderson got out of Yang's chair.

"Do what, Sarge?"

"There is a preformatted message in the system you need to send to the Commander and to the Pentagon, Flash precedence. The subject line is 'Major Incident in Space.'"

2 | *Monday, March 9*

0745 EST

Logan International Airport, Boston

"No, don't go that way. It's rush hour. Take the Ted and we'll loop back through the B School," Susan directed as Jimmy Foley drove the rent-a-car out of the Hertz lot.

"Oh, yeah, forgot. You know your way around here. Went to college here. And graduate school, right?"

"You did your homework," Susan replied as the car entered the tunnel. "Yeah, I lived in the freezer that was then Boston for seven icy years after growing up in Atlanta. Summer lasted a week up here. It's better now with global warming kicking in. . . . Now the real test of your knowledge: Ted Williams, the guy this tunnel is named after, holds a record for a season batting average . . ."

"Four-oh-six in 1941," Jimmy snapped back before she could finish the question.

"NYPD—shouldn't you be a Yankee fan?"

"I am. But Ted Williams was a Marine fighter pilot. World War Two and Korea." He held up his hand to show off a ring. "Semper Fi."

Susan silently damned herself for not getting around to reading Foley's personnel file. Rusty had simply assigned him to her, no questions allowed, but still she should have spent some time learning about the newest of her ten-person team. She wondered how much Foley had read about her.

"It's amazing to think what guys like Williams did without steroids," Jimmy added. "Think what they could do now if the league wasn't so backward in their thinking about PEPs."

"PEPs?"

"Performance-enhancing pharmaceuticals. Every other occupation is using drugs to make them better—why not baseball, why not athletes?" Jimmy asked. "Why the big fuss that the Chinese did gene-doping in the Beijing Olympics?"

"It's not natural," Susan replied.

"Tell me you don't use Memzax. All the trivia you have at the tip of your tongue, you must. You don't use Daystend when you have to stay awake for days in a crisis? They're PEPs."

"Of course I do, now that our staff doc prescribes them and the government pays for them. I couldn't afford Memzax on my own, and my health plan sure won't pay thirty dollars for a single pill," Susan admitted, "but in my job I need to have instant retrieval of lots of information. Memzax works, Detective."

"Okay, so in your job you memorize things and drugs are okay,"

Jimmy argued while driving. "An athlete's job is to send a ball sailing out of a park like that one there." They were passing Fenway on the Mass. Pike. "And they can't use drugs to do their job?"

"You sound like Margaret Myers," Susan said, and chuckled.

"Who's that?"

"So, Sherlock, you haven't done all of your homework on me. She was my dissertation advisor at Harvard," she said as they crossed the little bridge into Cambridge.

"Got me there, Bo—I mean, Susan. Damn these fuckin' drivers up here. I just went for L and S to get us out of this jam. Forgot I'm driving a rental."

"In fact, we're seeing her after lunch," Susan announced. "She's an expert on technology policy and the interaction between government and science. I thought she might have some thoughts about your theory on the six incidents. She knows somebody on every major research campus around the world. As Jimmy pulled the car up to a police line, she added "Okay, so I'll bite. L and S?"

"Lights and sirens. It's why we become cops. To get the lights and sirens." And then he smiled, again flashing dimples.

0805 EST

Kendall Square, Cambridge, Massachusetts

The police lines surrounded the charred hulk of what had been a modern, redbrick building. The windows were broken out and the brick singed around them. One section of outer wall had collapsed and bricks were scattered across the side street. The firetrucks were gone by now, but Susan spotted a large van with "State Fire Marshal" on the side. The March wind chilled the few who stood around the fire scene. Ice patches were scattered across the asphalt. Steam rose from a mobile canteen truck dispensing coffee. It was the kind of aggressively gray winter day that Susan associated with Cambridge, with forcing herself down snowy sidewalks to Harvard Square.

"Susan Connor, Intelligence Analysis Center, this is Lieutenant Tommy McDonough, Mass. State Police," Jimmy said, breaking into her flashback. The state cop actually looked a little like Foley, she thought. The two of them could have been investment bankers, in their black overcoats and red ties.

"Pleased ta meet yah. Let's go inside or we'll freeze like them firemen. The New Reactor Diner ovah there is pretty good. Warm anyway," McDonough said, pointing to a classic silver-sided diner on the other side of the traffic circle.

They squeezed into a tight, fake-red-leather booth and were quickly served coffee in chipped mugs. McDonough pulled out one of the newer PDAs and flipped up its screen to review his notes. "Friday night, after eleven. Initial explosion triggered secondary fires. First unit responding called in three alarms. Building fully involved. Everybody got out okay, but . . ." His voice dropped in volume. "Some of the staff that works there days arrived and tried to go back in. Kinda loosely wrapped, these MIT types. Digit heads."

He looked around the diner at the patrons, most of whom were hunched over laptops. "Fire marshal got an operating theory, and that's all it is at this point, that there was an undetected gas leak that really built up a big cloud before static or some other spark set it off. That blast knocked an exterior wall out and severed the water line for the sprinklers. They had sophisticated halon gas suppression in some of the labs, but most of the place went up quick, like a three decka, you know what I mean? Question is how come there was a big, undetected gas leak. Shouldn'ta just happened all on its own."

Foley, who had been taking notes into his own PDA, looked up. "That's good, Tommy, thanks. What'd the building do, what's its purpose?"

"CAIN. Center for Advanced Informatics and Networking. They were the U.S. end of an international project with Japan, France, and Russia involving gridded supercomputers. CAIN was also big in a project involved in reverse engineering the human brain. They're mainly famous now as the ones there that created the Living Software," McDonough said matter-of-factly. Susan was learning not to underestimate this clan of Irish cops.

"And all of that's gone?" Susan asked.

"Shit no," the lieutenant shot back. "Pardon my French. No, the Living Software thing wasn't just here. Others have it, too. The supercomputers here, well . . . the professors are trying to figure out how to get them outta the building and see if they can clean 'em up. Good fuckin' luck with that, huh, Jimmy?"

"No leads? Forensics on the gas pipes? Anything on the video-tapes? Pissed-off staff been fired or screwed over? Nut-job protest groups got a reason to hate the center?" Jimmy asked.

" 'Course we're runnin' all that kinda stuff down, Jimmy, but it ain't lookin' good, I'll tell yah. The pipes and all that at the blast scene are atomized. Cambridge cops had video, course, but nuttin' on it. No one went postal. Apparently, everybody loved to work there. Changin' the world, they said." McDonough scanned the diner again, then whispered, "Nut-job groups? Cambridge is nothin' but nut jobs, you ask me. People's Republic of Cambridge. But none that had it out for the center, not that we found."

"Could we put on hard hats and walk through some of it?" Susan asked.

"Sure, but listen, Jimmy, after that, my mother made me prom-ise to take you ovah her place for lunch. Wants ta hear about your dad. And see you, of course," McDonough said, putting away the PDA.

Foley looked questioningly at his boss. "You should do that, Jimmy," Susan said firmly. "Besides, I have to meet up with Professor Myers, and that's likely to go on and on. I'll hop on the Red Line two stops and we can meet up later at the Charles." She turned to McDonough. "This has been very helpful, Lieutenant, but there is one thing I do have to ask." She paused. "Why is it called the New Reactor Diner? Spicy hot food?"

"Hell, no, the food sucks here," McDonough bellowed, laughing loudly. "The diner's name's cuz these MIT nut jobs have a fuckin' nuclear reactor other side a the alley." In the nearby booths, a dozen heads briefly popped up from laptops and looked around as if sniffing the air for something. And then they went back down, down into cyberspace.

Susan thought about what could happen if another white van filled with RDX went down the alley. As they walked into the ruin of the building in yellow hard hats, a video-surveillance camera across the street zoomed in on their faces.

1055 EST

Summers Hall, Allston Campus

Harvard University, Boston

"So it's all very well to say that big government is bad and that big government backing big science projects is worse," said the woman behind the podium. "I know some of you think the American corporation is the highest achievement of efficiency that humanity has ever produced . . . but when you say all of that, my dears, remember not only that big bad old government created the internet but that the private sector would never, repeat never, have done so. There was no single company, no group of companies that either would have or could have accomplished it, including the single very large phone company we once had in this country."

Margaret Myers stepped out, taking the microphone with her, as she spotted Susan in the back row of the amphitheater-style class room. "The private sector found all sorts of things to do with the internet, and that has changed the way we live, but they would never have built it." Thinking of Susan's role in the Islamyah crisis, she continued, "The private sector would also have continued producing gas-guzzling cars, paying for overseas oil to make into gasoline, until the last drop of oil was pumped and the last dollar was spent on it. Only because of the government of Islamyah and its research and its investments in companies in the U.S., can we say that half the cars in this country are now powered by either hybrid engines or by ethanol from corn, sugarcane, and switch grasses.

"So your assignment for next week is a short essay, no more than two thousand words, on some technology problem of your choice that only a government can solve in the first instance, thereby creating opportunities for the private sector to build on. See you next week." Students immediately flocked around the short professor, asking questions, introducing friends, offering things for her to read. Susan thought her friend and one-time advisor looked older, more gray in her curls, her broad shoulders beginning to slouch. Still, she radiated a physical and intellectual strength and presence that lit up the room. Susan knew that some students would hang on, following Myers back to her office, so Susan signaled that she would meet her there.

The lecture hall and the professor's office were across the river on the Boston side, in Summers Hall, part of Harvard's new Allston Campus. The picture window in the office offered a stunning view of the old Cambridge campus, causing Susan to be lost in thought until Myers shut the office door behind her. The two embraced. "I hoped you would get a chance to work on the internet bombings when I heard about them," Myers began. "I can't help but think that there is something bigger about to happen."

"Bigger than severing the cyber connection between the Americas and the rest of the world? Bigger than causing communication satellites to disappear? That's already a big deal to some of us, Margaret," Susan replied. "We have a theory that China is involved. And now we think that other fires and explosions at scientific institutions over the last few months may be connected."

"Yes, of course, dear. And I know you know that the internet wasn't fully severed, just drastically reduced. I'm sure our Pentagon friends are busy even now trying to shift more of the load to their own military satellites." Myers dropped her lecture notes and papers on a coffee table already covered with other stacks of paper. "I know the theory that they are trying to distract us while they do something else, Taiwan maybe. But I can't help but wonder if we're looking at it wrong, if China might be doing it because they know more than we do about our technology, that we are about to leap ahead and leave them in the dust." Myers swept her arm across her desk, toppling a mound of books and journals, "Oh, no. That was my next book, sitting here in pieces. I'll pick it up tomorrow." She plunked down in a large wooden chair. "Susan, I'm afraid of those who want to whip up a war with China. We should share our technology with them, with everyone. That is the nature of scientific inquiry."

"Depends on the technology." Susan smiled and bent down to pick the books and paper off the floor. "What's this next book on?"

"Transhumanism," Myers said, rescuing a loose-leaf binder from the floor.

"What?" Susan felt a pang of disappointment. She had sought out Professor Myers for her understanding on the attacks, but she'd just been reminded that Margaret was often into some academic theory not necessarily related to the real world.

"I'm sorry, Susan. I know you spend all your time now running around the Middle East and saving us from bad guys. No time to keep up with things here." Myers dug out a journal and handed it across the desk. "I did a piece for *Sociology and Science* last fall. Transhumanism is the philosophy that espouses using genomics, robotics, informatics, nanotech, new pharma . . . to change humanity into a new species."

"New species? Or just one with the mistakes corrected?" Susan asked, flipping through the journal to be polite. "What's the concept?"

Myers sketched a graph on her whiteboard. Across the middle of the chart she drew a line. Below the line she wrote "Corrections," and above it she wrote "Enhancements." The arc on the graph passed through the line at a point indicating 2008, four years before.

"Something very big happened around 2008. We crossed over from just doing genetic corrections to creating genetic enhancements. That's where we are going now, to a human so enhanced, so improved, that some would say it is no longer human. Part carbon-based life-form, as you and I are, and part silicon-based, as this thing is." Myers whacked the computer console by her desk. "And the poor old carbon part will have been so transformed that it will be as far superior to us as we are to Neanderthals. You should catch up on the technological changes."

Susan unfolded a chart from the journal, showing the advances in several sciences and their convergence into a Transhuman over the next two decades. "Margaret, I have China blowing things up in the U.S. I don't have time anymore to keep up on all this crazy stuff, with what the Transwhatevers fear might happen someday."

Myers smiled her motherly look, then spoke softly and slowly, as if explaining about boys to an innocent young daughter. "Susan, this 'crazy stuff,' as you call it, *is* happening. Of course, the fundamentalists, Christian and Muslim, really hate it."

"That's not the only thing they have in common," Susan said, and laughed.

"True, but because of the political power of the fundamentalists in this country, stem-cell research was delayed and all sorts of rules imposed on federally funded research that prohibited work in genetics to enhance humans." Myers lifted a big publication from the National Institutes of Health. "Nonetheless, it is happening quietly in labs all across the country and overseas. Private research money, people skating around federal rules. A lot of it is now done in secret, or offshore."

Susan Connor was intently studying the large foldout chart, the arrows showing milestones of progress in genetics, nanocomputing, robotics, pharmaceuticals, information science, brain studies.

"That chart you have there is already out of date. Many of the key breakthroughs have taken place experimentally. Now it's a matter of scaling and integration. It's just that most people don't know how far the technologies have come, or don't see their implications." Professor Myers seemed almost weary. "Most people are focusing on the latest Hollywood murder scandal or on what's going on in Iran. Most Americans may know only about one or two scientific fields and don't see the combined effects of the several sciences that are now racing through advances."

"Racing?" Susan asked skeptically.

Myers seemed to get renewed strength when challenged. She rose quickly and went to the whiteboard and began sketching lines that were at first parallel, then intertwining, then spinning out in all directions. "This is what you have to internalize. Knowledge builds on itself, always has. Now armed with cheap, highly capable computers, the rate of progress in all of these fields is accelerating, building on itself, speeding ahead. And these fields are merging, reinforcing, enabling each other. The rate of acceleration today is five times what it was forty years ago when the internet was creeping out of the BBN labs up the street. In three years, 2015, scientific engineering will be blindingly fast, and in eight years, humans may not be able to keep up with it."

Susan's head was spinning; there were details, concepts that

Myers was assuming she knew. "Okay, okay . . . there's a lot of catching up I have to do. But let me bring you back to the internet bombings. Any thoughts on them? Who actually did them? What will they go after next?"

Myers sat back down. "The attacks will slow things down enormously. China may be able to catch up. We have been moving out faster than China in the last few years. They can't invent well, it seems. They can copy and understand theory, but that's not enough anymore. Labs in other countries around the world are collaborating, sending huge chunks of data back and forth, petabytes, on fiber-optic cables under the sea. Just look at the Globegrid Project. How, Susan, can you merge the three biggest civilian supercomputer farms in the U.S., with ones in France, Russia, and Japan to create into one virtual machine, as was planned, if there is now no big pipe to connect them? Note, please, that we left China out of the project because of U.S. paranoia."

"Wait, Globegrid. Was the U.S. end of that network going to be in CAIN, the building over at MIT that burned down Friday night?" Susan asked, looking at the soot on her shoes.

"The penny drops? Globegrid was to go online this month. Think what could have been done with all of those huge parallel processors working as one. Then Friday night, CAIN catches fire, and Sunday morning truck bombs take out the fiber-optic beachheads. Had you all really not put that together yet?" Myers asked incredulously. "The other two U.S. computers are at Stanford and UC San Diego."

Folding her hands together under her nose, Susan framed her question carefully. "What was Globegrid really going to do?"

Again, Myers pushed herself up out of the chair and began sketching on the whiteboard behind her. "Once the supercomputers were linked, a special version of the new Living Software would be added to them as the control program. It would be given the task of making the three supercomputers into one virtual machine. Living Software would then be proliferated throughout cyberspace to prevent another cyber crash like the one in 2009. A grid with that power could also solve the remaining problems in genomics and brain science. And that's what they intended to use it for. Their first task was to test the results of the consortium's work on reverse-engineering the human brain." Myers looked at her former student, who sat in front of her silently, glumly, with a facial expression that cried out, "I still don't get it!"

"Susan, Susan, Susan . . . don't worry. I didn't understand much of this either until the last year or so. You have to master so many disciplines simultaneously to get it, and even then you can't know everything that is going on in the labs now. Much of it has gone underground."

Susan stacked the last of the fallen books back on Myers's desk. "Underground? What about your principles of open scientific inquiry, about sharing information?"

"Some of the work on genomics and the human-machine interface activity have raised so much of a political stink that its gone quiet. We really should not have laws telling scientists what they can and cannot do." Myers moved the mouse to access a database on her screen. "There are two people here in Cambridge whom you need to see in order to understand the computer science part of this. Let's start there, while I put together a reading package for you on the other technologies, genomics, pharma. First, go see the boys up the river at Kamaiki Technologies, while I set you up on a date with a young man named Soxster, the best hacker in town."

"A date? Oh, no, no! Socks who?" Susan tried to stop Myers from calling the hacker. "Really, my social life is great. There's this doctor in Baltimore, a brain surgeon. I don't need any dates, expecially with geeks . . ."

Myers let her glasses slip down her nose so that she could look over them at Susan. "Do you really know who blew up the internet nodes for the Chinese? No. Do you have any real leads? I doubt it. Do you think they are going to stop there? I know you don't. Have you figured out where they will attack next? No because you don't understand the technology, either open or hidden. So you will go to Kamaiki and then you will have a beer with Soxster and be nice to him. Then, maybe, just maybe, he will tell you what you need to know."

1400 EST

Kamaiki Technologies, Technology Square

Cambridge, Massachusetts

"So . . . what you see below us is a live reflection of cyberspace, a multidimensional model of it. We're currently showing it geospatially, so you can see physical nodes in the same relationship to each other that they would be on the Earth's surface or on a map. You're standing over Virginia, Mr. Foley."

Susan Connor and Jimmy Foley were on a catwalk almost twenty feet above a surface in a cavernous, windowless room at Kamaiki headquarters in Cambridge. Below them, green and yellow lights shot horizontally to nodes, then shot up vertically, some almost reaching the catwalk. Thick, glowing green lights converged on northern Virginia, New York, and Boston. Tom Sanders, the chief technology officer at Kamaiki, hit a touch screen on the guardrail and said, "So. Now let's zoom back so we see most of North America." The surface below seemed to drop off quickly. "Sorry about that. Hope I didn't do that too quickly—some people get vertigo."

"If I understand you and all these lights, the internet seems to be really busy despite the bombings yesterday?" Jimmy asked.

"Yes. Much more so than during the '09 Cyber Crash. So that day, when we had Zero Day hacker attacks on Sytho Routers and SofTrust servers, almost nothing moved. The monoculture of their software being used by almost everyone cost the economy hundreds of billions. That's why the Living Software project got started, to generate error-free code. It's almost ready to deploy in the wild.

"Today, traffic within the Americas is normal, except for traffic trying to get to Europe and Asia, which just keeps trying and failing, for the most part. The packets that can't get through send messages back saying they're lost. That adds to the traffic load. But on a normal day there would be much more traffic. A lot of traffic from one point in Eurasia to another point in Eurasia normally goes through the U.S. Not now. So you know the old joke about the guy in Maine that says, 'You can't get there from here'? Well, we're trying to map where those places are that now can't get through and where it is they can't get through to." Sanders hit the touch pad and red dots starting blinking at locations on the surface below. "The trouble is that our sensors, Kamaiki's own servers on networks around the globe, are cut off. We have twelve thousand servers in Eurasia that we can't get to."

Susan stared down into the pulsing, blinking representation of cyberspace. "Kamaiki has sensors?"

"Well, you could call them that," Sanders replied. "So. We monitor the traffic loadings on the various internet companies' fiber lines from city to city, so we can help route our customers' traffic most rapidly and cheaply. Then we cache or store our customers' data on our servers around the world so that when somebody wants it, they just go to the nearest Kamaiki server to get it, instead of sending a packet all the way from, say, Yahoo in California to a user in Germany."

"I'm not sure I followed all of that, "Susan admitted, "but would you monitor traffic for MIT—are they a customer?"

"So, we're all from MIT originally. We give them a price break. I still teach there, in Course Six. Why?" Sanders asked.

"Well, I see one of the red lights is labeled CAIN. I guess that's because they're offline now, huh?" Susan said pointing below.

"Terrible tragedy. Sent Globegrid back years."

"Would you have been watching the traffic load going into CAIN just before it caught fire?" Susan asked.

"That's what they paid us to do for them, sure. So, we made sure that people trying to reach CAIN from anywhere in the world found the fastest, most reliable path through cyberspace," Sanders boasted.

Susan was understanding the importance of Kamaiki. Getting excited, she asked, "Can you run this thing backwards? Could we look at what was happening with CAIN just before it blew?" Susan asked.

"Well, sure, but I don't think . . ." Sanders started typing into the console. "So, about sixty-five hours ago, zoom in on Boston, zoom in on MIT . . ." The world below them seemed to spin. Streets and buildings appeared, with the internet coursing through and below them. "Other side of Kendall Square . . . here's CAIN . . ."

Susan, dizzy with vertigo, grabbed on to the catwalk's guardrail. "Can you tell us anything about the traffic going into CAIN?"

"So . . . country of origin. Red is Russia, old habit. Blue is France. Green is Japan," Sanders said as a hologram appeared hovering over the surface, with long lists of numbers spiraling down. "Those colors were from the other points in the Globegrid. They were doing test runs. The orange traffic is from within the U.S., other universities mainly. Some administrative, not sent to the Grid part of CAIN. Payroll, SCADA, and other things."

"SCADA?" Jimmy asked.

"Supervisory Control and Data Acquisition. It's the software program that runs digital controls for things like lights, heat, elevators. The devices communicate back to their SCADA system software manufacturer to tell it how they are," Sanders explained. "Here, I'll pull it out. So here are all the messages from MIT's central SCADA system in orange, turning the exterior lighting on, dropping the heat after hours, monitoring the video-surveillance cameras."

"What was that purple traffic a second ago?" Susan asked. "There's another one now."

"Well, it's hard to say without knowing the codes they were using and what system in the building that was going to, but it was going to an Internet Protocol, or IP, address. MIT is unique for a school. It has its own class A range. So 18, that's MIT, 280, that's CAIN, 090, that's probably the SCADA system's subnet, and then 113. Maybe the elevator or something," Sanders offered.

"The internet address of an elevator is 18.280.090.113?" Jimmy asked.

"Could be, or an air conditioner. Everything that is remotely monitored or serviced or controlled has an IP address. So the manufacturer can see how it's doing, diagnostics, fix it, whatever. This one is something that was probably made in China," Sanders said, hitting away at the console.

"Why do you say that?" Susan asked.

"Purple. On this program, traffic originating in China is shown

in purple. And let's see here, I will switch into MIT's network . . .
I can do that because I am faculty . . . so 090 was in fact the SCADA
system and 113 was . . . a Siemens pump and a Westinghouse valve
connected to the Boston Gas line . . . Oh, my God!" Sanders cried.

"Can you run a trace route, Dr. Sanders?" Susan asked.

"Ah yes. I can reverse the path that one of the packets took last
Friday, check the Border Gateway Protocal updates . . ."

The world below them pulled back from the close-up on CAIN,
showing what had happened five days earlier. The purple line ran
from the MIT router to the Horizon Communications router in
downtown Boston, across the United States paralleling Interstate
90, jumping through repeaters, to the Horizon Communications
router in Seattle. Susan grabbed on to the railing, her head swim-
ming at the speed of the changing landscapes below her. From
Horizon Seattle, the packets ran across town to the PacWest Sytho
router in a windowless telecoms hotel, out to the PacWest fiber
beachhead repeater on the Washington coast that would later blow
up, then under the Pacific, up onto a beach in Japan, through an internet peering point building in downtown Tokyo, through a
Sprucenet router to a Chinatel owned router, back out underwater
to China, up again to a beachhead, then through a Sytho router to
Dilan city, to an internet peering point building, and on to the
Dilan University system, and finally to an address on the university campus.

"We're gonna need to take that information with us, Dr.

Sanders," Jimmy said as he pulled out his PDA. "It's evidence, and I'll need to establish chain of custody."

1600 EST

Twin Oaks Estate, Woodley Park

Washington, D.C.

"Ambassador Rubenstein, it is an honor to welcome you to the Residence," Lee Wang enthused. "I don't believe you have been to this historic house before."

"Thank you, Ambassador Wang for receiving me in your home on such short notice." Sol Rubenstein gave his overcoat to the waiting butler. "And you're right, I haven't been here before. I had no idea there was a property with this much land in Woodley Park."

"Over seventeen acres, originally owned by a general in your revolutionary war, General Uriah Forrest. My children have a lot of fun with that name. They say, 'No, you are a forest.'" Wang led his guest out of the foyer. "The Republic of China's ambassador has lived here since 1937. Please come into the drawing room."

Seated in the large and bright yellow-walled room, Sol Rubenstein began somewhat sheepishly: "Mr. Ambassador, as you know, under the terms of the Taiwan Relations Act, we recognize you as the head of the Taipei Economic and Cultural Representative Office in the United States and not as ambassador of Taiwan. I am compelled to say this so that my friends at the State Department will not get mad at me."

"I understand. And yet you address me as Ambassador Wang?"

"I believe you were ambassador to Costa Rica, which recognized the Republic of China at the time. So I believe, sir, you are due that title on a personal basis," Sol suggested.

"Very good. And you were formerly ambassador to Turkey and Thailand, so that is why I call you Ambassador Rubenstein. Once one, always one." The butler reappeared with a tea service. "Please, would you like green tea or black?"

"Black. If I may, sir, dispense with the formalities, since I have never been very diplomatic. Most Americans aren't, as I'm sure you've noticed. We are, as you will have noticed in the media, in a tender period with Beijing and we cannot afford any mistakes right now." Rubenstein raised the fine china tea cup.

"I understand. We do not want to be a problem," Wang said emphatically.

"And we appreciate that very much," Rubenstein said, sitting back in the chair. "Now, what I really came here for: I know your government has very good sources in Beijing and in the PLA. I don't. And right now my President needs to know what is going on in their heads, without any spin. I would hope we could count on you for that."

Ambassador Wang seemed genuinely pleased. "Of course, Sol, of course. I will see what we can do. And you have my word it will be without spin, as you call it. 'No political influence in intelligence reporting.' Isn't that what you promised the Senate in your confirmation hearings?"

"You are a careful follower of what's going on in Washington, Lee." Rubenstein snickered.

"Before you go, I, too, have to say some formulaic diplomatic niceties. Please forgive me." Ambassador Wang picked up a piece of paper to read from it. " 'It is the policy of the United States to make clear that the United States' decision to establish diplomatic relations with the People's Republic of China rests upon the expectation that the future of Taiwan will be determined by peaceful means; to consider any effort to determine the future of Taiwan by other than peaceful means, including by boycotts or embargoes, is a threat to the peace and security of the Western Pacific area and of grave concern to the United States; to provide Taiwan with arms of a defensive character; and . . .' "

Sol Rubenstein leaned forward and waved his hand toward his host. "May I? 'And to maintain the capacity of the United States to resist any resort to force . . . that would jeopardize the security . . . of the people on Taiwan.' I am familiar with the Taiwan Relations Act. As a very young foreign service officer, I worked on the drafting group that agreed on the wording of our law."

"I know, but I am required to remind our guests here at Twin Oaks," Wang said, folding the paper and putting it in his pocket. "May I see you to your car, Sol?"

Back in the foyer, Wang opened a large, red-leather-covered volume on a side stand. "Will you be so kind as to sign our guest book?"

Rubenstein shot forth his hand to shake good-bye. "I'm afraid I can't, Mr. Ambassador. Since we do not formally recognize the Republic of China or your embassy, I was never here."

2250 EST

Off Brattle Square, Cambridge, Massachusetts

"Can I get you another?" the bartender at Red House asked.

"Not yet," Susan answered, and looked at her watch. Almost eleven. It had been a long day and she wanted nothing more than to walk down the alley and across the Square to her hotel room in the Charles. Rusty had been ecstatic with the results of their investigation so far. The indication that somebody in China had caused the gas leak in Cambridge had startled her, but Rusty seemed to accept right away that such an attack could occur.

Rusty had presented Jimmy's theory about the six earlier events at other research labs at the interagency wrap-up meeting that day. FBI and NSA were tasked to investigate whether there had been an unnoticed sabotage campaign by China against American high-tech facilities. We don't even get to follow up our own leads, Susan thought, sipping the chardonnay and staring across the room into the roaring fire. By the end of the week, the FBI would prove that

China was behind the attacks that the FBI had not even noticed, and the President would have to act. Lovely.

"Did they tell you the foundation of this house dates back to the 1630s?"

Susan frowned at the barkeep.

He tried again. "You know that Dutton vineyard you have there is the best of Dumol's chardonnay, at least for me," the bartender offered. "But then, I like my chardonnays a little malolactic."

"What's that mean?" Susan asked.

"Buttery tasting. You ask me, Dumol is as good as Kistler, but about half the price."

"Dumol and Kistler, are they from France?" Susan asked, really noticing the young bartender for the first time. He was thin, long haired, with thick glasses. Susan guessed he was a graduate student in literature or art.

"The part of France west of Napa. They're Californian. Sonoma Coast, Russian River." He laughed. "Not big into wines, I see."

"No. When I was a student here, I drank beer—Sam Adams mainly. Now that I've been working the last few years, I don't drink much anymore." Susan smiled at the bartender and thought of one other alcoholic drink she had started drinking, "Except I was forced to acquire a taste for single-malt Scotch, the Balvenie," Susan admitted.

"Forced? Pushy boyfriend?" the bartender suggested.

"No." Susan laughed. "My boss. It's kind of a rite of passage with him."

"Hope you don't mind me talkin'," he said. "Looks like you're getting stood up or something, although why anyone want to stand up such a—"

"Thanks." She cut him off. "Yes, looks like I'm stood up. The guy was supposed to be here at ten and it's past ten thirty. So maybe I will take just a little taste of the Balvenie and go. By the way, my name is Susan," she said extending her hand across the bar, "and I don't mind you talking at all. And I learned about a decent chardonnay."

"Kistler is the best," the bartender said, shaking her hand. "And they call me Soxster."

"You son of a bitch!" Susan shot back. "What were you doing, checking me out before you'd introduce yourself? You bastard!" She quickly gathered up her coat and bag to leave.

"Hang on, please don't go," Soxster said, backing away. "You're like a cop or something. 'Course I wanted to check out what was goin' on first."

"I'm wasting my time. Maybe Margaret was wrong about you," Susan said, moving toward the door.

"No, really. I'm sorry. Listen, let's just go up to one of the dining rooms upstairs. Here, we can bring the Balvenie," he said, grabbing a bottle off the rack. "I'll tell you what Margaret wants me to explain." He headed up to the second floor. Susan thought following this weird guy upstairs was not something she should do, but Red House was still filled with late diners and Megs was usually right about people. Besides, she thought, I did take all of that self-protection training; I could probably throw this guy right out a window if I had to.

They climbed up the rickety, narrow stair to the second floor. In one of the three small dining rooms graduate students were still drinking their professor's wine and arguing with him about Kant. The fireplace still burned in the next dining room, although all that was left of the dinners was their debris. Soxster pulled two chairs up near the fire.

"I just have to be careful, you know. There are all sorts of weirdos and spies and shit. Not that I don't trust Megs, and she did say I could trust you and all, but gotta be careful. She said you were with a government research thing. Sounded spooky."

Susan calmed down and had to laugh at Soxster's attempt at security. "Fine, whatever. I work at the Analysis Center in Washington. We do research into things that the government needs to know about, threats mainly. I wanted some help. We're working on the internet attacks and wondering about the CAIN explosion, too. Margaret somehow thought that you would know something that—"

"Yeah, man, the internet attacks. Surprised me, too. Kinetic kills. I thought it was going to be cyber," Soxster said nervously as he poured two shots of the Scotch.

"So you expected attacks on the beachhead routers and switches?" Susan asked, taking the glass.

"Expected something. Not that. The way they've been hiring black hats and gray hats the last year or so, something was up." He sipped the whiskey and rasped, "Coulda made me some real money, but I don't break the law and I like to know who I'm working for, you know?"

"Somebody's been hiring hackers?"

"Yeah. Half a million bucks a year and more, plus five-star room and board somewheres nice. Problem is you don't know where," Soxster said, parting the curtain and looking out on the cold night.

"How did you hear about this?" Susan pressed.

"IRC, hacker chat rooms, e-mails. At first just rumors from some of my more interesting contacts and friends. Then some other folks and I started to be approached over SILC, IRC, some closely guarded private mailing lists. You know, encrypted e-mails through anonymous relays. They seemed to know all the usual suspects, everybody that can get in places, slice and dice code."

"You know anyone who joined up?" Susan asked.

"Hell yeah, one guy used to hang with us, but we didn't trust him. He was breaking the law. Haven't heard from him or seen any of those guys on the Net for months. It's getting a little lonely out there," Soxster said, and laughed.

"Think you could help us find some of the hackers who've been hired?" Susan asked.

"Yeah. We could try, but what was it you said a little while ago about CAIN? Megs just mentioned you were working on the truck bombs, the beachheads. Sign me up if I can help you on CAIN— that was such a disaster. I'd love to get the guys did that."

"Why? Was CAIN so much more of a loss than the beachheads?"

"CAIN made the Living Software. It can fix everything. Look, since the internet began, earlier even, man has been writing code. And a few chicks, okay. But humans suck at coding after a million lines or so. Errors, sloppy drafting, stupidity. You get up to fifty million lines like in the Sytho routers and SofTrust operating system, they're like Swiss cheese or a colander. The code hangs up, breaks down, anybody can hack it, nothing can work seamlessly with it. Problem was almost all the PCs were running SofTrust and almost all the routers were Sytho. There was a monoculture. So somebody figured out two Zero Day worms, surprise attack hacks, and we got the Cyber Crash of 2009."

"And why isn't Living Software going to be just like that? Won't everybody use that and make it a monoculture? I don't know much about it," Susan was chagrined to confess.

"Shit, no. The Living Software kernel generates flawless code to do whatever it is you ask it to do. It's software that writes software, flawlessly. None of the millions of mistakes like in SofTrust. And the kernel clones itself. So all the kernels talk to one another on the Net, so that they learn what has already been done. They learn, like in Open Software, and fix past mistakes. They know how to plug and play with each other's work like its like one big organic code." Soxster was definitely excited. He took another gulp of the Balvenie.

"So when Globegrid was connected, it would have been the

smartest thing that ever existed. All that incredible processing power, working in parallel, with Living Software writing new code, monitoring what it wrote. Even if ninety percent of the Globegrid was working on studying reverse-engineering the human brain and the genome, with just ten percent running on the world's software problems, they'd all have been fixed. All anyone has to do to be part of it is just buy a Living Software kernel. So we'll still get there. Just take longer without Globegrid."

Susan rose and stepped closer to the fire, feeling its heat on her back. "Living Software, when paired with the Globegrid, would have put hackers out of business. You're a hacker."

"Yeah, it's my hobby. Hacking means slicing and dicing computer code, not doing things that are illegal. The media uses *hacker* to mean cybercriminal, but few of us are. With flawless software available, I wouldn't have to go 'round finding stupid mistakes in programs. I could ask the Living Software for new software to do all sorts of shit. Make the world a lot better place." He looked out the window again. "Not only put hackers out of work. Woulda put a lot of government types out of work, too. How do you think all the electronic spy agencies around the world get in to systems? Through glitches in the software, mistaken or intentional. The same way I . . ." Soxster turned from Susan and looked to the window.

Susan was taking notes on her PDA. "The world was about to change in a big way, and suddenly the computers that were going to do it, at least some of them, burn up. The fiber-optic connections that would have linked the supercomputers globally get cut. Then, just for extra measure, the satellites that might have been used as a backup disappear. Would China want to do that?" Susan asked.

"Maybe. China has been trying to lace our computer networks with back doors for years, but they can't keep up with some of it. Could have felt left out. Maybe they didn't want a U.S. software monster taking over the world, again. But maybe it was NSA. Your own spy agency might not have wanted the world to have flawless software. How would they hack into places?" Soxster said, putting his glass down on the mantel. "Look, so why don't we invite him in? He's going to freeze to death out there."

"Who?" Susan asked.

"The big guy in the doorway across the alley. He's with you, isn't he?" Soxster said, parting the curtain. Susan stood next to him and saw Jimmy hovering across the narrow alley in the doorway of a dress shop.

She bent over and cracked open the old window, shoving it up about a foot. "Foley, come on up. You'll be frozen into a statue out there."

Two minutes later, Jimmy was warming himself by the fire. Soxster offered him three fingers of the Balvenie, which Foley quickly gulped down. "I was just passing by . . . ," he tried.

"Yeah, whatever. What's that you're packing, dude? Looks like a Sig," Soxster said, pointing under Foley's jacket. "Those things are mean mothers."

Foley gave him a questioning look.

"Jimmy, Soxster was being very helpful. He was telling me about how the world would have changed if CAIN and the other nodes on Globegrid had propagated the Living Software," Susan interjected, getting the subject off Jimmy's gun.

"The whole world would have changed, huh? Isn't that just a touch melodramatic there, buddy?" Jimmy asked, reaching for the Balvenie bottle.

"Hell no, man. The Singularity might have actually happened. The Borg, the Terminator, the Matrix!" Soxster gestured wildly, half mockingly.

"Okay, okay," Jimmy started waving his hands, too. "The Borg, Terminator, Matrix. Got all that. What's the Singularity?"

"Kurzweil. Brilliant local guy." Soxster was on a roll. "*The Age of Spiritual Machines* was seminal. Back in '99, he theorized about what would happen when computers became smarter than humans, in like five years from now. Then he wrote *The Singularity Is Near*. His theory, seven years ago, was that the only way mankind would be able to compete with smarter computers was to merge with them and that this would set off a period in human history where change would happen so fast and be so profound that we would not even be able to comprehend it—where humanity would be altered to the point at which we would not be able to understand the present in terms of the past. So far, the only thing Kurzweil was wrong about was the timing. With Globegrid we could get there tomorrow."

"Science fiction," Jimmy sneered. "I read all those plots, saw the movies. Machine versus man and man loses. *Matrix, Terminator.* Bullshit."

"Maybe, maybe not. But it certainly sounds like everything was coming into place to find out," Susan suggested. "The Globegrid spreading Living Software sure sounds like the thing that this Kurzweil guy was afraid of."

"He wasn't afraid of it," Soxster answered. "He wanted it. Thought it was the next step in evolution. But, an odd coalition of right-wing nutbags, evangelicals, and spiritual humanists did get pretty worked up about it."

"And Megs Myers thinks that there is another whole layer of technological advance that the public can't see, gone underground, modifying the human genome," Susan interjected.

"Whatever. The fact that the Globegrid was going to go live sounds like motive to me. Blow up the computers, cut the connections. Slow the acceleration of technology. Give China time to catch up," Jimmy insisted.

"Save China or save the human race?" Susan interjected.

"Or keep it sick and stupid," Soxster shot back. "Look, even if the Singularity did not happen in one flash when Globegrid went live, the point is that the things that Globegrid is going to do in genomics and brain study will change the world," Soxster asserted. "They are into reverse-engineering the human brain, downloading the brain, adding memory boards to the brain with nano, altering the genome to create a self-diagnostics and healing system in our bodies. They're going to change the world, dude."

"Who are the 'they'?" Jimmy asked.

"You guys. The government, man, all those letter agencies.

DARPA, NIH, and NSF giving billions to all the profs in Cambridge and California to do this shit," Soxster smirked. "It's the guys that run those federal agencies that are moving technology fast while the politicians and the clergy and all have no clue."

"And I'll bet we're leaving China in the dust with some of that research, just when they thought they were catching up. Motive," Susan thought out loud.

"I know some of the stuff that DARPA's doing will definitely leave China, Iran, everybody in the dust," Jimmy interjected. "Guy I knew from when I was in the Marines is in this program at Twentynine Palms where you wear a spacesuit-like thing that makes a grunt infantryman into Superman."

"Twentynine Palms. That's a place?" Soxster asked.

"Yeah, California desert," Jimmy replied. "Why?"

"I thought it was a program. One of the hackers I know from the Dugout, TTeeLer, before he disappeared last year, said he was going to keep an eye on the 'two niner palm program' for whoever it was hired him."

"Keep an eye on, not be part of?" Susan asked. "So we may know where one of the hackers disappeared to? We need to find him." She stretched and yawned, looking suddenly like an eight-year-old past her bedtime. "It's possible, then, that China hired American hackers, maybe without them knowing they were working for China? We're making progress today, boys. We have leads on who did it and ideas about what they might hit next."

"Yeah, we may be making progress, but the Bureau ain't. Tommy McDonough told me that the FBI can't get anywhere with the Vehicle Identification Numbers on the truck bombs," Jimmy said, smiling. "VINs are supposed to be a unique number on every vehicle, seared into the chasis frame by lasers. Turns out all the bomb trucks had the *same* number and so do a lot of other trucks."

"So we've got somebody at Dilan University in China fooling around with Boston gas lines and blowing up a node on Globegrid. Hackers hired for big bucks and then disappearing. This stuff on the VINs. Not a bad start for one day's work," Susan said, picking up her coat and heading for the door. "But its not going to be enough for Rusty. Not enough until we stop whoever it is that's smashing our crown jewels. Hopefully, before they smash some more . . ."

As Susan walked down the warped stairs in Red House, the cop turned to the hacker. "Sox, there's almost half a bottle of whiskey left there, man, and I still don't understand how a bunch of different trucks can end up with the same VIN."

The hacker's smile looked evil in the light and shadows from the fireplace. His hand went out for the bottle, "So let me tell you how you hack VINs, flatfoot. . . ."

3 | *Tuesday, March 10*

0730 EST

Ballston Neighborhood

Arlington, Virginia

"Ten-minute delay on the Orange Line due to a security sweep at Rossyln . . ." the public address system was repeating as Dr. Freda Canas stepped onto the up escalator at the Ballston station. "Be sure to report any suspicious activity. If you see it, say it." Freda hated to be late to anything, and she almost never was, but the Washington Metro was getting fairly unpredictable. She was especially concerned about being late today, the second Tuesday of the month. She knew that Dr. Harry Shapiro and Professor Ahmad Mustafa would already be there. She also knew they would not start talking about the research until she arrived, but it was embarrassing to be the last one arriving when your office was the closest.

Two years earlier, they had chosen the Pancake Factory as their meeting place because it was two blocks from her office at the

National Science Foundation on Wilson Boulevard and four blocks from DARPA on Fairfax Drive, where Shapiro worked. Dr. Mustafa's National Institutes of Health office was fifteen miles away in Bethesda, but his town-house home was only a five-minute walk from the big blue-roofed restaurant. Freda had dubbed the informal coordination sessions "Science and Syrup," but she joked that the name hadn't been sticky enough. It had become known to their staffs as "The Billion-Dollar Breakfast." Today's was more important than most, because they were going to talk about the Work-Around Plan, how to go ahead with Globegrid despite the internet connectivity problems. As Dr. Freda Canas, director of the National Science Foundation, left the Ballston Metro station, a surveillance camera scanned her face. She hurried to the restaurant.

"Adding an extra pair of chromosomes to the embryo will allow us to modify the genetic makeup of children without upsetting the delicate balance developed over eons in the other chromosomes. They're like genetic scaffolding, you can add any number of characteristics with little risk," Dr. Mustafa was saying as Freda arrived at their usual spot, the large corner booth. "Ah, Dr. Canas, we have already taken the liberty of ordering your usual, with the blueberry sauce." Freda Canas placed her laptop on the table and began unbundling her scarf and parka. "So much for globe warming, huh, Freda? It must be twenty Fahrenheit out there this morning,"

Mustafa chided as the door opened and a student with a large backpack walked in.

"Ahmed, I've told you it's no longer a theory. We know. The National Science Foundation runs Antarctica for the U.S. My stations there can't keep up with the glacial movement. Big shifts that used to take generations," Freda asserted.

"The Navy has asked us to do a model that will show where the coastlines will be ten, twenty, and fifty years from now," Dr. Shapiro joined in. "It ain't pretty. Under the worst-case scenario, fifty years from now, half of Florida is under water."

"Maybe the future humans will evolve their gills back, Harry, or maybe we will have to add them back to the human genetic code," Mustafa joked. "Changing topics, Harry, tell me—whoever hacked the commercial communications satellites over the Pacific, why didn't they hack the DOD birds, too?"

"Thank you for asking. Our birds now use an unbreakable encryption for station-keeping updates, quantum cyphers shot up to space by laser," Harry Shapiro said, scribbling a depiction on a napkin. "And who came up with that, you ask? Why, DARPA, of course. Ahmad, you can be my straight man anytime."

Mustafa chuckled and said, "Just call me Ed McMahon." His smile faded as he saw the look on the face of the man heading toward the corner booth, young and clean-shaven, but a wildness in his bulging eyes. Ahmad Mustafa thought somehow the man might be Pakistani. He noticed how the man was struggling under the weight of the backpack. Suddenly and too late, Dr. Mustafa knew.

To the Arlington Police video-surveillance camera atop the traffic light across the street, the flash was yellow, then orange. The flash jumped out through the picture windows of the Pancake Factory, across the parking lot, and into Fairfax Drive, as large chunks of blue roof tile shot up and out. The camera could not hear the noise, but windows shattered in the tall buildings within two blocks, and plate glass rained on the sidewalks.

What the camera saw, its intelligent surveillance software converted to digits, was ones and zeroes. It moved them to a WiFi transmitter sitting above on the traffic pole. From there, the digits moved through the air on a radio frequency, 802.11, to another WiFi box on a light two blocks away. They flowed down the pole on fiber-optic cable that ran into a router under the street. From there they shot up Fairfax Drive on fiber to Clarendon Boulevard and east to Arlington Police Headquarters. In the headquarters, the digits were routed to an intelligent surveillance server. The server processed the digits and ran the image they created against the way the pancake house normally appeared. It ran the image against other known images and recognized that what it saw now was not normal; indeed, it was not good. Then the analytical software sent a signal to the large flat screen in the center of the police operations center. The image on the screen quickly changed from the normal scan of traffic on the Key Bridge into Georgetown. Now the screen showed a single word in large orange font: ALERT.

Less than one second had elapsed since the flames shot through the windows of the restaurant.

A computerized voice spoke the word "Alert" twice over speakers in the room. Then the large screen dissolved to a feed from the camera across from the blast. The camera showed a dust cloud billowing out of all the windows of the pancake factory. There were fires inside and fires in cars in the parking lot. A man was staggering out of the doorway, coughing, choking, bleeding. One corner of the restaurant was missing, the wall having been blown out by the force of the blast near the big corner booth.

Then a chunk of blue roof tile that had shot up from the building came down on the camera. The video feed from the blast site died. In the operations center, the image of Key Bridge traffic reappeared on the screen.

0755 EST

The Freedom Garage

Sillsbee Street

Lynn, Massachusetts

"I'd better call Connor," Jimmy said, touching his earpiece. "I told her I'd meet her and the professor for breakfast at eight. Obviously not going to make that." Tommy McDonough nodded and climbed out of the undercover State Police step van to check on the parking lot. Soxster took the opportunity of both cops being busy to grab the last chocolate-glazed in the Dunkin' Donuts box. His hand was shaking.

"Susan, listen, I'm up the coast a little way in Lynn. Soxster and I pulled an all-nighter over at the Dugout—it's like this secret geek clubhouse he and his gang have over in Watertown . . . Anyway, look, what we found was a lead to who may have provided the pickup trucks used in the beachhead bombings. The computer address of whoever hacked the Nissan truck factory comes back to a garage in Lynn, so I got Tommy to get a warrant and we're goin' in."

"So you're saying that while I slept, you figured out who the Chinese hired in America?" Susan did not sound entirely happy about it.

"Maybe. There are some Russian mob guys up here running a chop shop, but they have this young Russian hacker who looks like he figured out how to get into the VIN system and create a bunch of trucks all with the same numbers on the frames. Then they have the trucks delivered to them with paperwork that says they all have different VINs. Soxster got into the kid's computer last night. . . . Anyway, no need to go into the details of that part. We're saying we had a confidential informant on the warrants we're going to get —"

"Have you checked Soxster out before making him part of our team?" Susan asked testily.

"Yeah, of course, ran an interagency name check. Turns out he consults for the National Security Agency. He's clean." As he spoke, Jimmy looked out of the small window in the van and zoomed in on a white Ford pickup near the side door of the garage. Then he blinked and looked up at the digital clock just over his head, above the bank of television monitors in the van. "Gotta go, but I'll catch up with you. Okay?"

As he disconnected from Susan, Jimmy switched to the police tactical radio band. "In three, two . . . Go, go, go!" On the monitor, he saw what looked like dark-blue-suited football players or ninjas burst from the back of the Ford van across the street. On another screen, a second wave of State Police SWAT officers were leaping from a trailer truck in the front yard of the Freedom Garage.

Brrrttt . . . brrttt. The muffled sound of automatic-weapons fire could be heard even across the street and inside the command truck. "Stay here. I mean it," Jimmy yelled at Soxster as he jumped down off the stool and exited out the back of the truck. "You're still a civilian." Jimmy sprinted across the street to the garage, unholstering his side arm as he ran. He was wearing a raid jacket windbreaker that had four large letters on the back: NYPD.

As he entered the garage, he saw the dead man, his blood sprayed across the wall, his AK-74 on the floor nearby. There was always one dummy, Jimmy thought. As the SWAT officers began to handcuff the men they had pushed to the floor, Foley joined his cousin, Tommy McDonough, in the office at the rear of the four-bay garage. McDonough and three other detectives were grabbing up mobile phones, computer flash drives, and laptops as two men on the floor babbled in Russian at the SWAT officers above them. "Treasure trove, Jimmy," McDonough smiled, "although it's probably all Cyrillic."

Jimmy knelt over the larger of the two men on the floor. He

spoke in Russian to the prone suspect: "Who are you working for? Who got you to buy the seven white vans last month? Who took them off you? Tell us that now."

"They will kill me," the man grunted in Russian as a SWAT officer's boot ground into his back.

"Either way, we're going to tell the TV news guys out there that you cooperated," Jimmy said in English. "If you don't cooperate, it's Immigration. If you do, it's Witness Protection. Decide now or it's straight into that Immigration truck outside. Now!"

The man on the floor hesitated briefly. "Yellin, Dimitri Yellin," the Russian spat out. "But it must be Nevada I go to. Not Nebraska, Nevada."

Foley and McDonough walked out of the office into the clerestory work area, filled with welding tools and grease. "Whaddya get, Jimmy?" the state policeman asked. "Didn't follow the Russian jabber too well there."

"He gave up the head of one of the big Brighton Beach operations. New York Ukrainian mob. Means they probably sourced the trucks up here, filled them in Jersey, had their grunts drive them to the beachheads and then escaped in a backup car or on a bike."

"I don't get it," McDonough complained. "The Russians, the Ukrainians make a killin' on internet fraud. Why they want to go and blow it up? Doesn't add up."

"Yeah, but maybe Yellin doesn't make money in cyberspace," Jimmy thought out loud. "Or maybe he got paid a boatload to blow up seven little buildings without any people in them and that's better than credit-card fraud. Anyway, tell the FBI what you found. Let them ask this Russian. I'll warn NYPD it links back to the City."

Two SWAT officers carried the Russian out of the office. "Nevada, remember you promised Nevada."

"You say Novosibirsk?" Jimmy asked as the man was dragged away. "I knew those two years out in Brooklyn polishing my Russian wouldn't just be useful for the borscht and blini recipes."

0810 EST

The Charles Hotel

Cambridge, Massachusetts

"Just got off the phone with my boss," Susan said, sitting down for breakfast with Professor Myers at Henrietta's Table. "There's a possible terrorist incident just outside of D.C., but at a pancake house. Weird."

"Did you know the nine-eleven terrorists stayed at this very hotel eleven years ago?" Margaret Myers observed, then her face turned ashen. "Did you say pancake house?

"Yes."

"This is the second Tuesday in the month, isn't it, Susan?"

"Yeah, so?"

Myers bit her lip. "It's the Billion-Dollar Breakfast. The heads of the DARPA, the National Science Foundation, and the National Institutes of Health get together every month, second Tuesday, for an informal research-coordination session. They do it at a Ballston pancake place . . . Oh, Freda." She lowered her head.

"More crown jewels," Susan said to no one in particular. "I'll find out if your friends survived." She typed in a message on her BlackBerry.

Myers looked up. "You've got to stop these people. They're moving fast."

"Megs, I was thinking about what you said yesterday. Here's a theory that came to me while I was running along the river this morning. You taught a class once on why the Soviet Union gave up the arms race. Remember?"

"Of course. The Americans and the Soviets had been in a high-tech arms race for years. Then, by spending like crazy, the Americans pulled way ahead. Some Soviet military leaders, Marshal Ogarkov initially, realized that the gap had gotten so wide that the Soviets could not afford to catch up. So they gave up and Ronald Reagan got credit for winning the Cold War." Myers paused. "That is, of course, the overly simplified, one-minute version of a three-part lecture."

"Right. So, Megs, what if Chinese intelligence on U.S. high tech is so good that they uncovered a lot of the breakthroughs that are about to happen, some of it the work in genomics and brain-computer interface that has gone underground because of the right-wing politics? Things the national-security policy types in D.C. don't understand or even know about."

Margaret Myers was silent for a minute. Susan knew that

Professor Myers was digesting the idea and spinning it out into half a dozen alternative hypotheses. Finally, she replied, "Yes, a possibility. China would try to steal the information and bring the technologies back to their scientists, who might fail to be able to replicate them. Did I ever tell you the story of the first Chinese jetliner? Exact copy of the Boeing 707. Looked just like it, but they got the center of gravity wrong and the damn thing could not fly. Long time ago, of course, but they still have problems with creativity, project integration, and management."

Susan was pleased at the response. "So you think it's possible that . . ."

"Yes, Susan, yes. If the Chinese had discovered a U.S. technology edge, instead of choosing the path of Marshal Ogarkov and Mikhail Gorbachev and giving up, the Chinese might decide instead to eliminate some of the U.S. labs until their own scientists could catch up, which eventually they probably would."

"That's motive. We're making progress on who the Chinese might have used to actually do the attacks on Sunday. Jimmy's got proof of Russian organized-crime involvement from Soxster. Soxster also thinks the attacks might be from our own NSA." Susan shook her head. "Other than that, Soxster's good, by the way. You were right about him. Jimmy and he have already bonded in some bizarre way and are up in Lynn busting Russians."

"Russians in Lynn?" Myers sat still, thinking. "The concept of layered deniability. You find who did it and you think it's Russia who is attacking us, but that's only the first layer."

"That's what we think. China hires Russian organized crime to do their dirty work in the U.S. If they get caught, our first suspicion is that it's the Moscow government that's doing the attacks," Susan agreed. "Layered deniability, that's a good term for it. Mind if I steal it for my report?"

Professor Myers smiled permission. "What else have you developed so far? What are the facts? Facts before hypotheses, remember?"

Susan was thinking again that Margaret seemed overly pedantic. She was glad that she had decided not to be an academic herself. Thank heaven for that recruiter. "We've told FBI and CIA about the message traffic from Dilan University in China that may have led to the CAIN building blowing up. Now we have this Russian crime group that got the trucks and explosives to blow up the beachheads. Soxster says someone was hiring hackers last year and one of them, named TTeeLer, told him he was going to a place in the California desert, Twentynine Palms," Susan rattled off. "And Jimmy, amazingly, knows somebody who is working there on some high-tech project."

"It's the Twentynine Palms Marine Corps base, dear. I know about it, too, because there is a major DARPA project there on exoskeleton suits and performance drugs. Meant to create the superwarrior, strength of ten men, can't be killed, and each man plugged into the Pentagon grid," Myers recited from an article she had read. "If the wrong people hack into that technology . . ."

"Or try to blow it up to prevent it . . . ," Susan added. "You see a pattern yet? Where might they strike next, whoever they are? We have to stop showing up after shit blows up."

Myers chuckled softly. "Always the easy questions from you. Just like in the seminar." The professor closed her eyes and, after a moment, spoke. "With CAIN a pile of rubble, the people who will take over the work on Globegrid are in Silicon Valley. The joint Carnegie-Stanford computing center at the Googleplex, the old Ames NASA site at Moffet Naval Air Station. Maybe you should tell them they might be a target, too, if this keeps happening. But I would warn the DARPA people, too, at the Marine base. Lots of nasty things out in that desert."

Susan looked down at her vibrating BlackBerry. "Margaret, I'm sorry. Freda and the other two directors. They all died instantly."

1502 EST

On Guard Alarm Company

Moonachie Avenue

Teterboro, New Jersey

"Of course, I dropped everything and came to meet you, General. You say you have another job that will pay like the last one, I come right away," Dimitri Yellin said, gesturing with his hands as he talked.

"Don't call me General. I am Mr. Cunningham," the man replied.

"You look like a general I once knew in the Spetsnaz. You know what this means, Spetsnaz, I think, Mr. Cunningham?" Yellin picked up the cup of tea. "But I don't understand why we must meet in person always with you."

"I am not Russian, nor Spetsnaz. And I don't trust some things to the phone, or the internet, or to subordinates," the man replied. He placed his own cup of coffee back down on the conference room table.

"I know you don't trust the internet. You hate it, you had me blow it up, some of it! And we did, flawlessly, no? But now I can't get through to Kiev on the free phone . . . ," Yellin lamented. "But for that price—and in gold no less, deposited in Kiev—I can put up with such inconveniences. So, what is the new job? You want me to run this alarm company for you? I already own three others. They make money like nobody's business. You just sit and wait for an alarm to go off. Then you call the cops. Seventy-five dollars a month, automatic to their credit cards."

"It's just a front, Dimitri, not a real alarm company," the man calling himself Mr. Cunningham replied. "But I don't hate the internet. I get some very useful information from it." There was a noise outside the conference room, and Yellin glanced at the door. "Like the FBI's message system, which they think is encrypted, too. Never good at computers, the FBI."

"Then maybe you can tell me, Mr. Cunningham, does the FBI or do you know what happened to the Atlantic Star?" Dimitri Yellin took a brown cigarette out of a silver case. "My people have not heard from the ship since Sunday night. It has some of the people I used on this operation for you, it was bringing some of my cash back to Ukraine."

"FBI would not know where it is, Mr. Yellin, but I can have my people look into the Coast Guard's records. It's very rough in the North Atlantic this time of year, you know."

Another noise made Yellin look concerned. "What is going on out there?"

"Don't worry. Our men are out there," the man who was not Spetsnaz replied. "Freedom Garage in Lynn, Massachusetts. You know of it, Dimitri?" the man asked.

"Yes, my cousin's. We got the trucks there. We made sure that they all had the same identification numbers. I told you they would be untraceable," Yellin insisted, "totally untraceable."

"Then why, Dimitri, why do the FBI computers say that the Bureau raided the Freedom Garage today and why do they have your cousin in custody in connection with the beachhead bombings?"

Yellin began to stand up but grabbed at his chest and fell against the table, gasping. His skin suddenly had a bluish tint. He crumpled, hitting his head on the table and then on the floor.

"Cunningham," on the other side of the conference table, finished his coffee and then spoke into a microphone inside the arm of his jacket. "Please join me." Two men entered the conference room. Both wore blue sport coats and green ties. Both stood over six feet and looked like college football players. "No problems out front, I trust?" the Cunningham man asked.

"No, sir. There were only six of them. Just his Caddy and an old Suburban, sir."

"The bodies all go in the cargo hold on the 737. I'll fly out of here first in the Gulfstream. And you know to leave their cars in the long-term lot at Newark Liberty?" Cunningham asked as he stepped over the body.

"Yes, sir."

"And make sure this place is wiped clean. No prints, no blood, no hairs. . . . Untraceable, totally untraceable," the man said as he left the room.

"Yes, sir, General, sir."

1600 EST

The Forum

Kennedy School of Government, Harvard University

Cambridge, Massachusetts

". . . organizer of the million plus rally in Washington last October, coming off a great performance in the New Hampshire primary, and now considered among the three front-runners as the race goes forward, Senator Alexander George," the Dean intoned.

The students, faculty, and neighborhood regulars gave polite applause from the floor and from the seats rising up three stories in tiers on the sides of the Forum. Margaret, Soxster, and Susan were in a box seat near the top tier by the television klieg lights. "Here we go," Myers said from behind her hand.

"Thank you, Dean. And thank you for the invitation. Bein' from Dixie, I never really expected to be invited to anything in Cambridge, Massachusetts, but here I am . . .

"I know you, like me are deeply concerned about the bombings yesterday. And you may have heard the speculation today that the Chinese may be behind it. I think we all, as one people, should tell China that if it was involved, it will pay a price. And I demand that the President tell the Congress and the American people what he plans to do about it."

There was no reaction from the audience. The senator continued, "I see the campus newspaper today said I was against the pursuit of knowledge. Nothing could be further from the truth. The truth, *veritas,* the motto of your school. The truth is that I, like most Americans, value the pursuit of knowledge, but as a means, not an end. As a means to understanding this marvelous world that God created for us.

"When I oppose the teaching of the Darwin theory, I do so because I want our children to have more knowledge, not less, to know that there are other explanations. When I oppose stem-cell research, it is because it is misplaced research, attempting to make scientists into godlike creatures without any limits. Disease prevention and repair, yes, but not enhancement, not supermen. Yes, I am opposed to the pursuit of knowledge when the end is breaking God's codes so that man can pretend to be God.

"And now, with the advent of expensive designer drugs to enhance human capabilities, with the manipulation of genetic codes not to kill disease, but to improve performance . . . I say we are crossing a line that should not be crossed." There was a smattering of applause from the few supporters who had accompanied the senator.

Soxster audibly sighed.

"As citizens of this republic, we are allowed to not believe in God, but we all should believe in democracy. When we set out to make the rich smarter and stronger than the poor by offering to the wealthy these expensive drugs and genetic alterations, we undermine democracy. I have always thought that the size of a person's income did not tell me about his IQ , but that will soon no longer be the case . . ."

"Good argument," Professor Myers said softly. "Gets away from the purely religious justification."

"Do we want to throw out an egalitarian democracy for a Platonic republic with a caste system of gold men, silver men, and bronze? Because, make no mistake about it, even if we spent the entire GDP on these human enhancements, we could not afford it for all of our citizens. Who will decide who gets them? The almighty dollar will, just as it decides today who will get a facelift. But a facelift and a brain lift are two different things. . . ."

"And guess which one he's had," Soxster said too loudly. There were chuckles from others in the third-floor seats.

The Senator was unfazed, or did not notice. "So I propose a moratorium on certain research and certain products until we have a plan for how we as a society can preserve our democracy and how we can together decide what it means to be human. . . ."

The applause was only slightly stronger than it had been earlier. "Have to hand it to the man, coming to a university to propose a moratorium on research," Susan said as they stood up to leave, not waiting for the question period. "Like how he went to Congress to oppose lobbying . . ."

"Gaudium said the same thing last year here at the Forum," Margaret Myers noted. "Only in more technospeak."

"Who?" Susan asked as they walked back into the classroom area.

"Will Gaudium, creator of Jupiter Systems back in the early nineties. Serious cyberguru," Soxster explained. "Now he's scared of the Singularity or nano-ooze or a mutant gene. Wants to freeze research, just like Senator Foghorn down there."

"Nano-ooze? You mean like in the novel where nano-bots replicate themselves and can't stop, and they eat up everything, converting it into more nano-bots? Gray goo? That's nuts," Susan said, and laughed.

"Not to Gaudium," Myers replied. "He's spending some of his considerable billions to do public education on these issues."

"You ought to go hear him at Infocon Alpha in Vegas," Soxster suggested. "He's the keynote speaker this year at the hacker convention. Oughta be a blast. I'm going. And we may be able to learn more there about the hackers who have been hired by the big-money guys, China, or whoever they told them they were. From what I can tell so far, they been probing some really important networks, infrastructure stuff that makes the country run. They've also been running scams to pay for some of their big salaries."

"What kind of scams, Sox?" the professor asked as they walked together.

"Phishing to get bank account passwords and credit cards, then taking small amounts from thousands of accounts and transferring them to banks in Antigua, Vanuatu, places like that."

"Phishing, Googleplex, Infocon Alpha." Susan shook her head. "I feel like I fell down a rabbit hole."

Margaret Myers stopped and looked at Susan and Soxster. "Maybe we have. Maybe we all have. Curiouser and curiouser."

1926 EST

Room 1211, the Charles Hotel

Cambridge, Massachusetts

Susan Connor and James Foley had rooms on the same floor of the Charles Hotel, looking out toward the courtyard and the river beyond. In between their two rooms was a third, staffed by two Air Force communications specialists assigned to the Intelligence Analysis Center. The two sergeants had converted the hotel room into a field communications and support site for the two IAC officers. The sergeants had been receiving and sorting intelligence reports from IAC headquarters back in Foggy Bottom. A small satellite dish sat on an end table, pointing up into the southern sky.

"His office said he would come on the secure vid at 1930 hours, miss, which is in about two minutes," the senior sergeant told Susan.

"Thanks, Walid," Susan replied, putting on her headset and sitting down in front of the twenty-eight-inch computer screen. Jimmy followed, sitting next to her. The sergeant flipped on a white-noise machine that created a sonic field projecting at the window and the entry door. If anyone was attempting to listen, they would hear only jumbled sounds of Susan and Jimmy. The voice coming from IAC headquarters would be heard only on the headsets, which decrypted the incoming signal and encrypted what was said on this end before it was transmitted to Washington.

Rusty MacIntyre appeared on the screen, somewhat blurred as he moved quickly into the room. He wore no headset. His office on Navy Hill was in a secure building above the Kennedy Center and the Potomac. The image sharpened as MacIntyre sat in front of his screen. Susan could tell from the puffiness under his eyes that her boss had not been getting much sleep. "Good to see you guys, Susan, Jimmy. I just got back from the daily coordination meeting on the investigations. We look good, thanks to you. Really nice work so far. What you found out about the Chinese using the internet to open the gas valve at the MIT computer science center was great. NSA is still trying to figure out exactly what terminal they used at Dilan University, but we may have to put a CIA asset on the ground to find out. For now, NSA's thinking is that the university computer is just a relay anyway to the real origination point, probably in the People's Liberation Army's Information Warfare Brigade at Wuhan. That's their best cyberwarrior group."

Susan didn't respond, and there was a moment of silence on the line. "Sir, what about the other high-tech facilities that were hit before the MIT center? Should we go to them, too, and see if there is a connection?" Jimmy asked.

"No, Jim, no need. I convinced the FBI that we found a pattern that they had missed. They now have hundreds of special agents going to those other sites to see if they are connected to this Cybomb case." Rusty was clearly enthusiastic. "They even had to admit that the Russian mob guys you found in Lynn were connected to Cybomb. It's pretty clear now that they were involved, at least with the trucks that were used to blow up the East Coast beachheads."

"We came to the same conclusion," Susan interjected. "The Russian mob's involvement does not mean that it's Russia. These guys are just guns for hire."

"Thinking is here, Susan, that the Chinese may have hired the mob, maybe using a false-flag operation, a front, to do the dirty work and cover their own tracks." MacIntyre continued, "Anyway, the Bureau has a BOLO out on the guy who your man in Lynn coughed up, Dimitri Yellin. He's the boss of the Ukrainian mob in the New York–New Jersey area, but he has been pretty scarce this afternoon since the Bureau started looking for him. Maybe tipped off by local cops who saw the bulletin."

"If he was tipped off, sir, it was by somebody in the FBI, not local cops, not NYPD," Jimmy shot back.

"No offense intended, Jimmy," Rusty laughed. "Just a matter of time 'til he shows up. And then we get to ask him who hired him to blow up the beachheads."

Susan, her fingers twisting her lower lip, looked up at the screen. "Anything more on the pancake house bombing? Has everyone accepted that it was targeted to kill the heads of DARPA, NIH, and NSF?"

"Yeah, pretty much. Seems like half the world knew about these monthly Billion-Dollar Breakfasts," Rusty said, flipping through his notes. "But Defense Intelligence now says that the Hunan Kitchen restaurant a block away is probably a Chinese intelligence front. They've asked the Bureau to see if there is a connection."

"The bomber was vaporized. Video-surveillance cameras in the area worked well. They're running images of people seen in the Metro station and on the sidewalk above just before the blast. One possible lead is a guy with a backpack who looks a lot like an Iraqi Revenge Movement terrorist," Rusty said, and leaned back in his chair. "I hope we're not going to get another round of them attacking in the U.S."

"Okay, well, we have some ideas about how to follow up what we have learned up here. I think now that whoever is doing this knows more about the state of our technology research than we do. A lot of science is speeding ahead at a breakneck pace, but much of it is hidden to avoid political problems with the radical right," Susan offered. "So we're going to go looking for it before it gets attacked. Might mean going to the West Coast first, to a computer center that might be a target. Should take about three days."

On the screen Rusty looked tired and, unusually for him, he didn't seem to be listening closely. "Whatever you guys think. So far you're the only ones producing any solid leads and I can tell you from Sol Rubenstein that the President has been seized with this, he's doing nothing else. If it is China, we are going to have to respond, and God knows how they'll react to our response. Could get into a tit-for-tat cycle that keeps escalating. Ugly. And destroys the economy worse than this current flap with the international stock markets being disconnected. The real fear at the White House is not only that this shit'll keep happening, but that it'll make us look like fools because we can't stop it and can't even prove who's doing it. Sol's got a meeting with the Principals coming up tonight."

"Rusty, has the media connected the pancake house explosion with the beachhead bombings and the satellites' disappearing?" Susan asked.

"Not yet, not really, but they will pretty soon. So far the media is saying that the Cybomb case, even including the three missing satellites over the Pacific, hasn't involved many fatalities, which is true as far as we know," MacIntyre noted. "And that's why some people think it's a pretty low-risk way for China to send us a message."

"But eight people died at the pancake house, including three of our leading scientists, and another fourteen died in connection with all the lab fires Jimmy found," Susan countered.

"If they're all connected," Rusty said, again looking at his notes from the interagency-coordination meeting. "One other thing that came up, and keep this close hold. Without those three commercial satellites over the Pacific, the Commander-in-Chief Pacific says he would be, quote, unable to perform key warfighting missions adequately, unquote. One assumes the Chinese know that about us too. Anyway . . . I have to go meet Sol after his session in the bunker. Keep me posted." The image faded on the screen, replaced by the Intelligence Analysis Center logo, spinning on a blue background.

Jimmy quickly shot Susan a look. "We're going to the West Coast?"

"Silicon Valley," Susan said. "Near the Googleplex. One of the Globegrid supercomputers that has not yet been blown up."

Jimmy stood up. "Sunny California sounds like a good idea about now." He looked across the brick courtyard toward the cold river. "But tonight, let's go downstairs, there's something I want to show you. I got some tickets that weren't easy to land."

"What? I've got reading to do that Margaret gave me," Susan protested. "And you keep trying to butter me up by cooking for me and now buying me tickets to . . . to what?"

"McCoy Tyner is playing downstairs at the Regatta Club tonight," Foley said, flashing two tickets to the jazz club. "I've always wanted to see him. And I don't want to go alone."

"Who?"

"McCoy Tyner. He's almost seventy-five, but he's the greatest living jazz pianist. He did all the original work with Coltrane. Jesus, Susan, isn't jazz the Afro-American classical music?"

Susan stared at him. "If we are all supposed to be stereotypes, why aren't you going to hear some bagpiper?"

"Touché. You'll like it, though, and we both need to relax a little. You never think of the answer when you're trying too hard. We need perspective—and a Balvenie?" Jimmy smiled.

"You'll do fine alone at a bar," Susan said, her resolve weakening. "Somehow I bet you never had a problem with that."

Foley shook his head in disagreement, "It's not like that. I'm married and, yes, happily. But when I'm alone at bars, traveling on work and whatnot, well, sometimes I do fall into old habits, and then I have to stop when I realize what's about to happen. It confuses the woman and it leaves me, well, wishing I hadn't started."

"So you want me there so you don't get tempted? Gee, thanks for the compliment."

Jimmy ran his hand through his hair. "No, no, it's not like that. It's just you said you had a guy, and I thought since neither one of us is on the market, we could just relax and talk about something other than work, listen to some great American music, have a drink, and unwind." The irresistible little-boy smile appeared.

Susan sighed in resignation. "Well, since you already bought the tickets . . ."

1930 EST

The West Wing, the White House

"I liked it better when your office was aboveground, Wallace," Sol Rubenstein complained to the National Security Advisor. "This feels like some post-Armageddon redoubt where the survivors wait for the nuclear winter to end before they can reemerge onto the surface of the earth." Two Navy stewards carried in pizza and colas. "Strangelovian."

"You watch too many movies, Sol." Wallace Reynolds chuckled, "I'm not so sure the Director of National Intelligence should have so much time on his hands that he can see as many movies as you do." Reynolds passed the peppers to Secretary of State Brenda Neyers. "Besides, it's more important that the National Security Advisor survive any attack on the White House than that I get to see the sun."

It was the National Security Advisor's turn to host the weekly after-work dinner with the Secretary of State, the Secretary of Defense, and the Director of National Intelligence. They met in his office in the new National Security Council (NSC) staff center, fifty feet below the West Wing and the Eisenhower Office Building, inside the White House compound. There the Situation Room staff monitored world developments, interagency working groups met in person and on secure video conferences, and the NSC staff prepared presidential decisions and monitored their implementation.

"Movies are my escape from you three," Rubenstein admitted as he lifted anchovies off his slice. "And they give me insight into what people are thinking. You should try it, Brenda, sneak into the back of a cinema after the lights go down. Try the multiplex in Georgetown. It's showing a Schwarzenegger festival this week. Your protective detail will love it."

"Just my kind of stuff, Solly, the Guvenator as a robot. I saw enough of that in reality as a congresswoman from California," Secretary Neyers replied, and poured her Coke.

"Let's get started. Bill, what's the latest on the Chinese military alert?" Reynolds asked, turning to Secretary of Defense William Chesterfield.

"Seems like it might just be a drill, an exercise, now, but Pacific Command got pretty worked up during the day today. Most of the Chinese fleet put to sea and their strategic missile forces were communicating a lot, but we think now it was just a test to see how quickly they could respond to an alert message."

Chesterfield flipped through briefing notes that his staff at the Pentagon had prepared for him. "Probably long planned and not connected with the disappearance of our satellites and the internet beachhead attacks. By the way, it turns out the economic effect of the satellite losses is less than we thought because there was excess capacity, some of it Chinese. But, your question, the Chinese exercise coming right now could be a coincidence."

"Coincidence, Bill? I don't trust coincidences in this business."

The National Security Advisor squinted as he looked across the table at the Secretary of Defense. "What do your guys say, Sol?"

"Coincidences happen, and we do have to be careful not to shape all the events we see through the prism of what is on our agenda. Nonetheless, the coincidence here could be that the Chinese had plans for a no-notice alert to their military and decided to run the test now to signal us," Rubenstein replied. "Or it's not about us. It's just more of the saber rattling against Taiwan in the lead-up to their new parliament coming into session."

"Signal us what? The signal doesn't work if we don't get it. I may just be a dumb former congresswoman, but I, for one, don't get it," Brenda Neyers shot back.

"To signal Taiwan's new leader not to make good on his Independence platform. To tell us that they know we may think they are behind the attacks on our cyber infrastructure and we should not try any response because it could quickly escalate?" the National Security Advisor asked. "Is that what you're thinking, Bill?"

"Could be both. If it's about Taiwan, there are over sixty years of U.S. pledges to defend Taiwan from China, including the Taiwan Relations Act passed by Congress. If they go after Taiwan, we have no choice. Bill Clinton sent two carrier battle groups there the last time things were heating up." Defense Secretary Chesterfield looked over at the Secretary of State and then continued, "But if it's about us, and after all, it's always about us . . . look, they know that we are trying to figure out who blew up the beachheads, hacked the Pacific commercial satellites and sent them hurtling toward Pluto. They know they must be a suspect. Therefore, they shake the cobwebs out of their military and at the same time their maneuvers remind us that they have modernized their forces. If we try anything against them, it won't be a walk in the park. That's what they're signaling," Secretary Chesterfield said, sounding like he was still teaching at Princeton. "Or they could have learned about our own big Pacific exercise upcoming and want to get in place first."

"We know that they know that we know what they might have done. Good god," Neyers said. "And people wonder how nations fall into unintended wars. What big Pacific exercise of our own do we have coming up?"

"No one's talking about a war here, Brenda, just a big show of force by Pacific Command beginning next week," the National Security Advisor admonished. "Sol, what do you have on the investigations? Is there a Chinese hand or not? The President wants options from us if it is China. He's meeting with his economic advisors again in the morning. The stock market's down twenty percent since the opening Monday, worse on the NASDAQ. And the media is beginning to turn on us for not knowing what's going on." The two Navy stewards reappeared to clear the pizza plates and bring in the apple pie à la mode. Conversation halted until they departed. Rubenstein then went over his report.

"As my friends at the FBI would say, Wallace, the investigation is ongoing. But, not being them, I will actually tell you what's going on. I have four points in today's intel summary. First, on the internet cable beachhead attacks Sunday, it now appears that a Russian organized-crime figure was involved. He was last seen on video monitors on the George Washington Bridge going into New Jersey on Tuesday. His car was later found at Newark Liberty Airport. NSA discovered that this fellow Yellin had a very large amount of money deposited recently into an account he controls in the Ukraine. Now he's gone to ground.

"Second, on the Pacific communications satellites, we assume they were hacked by phony signals. They would have to have originated from somewhere in the western U.S.; we don't know where. The attack was smart, sending the satellites out of orbit and toward Uranus, Neptune, Alpha Centuri, your choice.

Number three, on the suicide bomber, it came back as a positive match with a known Iraqi terrorist. Can't explain that," Rubenstein said, ticking through the bottom lines of in depth reports in his briefing book.

Defense Secretary Chesterfield looked exasperated. "I have to testify before Senate Armed Services tomorrow in closed session. I wish I understood all this cyber stuff better. I thought it was just for nerds. Who knew how important it was? Don't you guys know anything more about what happened?"

"We may know more, but it's speculation. China may not just be trying to get us to back off from helping Taiwan. They may be after our technological lead over them. My officers also identified a pattern of fires and accidents at major computer facilities and bio labs over the last few months," Rubenstein responded. "If you add these all up, strip out some attacks or accidents at bio facilities, it looks like a Chinese attempt to take apart our cyber networks and to prevent us from implementing some of the fixes the President approved after the Cyber Crash of 2009. Those fixes might prevent Chinese industrial espionage on us, among other things. FBI is investigating a gas-leak explosion at one major computer lab that may have been a result of hacking into the gas line's computer controls, someone hacking in from China. CIA is sending someone in to see if we can trace who in China."

"Russian mobsters, computers that we all know can be spoofed. All of that does not yet sound like you could go to the UN and prove the Beijing government had attacked us," Neyers observed.

"Doesn't mean it didn't either, Brenda," Secretary Chesterfield shot back.

"They're being careful," Rubenstein interjected.

"Careful of what, Sol?" Reynolds asked.

Rubenstein closed his briefing book, signaling that what he was about to say was his own personal analysis and not what his staff had given him. "Careful not to kill. Only about ten people or so have been killed in all of this thus far, and two of them were suicide bombers, which by the way is not a traditional Chinese practice, suicide bombing. They probably hired the Russian organized-crime gangs and the Iraqi suicide bombers to operate in this country, but I can't prove that to the UN or even to us yet. In any event, there has been little killing. Maybe they do just want to signal and not really piss us off. Careful also to cover their tracks to keep deniability."

The National Security Advisor looked around the table to see if anyone had anything more to add. Then he said his piece: "The President wants to give a prime-time speech on Monday, six days from now, to try to explain what has been happening and what we're going to do about it," Reynolds said, looking straight at Rubenstein. "I hope we have something for him to say by then about who is doing this and how we know." The National Security Advisor then looked at the Secretary of Defense. "And Bill, you will have options for him." The SecDef nodded. "Good," Reynolds continued, "then we will meet Sunday to go over what we will all say to him at Monday morning's National Security Council session. Anything else?"

Brenda Neyers pushed back from the table. "Having nothing else go wrong this week would be good."

The four leaders of America's national security apparatus looked quietly at one another and the remnants of their meal. Wallace Reynolds looked up from his half-eaten slice of pepperoni pizza. "Or they could just go on destroying our technological edge bit by bit while we try to prove who they are and try to stop them. If they keep going, all we would have left going for us would be our amber waves of grain. That would really piss me off. To say nothing of my boss, upstairs, who will not let that happen."

2115 EST

The Metropolitan Club,

Washington, D.C.

"Sorry to be late. They kept you waiting in the lobby? You really ought to be a member yourself, you know," Sol Rubenstein prodded his protégé, as the two men sat down in a secluded corner of the second-floor drawing room. "Founded one hundred fifty years ago next year."

"Are you kidding? Initiation fees, monthly dues. I don't make that kind of money anymore, Sol, I'm in the government. You joined when the club was almost new," Rusty MacIntryre protested. "Besides, its stuffy and aristocratic, and I'm working class and democratic."

"Well, it is just a block from my downtown office in the White House complex, and the meals aren't too bad here now. New chef." Rubenstein settled into a commodious armchair. "And at the White House, all is not well. They were worried about the reelection anyway after Senator George flooded the mall with a million plus people last October protesting stem-cell research, evolution, and genetic engineering. Now, with the internet attacks Sunday and then the terrorist bombing in Arlington . . . Senator George is going to be able to play the security card. Scare people into voting for him the way Bush did in 2004."

"Maybe there will be a nice, big crisis to unite the country behind the President. I keep expecting clear signs that China intends to move against Taiwan after the Independence Party got elected," Rusty said, passing their drink order on a little card to the waiter.

"That was four months ago. So far, no retaliation. Maybe they think their economy would suffer too much from a showdown with Taiwan and us," Rubenstein suggested.

"You're the China expert, Sol, but I doubt it."

"No, you're probably right. They like to get all the pieces in place first. And we are one of the pieces. If they are going to do something militarily, scare Taiwan or even invade it, they will want us out of the picture first." Rubenstein stopped as the waiter returned with his Armagnac and Rusty's Balvenie. "And that's not likely to happen. The President wants options from the Pentagon and is planning a speech Monday night."

Rusty sniffed and inhaled the single-malt. "Atritting our comms in the Pacific by sending the commercial satellites off to Uranus fits the pattern of China trying to get us to back off, as does preoccupying us with terrorism against our technological base here at home. Its a form of deniable escalation dominance. It says we know how to get at things that you really value and we can do more unless you stay out of our way."

Sol Rubenstein, Director of National Intelligence, swirled the brandy. "Armagnac is two centuries older than Cognac. Did you know that? China is two thousand years older than us as a national security bureaucracy. Did I ever tell you about my investigation into their industrial espionage here?"

"There is still a lot you haven't told me." Rusty smiled and readied himself to hear another story that he knew could not be found in writing anywhere. It was priceless having Sol as a mentor.

"About seven years ago, I headed up an Intelligence Community team: NSA, FBI, DOD, Homeland—to quietly look into allegations from industry that China was engaged in massive economic espionage, stealing formulas, proprietary information, from U.S. companies. Of course, they were. But how they were doing it was what was most disturbing." Rubenstein stopped and sighed as he recalled the case. "They had placed Chinese nationals in many of the companies. Smart guys who had graduate degrees from MIT, Stanford. They had also created U.S. companies that supplied parts for sensitive projects and learned all about the projects. Not so unusual. But then there were companies that they had penetrated where there were no Chinese nationals or front companies in the supply chain."

"I never heard about this effort," Rusty admitted. "So how had they gotten into the other companies' sanctum sanctorum?"

"Well, you weren't supposed to know about it. Sometimes—not often, but sometimes—we keep secrets. The Chinese had gotten into the other companies through the products that they were using in their computer networks. Things like computer firewalls, intrusion-detection systems, all sorts of gizmos I don't understand. But I understood this much: They all had parts made in China, sometimes the whole things were even assembled in China. And these gizmos had back doors, Trojan horses, put in their computer code and in the hardware. The U.S. manufacturers never even knew. In one case, they got into software being written in the U.S. by hacking into the U.S. company's research lab in Shanghai and then tunneling through the company's own network back into the U.S. headquarters." Rubenstein gave MacIntyre a bemused look.

Rusty MacIntyre took another sip of the Balvenie and waited for the conclusion to his bedtime story.

"I figured out that it was their station chief here in Washington that was running most of the program, so I had him tailed, harassed by the FBI. The Chinese got the point and recalled him. FBI and DOD went around to the Defense contractors and cleaned things up as best they could. Checked on the supply-chain companies, the Chinese nationals with access to the plants, and the like.

"But we never uncovered the full extent of the back doors. There are probably a lot of back doors still out there in the big telcoms' switches and internet routers. They were also in the big electrical components and video-surveillance systems. The decision was made that we couldn't find them all, replace everything. Couldn't prevent them from reinstalling the Trojans. Big economic cost. Maybe some panic. So there may be a little of it still out there. There may be a lot." Rubenstein's eyes were looking at the carved molding along the edge of the high ceiling.

"If I understood what you just said, Sol, Beijing could pull the plug on us anytime they want to?" Rusty asked, sitting up in his chair.

"Possibly."

"Then why, if they are so deep into our networks, why don't they just let them keep running and then continue to steal our intellectual property and copy it? Why blow it up instead? I don't get it," Rusty asked.

Rubenstein's eyes met Rusty's. "Maybe because some things are hard to copy and maybe they think we're getting too far out ahead of them again technologically. They can do knockoff jeans with a *J*, not knockoff genes with a *G*. Or because they are planning to finally solve their Taiwan problem and they want us down for the count while they do. Or because they are not a unitary actor any more than we are. Or because I am wrong. Never exclude that possibility, Mister Director of Analysis."

Rusty laughed. "I never do, but it's such a low probability." He polished off the Balvenie. "If I were the President, thinking about my options with China, I would want to have heard your bedtime story."

Sol Rubenstein signaled for the waiter to bring another round. "That's why I was late."

2115 EST

The Regatta Club

The Charles Hotel

Cambridge, Massachusetts

At seventy-four, Tyner's fingers glided across the ivory like the fast, cool waters of a rushing brook. The crowd in the packed club seemed to be extensions of his piano, nodding and moving in time with his music. In the dim red light, Jimmy showed Susan to a table stuffed in a corner. Tyner finished a bar and passed off to the drummer, as the crowd applauded. The percussionist began a riff. Susan leaned across the small table and whispered, "Thanks for doing this—we did need a break."

"Well, I never really got to tell you that I was sorry that Rusty stuck you with me, the one-year-tour guy with no federal experience, unless you count the Marines," Jimmy Foley replied. "But I can't say I'm unhappy; I'm learning a lot already. But tell me one thing: Why do you do it? You could be making a bundle in investment banking, like my wife is, or law, or consulting."

"That's easy. I like to sleep late," she admitted. "If I were just working for money, I'd sleep in all the time. This stuff gets me out of bed real early, because it matters. It matters more than just about me and my bank account."

Jimmy did his little-boy-smile thing. "Yeah, I can see that. Me? I'm just in it for the pension. Get my twenty in, move to Florida, get a young bride, and fish, play golf."

"You already have a bride!"

"Yeah, she's my first wife, but she won't be young by then," Jimmy said, and chortled.

Susan mouthed a word back at him: "Asshole." Then his infectious smile caused her to laugh. "Listen, I'm actually glad to have you on this case. I usually do analysis of things overseas, and this is shaping up to be more domestic, at least partially. And I'm really not too good at raiding Russian mob dens."

"That's easy. Just let the SWAT guys go first; they love it. They were all linebackers in high school." Jimmy looked around for the waiter. "But tell me where you see this case going. The way the news guys are talking on TV, if we prove this is China, there could be war. I've been to war, and I'm not sure we need another, especially when they got us outnumbered four to one."

"I didn't look closely at your file," Susan admitted. "Iraq?"

"Twice, although I found a way of shortening my second tour by being in a Humvee that hadn't been fitted with armor yet. Not that I'm at all bitter about civilians sending us off on some wild-goose chase without proper equipment, but don't get me started," Foley replied, letting down the always happy guy facade.

"Sounds like we agree about Iraq," Susan said. "My little brother, who is about five inches taller than me, went there, too. Army doctor. He gets so mad talking about the things he saw in that hospital. You two must be about the same age, thirty-three?"

"I will be in July," Jimmy admitted. "So you get why I'm not so happy with this assignment of proving China did it, if the result is more guys having to go off to war. I was listening to the news before I came down. Senators and representatives all demanding we do something."

Susan put her business face on again. "We prove what the evidence tells us, not what the TV and the Pentagon and Congress all assume. We can't go to war on an assumption, like we did with the WMD. You know, Rusty damn near single-handedly stopped us from going to war with Islamyah. Now they're one of our biggest allies, cochair with us of the new International Alternative Energy Agency. Even if we prove the Chinese attacked us, there doesn't have to be war. You can bet back in D.C. Sol and Rusty are plotting how to defuse things."

"Could be a tall order," Jimmy Foley replied, "like getting a drink in this place."

Another round of applause spread across the room as Tyner played his standard, "Just in Time." Two Balvenies suddenly appeared on the table. As Tyner concluded the set, the room filled with applause and cheers. "Well, that's an appropriate song title," Soxster said, pulling a third chair up to the table.

Startled, Jimmy looked across at his new friend. "What the hell? How did you get here?"

The lights in the jazz club came back up. "You call yourself a detective. I'm wearing a waiter's outfit and carrying two Balvenies and you ask me how I got in? It's sold out, man, but they never stop someone who is serving drinks. Old trick. Anyway, I think we may be closing in on this thing Just in Time, like the song . . ." Soxster was talking fast.

Susan was shaking from laughter, more at Jimmy's reaction and the incongruous circumstances than at Soxster. Finally, she got out, "What's up, Sox?"

"What's up Jimmy's socks is an ankle holster, Walther P99C. Think I didn't notice, Jim? Anyway . . . ," the hacker sped ahead, "I've been trying to make contact again with any of the guys who got hired off the Net last year, like you asked me, and I found one of them, TTeeLer. He's got a new handle, but I knew it was him in the secure chat room by an exploit he suggested and the way he explained it to this guy. So I asked him to join me in a private chat and he used TTeeLer's PGP key, which I already had—"

Foley, who was still recovering from the mood change, interrupted. "So what, man? Get to the bottom line."

Soxster screwed his face up at Foley. "Dude. Chill. TTeeLer got out because he thinks they're going to do something, kill a lot of people in March. He's hiding out, says they're trying to track him down because he left without permission."

"Who are 'they' Soxster?" Susan asked slowly.

"He wouldn't say."

"Okay, where are they?" Jimmy pressed.

"He wouldn't tell me anything else. Got offline fast once he knew I had figured out he was TTeeLer," Soxster said, taking Jimmy's drink.

"Great. Somebody who hired a lot of hackers last year is going to do something sometime this month that will kill a lot of people somewhere. That's actionable intelligence," Jimmy grumbled.

"Wait a minute." Susan waved her hands downward, trying to get the two men to slow down. "Isn't this the guy you said got hired to keep an eye on the two-niner project in the desert?"

"Yeah, that was TTeeLer," Soxster replied, and then, slowly, a smile spread across his face. "Yeah. Good memory, Susan, wow! Those PEPs must really work." Then he polished off Foley's Scotch. "I put these drinks on your room tab, Jimmy, okay?"

Before he could respond, Susan jumped in, "That does it, Jimmy. While I go to Silicon Valley in the morning, you go to the desert and try to find where this hacker was and what he was up to. They're going to kill a lot of people," Susan repeated, "whoever *they* are."

"In March," Jimmy added, looking into his now-empty glass. "And this is already March."

4 | *Wednesday, March 11*

Randall Ackerman carried his Starbucks grande mocha skim latte in his right hand and the *Financial Times* and *Wall Street Journal* under his left arm as he bounded into his thirty-third-floor office at Paragon, the hedge fund his father had started eleven years earlier. Now, under Randall, it managed seventeen billion dollars in assets.

"Morning, Asimov," he said to the silvery doglike robot standing by the window. It barked once in reply. "Let's begin," he said to the bot. It was what he said to the machine every morning. The bot barked twice and activated Randall's office systems. A large flat-panel screen lit up on the wall, stock market data in several windows and a cable news channel in another. The overhead lights glowed on. The bot had cost him twenty-five thousand dollars and he thought that every penny was well spent. This fourth generation bot dog was not a toy. It was his assistant. "Book a table at the Four Seasons for four people at one," he said to Asimov.

Asimov was also a symbol of Randall's own success. Only the most technologically savvy and financially prosperous had a canine assistant, or as the Kiasanjay company called them, Cassys. In the thirteen months they had been on the market, only thirty thousand had sold. Nine thousand of them were in Manhattan, Stamford, and Greenwich.

Randall Ackerman spread the papers out on the glass table that served as his desk. "Asimov, ask Bartlett to join me."

The Cassy turned toward its master. And growled. It was a low, guttural sound that was used to warn off trespassers. "Who's there, Asimov?" Ackerman asked, looking up from the papers. "What's wrong, boy?"

The dog barked and leaped up onto the coffee table, scattering the magazines. It barked twice more and then leaped the three feet from the coffee table up onto the surface of the glass desk, hitting the cup of grande mocha skim latte, which emptied its hot liquid onto Randall's shirt and lap. "Ahhhh! What the fuck! Asimov!" Randall jumped up. "Asimov, system off! Off!"

The dog bot was growling again, at its master. "Asimov, shut down!" Randall screamed. The dog did not comply. "Damn it, search for: First Law of Robotics!"

The canine's simulated human voice annunciator switched on: "Search results: Data set not found." Asimov stepped back to the corner of the glass-topped desk and barked loudly three times. It then ran the length of the table and leaped into the air, toward, then through the plate-glass window, shattering the glass as it shot itself into the air thirty-three stories above Madison Avenue. Then Asimov, and pieces of glass, fell to the street and sidewalk below.

Stunned, horrified, Randall Ackerman moved slowly to the window, suppressing his fear of heights. He felt a blast of cold air shooting through the hole in the glass. As he looked down Madison Avenue, he saw a window break in the building across Fifty-seventh Street. Another Cassy shot out of that window and arced out over Madison Avenue. He watched, incredulous, as the silvery dog bot smashed into a yellow taxi below, shattering the advertising screen on its roof.

"Asimov!" Randall called out. Then, "Bartlett!" No one answered. He patted his coat, found his PDA, and then hit the speed dial for his lawyer.

1145 Pacific Standard Time

Moffett Airfield, Silicon Valley

California

"It's so big that clouds form and it rains inside," the Space Agency guard said to Susan while he was waiting for her name on the facility's guest access list of his computer screen. "They built it to house blimps when this was a Navy air station. Then NASA took over for the Ames Research Center; now Google rents a big chunk of the base for the Googleplex. You're going to the Stanford-Carnegie Advanced Informatics Facility, SCAIF. Turn right and it's all the way down at the end of the road. Big building, no windows. Have a good one," he said, handing over a badge for her and a Visitor sign for the dashboard of her rented Nissan battery car.

SCAIF, a joint operation of Pittsburgh's Carnegie-Mellon University and California's Stanford University, was one of three American supercomputer hubs that were to be part of Globegrid. Another one, CAIN, in Cambridge, had blown up. The fiber-optic connections needed to link them to their counterparts in Europe and Japan had also blown up, or at least the U.S. ends of the fiber had. Susan expected security here to be heightened, but the NASA police guarding the campus seemed relaxed. In addition to the guard at the gate, there had been a NASA police car inside the perimeter. She wondered about the NASA police. They were probably like the National Zoo police, the Library of Congress police, the Washington Aqueduct police, and the twenty-one other federal police agencies she had counted in the nation's capital. Now, as she approached SCAIF, she saw another NASA patrol car parked prominently outside the building, in front of a row of concrete Jersey barriers. Not enough to stop somebody serious, Susan thought as she walked in.

Susan had taken the first flight out from Logan to San Francisco, and as she finally got to her destination at SCAIF, she remembered what its twin facility in Cambridge looked like as a burned-out hulk. Walking into the California computer center, she wondered exactly what her office had said to get her the appointment on such short notice.

"I'm Dr. Walter Heintel, deputy director at SCAIF," the tall, bald man said, thrusting out a hand awkwardly. "Our director, Dr. Stanley Goldberg, can't be with you today, budget meeting up the road at Stanford, but he said to tell you anything, show you anything you want. You must be with the National Science Foundation?"

"No, but I am with another research arm of the federal government, the IAC," she said, quickly flashing her credentials. "I was hoping you could tell me more about Living Software and Globegrid, and also the Human Brain Reverse-Engineering Project."

They sat in a small, dimly lit conference room inside SCAIF. The left wall was glass, and through it Susan could see what she assumed the inside of a laptop would look like through a microscope. Blue lights glowed and blinked down identical, three-story-high stacks of gray boxes. She counted twelve rows, each perhaps as long as half a football field. Catwalks wove among the machines, as did bundles of orange cables. She saw no humans.

"Well, where to begin?" The professor looked away, as if to see the answer on the other wall. "Stanley, Dr. Goldberg, has really been the man on Living Software since the Cyber Crash, but simply put, once we go live with Globegrid, we will propagate Living Software into any network that opens itself up to receive it. So, LS will determine the task being done by existing software and it will create new, alternative, glitch-free, efficient, secure software to do the routing and to run the servers. The new software will then run on a test bed, and if the network operators like it, they can buy it for a nominal amount that will be paid to the manufacturer of the old software and to Globegrid. We have had self-modifying code for years in worms, but this new code is for a good purpose. Of course, privacy and security rules will mean that sensitive information cannot leave a network. Living Software won't export anything from the networks it fixes and rewrites, just diagnostic data about itself."

"Any idea who would want to stop it? China? Russia? Iran?" Susan asked.

"Maybe bad software manufacturers? No, just kidding." Heintel laughed nervously. "We are dreadfully sorry about CAIN and everything that has happened this week, but Stan is still planning to go live with Globegrid and Living Software by the end of the month. We had hoped that all six computer centers would be linked to save computing time and to ensure that we produced the same result to the same problem everywhere, but we think we can use the two U.S. centers, here and San Diego, with a smaller facility in Pittsburgh, and then we can fly copies of the memory to Japan and Europe every few days and we will sync every five days or so."

"Who knows you're still going ahead?" Susan asked.

"People at all the remaining five centers and in Pittsburgh. Only about a thousand or so staff of the Globegrid project. We don't want to announce it until we are sure we can do it and we have a specific date. It will probably be March twentieth."

Susan sat silently for a moment, then asked, "Have you personally read and understood the code for the new Living Software?"

"Pieces of it. No one individual has read all of it. My dear, no one person has read all of any operating system for years. Too many lines of code, seventy million lines in most operating systems," Heintel shrugged, "and eventually what LS writes will get too complex to read and understand with the naked eye anyway. You'll need a reader application as it evolves."

"Software to read software. I get it—why not, since software is writing software?" Susan said aloud, but apparently to herself.

"So. Can I tell you about the Human Brain Reverse-Engineering Project—that's my baby," Heintel volunteered. He flashed images on the large screen that was the wall at the front of the room. "We just completed the project last November. It's so exciting, I'm sure you saw all the press about it. It's like when they finished decoding the human genome and, who knows, maybe as important, or almost. We know now what every part of the brain does and how. We can implant electronics in the ear, eye, and elsewhere directly into the brain, and send signals that are converted to the biochemical language of the brain. And we can go the other way now, taking biochemical signals for memory and turning them into ones and zeroes for copying and storing in silicon, in electronic computers. So, phase two will involve nanotechnology inserts, but we need another five years before we can test that in humans."

Susan was embarrassed; she had really not noticed all the media coverage of the brain project last November. She had been on a vacation hiking through New Zealand with her boyfriend, Sam who had just accepted a job at Johns Hopkins Hospital in Baltimore. Rusty Macintyre had ordered her to take a month off, and she and Sam had camped, fished, and sailed for three weeks. Then Sam had gone went back to surgery and she to IAC. Last month, they'd been together all of three nights. In Baltimore.

"And exactly how would the Globegrid help?" Susan asked.

"Well, it will give us the computing power and the software to accelerate the research into the nano program and other things we have not really cracked yet, like the consciousness problem, connectivity, other things . . ." Heintel almost mumbled.

"The consciousness problem?" Susan asked.

"Yes, you see we have successfully downloaded the short-term and long term memories of almost three hundred human subjects. We can send sensor inputs like what their brains receive to a processor, but we haven't really been able yet to get a computer to take those inputs and, well, puts them all together. We need to develop an application or program that is the master control, something like human consciousness. We can't find a single place in the human brain that is the locus for consciousness."

Susan didn't know whether to be disappointed or reassured. "And the connectivity problem?"

"So, there we are in better shape." Heintel beamed. "My own work is in this area. We have built converters that will take a series of standard Internet Protocol–formatted packets of data and convert it to the appropriate biochemical-electrical message that the brain will understand and process, and vice versa. Add a WiFi transceiver connected to the internet and you could literally think an e-mail message, see it on your visor, and send it, or think a Google search and then see the results by using wraparound visualization glasses. The Google guys down the street love it."

"You're serious?" Susan breathed.

"I know, and it was only what, just eight years ago that we first used the thoughts of paralyzed patients to move computer mouses and keyboards? Then we had the little brain-connected appliances that stopped depression and the like." Sensing Susan's apparent concern, he added, "Of course, no one will be connected directly to the internet for a while. The subjects we have will be tied into a closed, firewalled sub-network on Globegrid, but the subjects will be able to search some files and send each other text messages. And Living Software can learn from what they, the humans, see and do. That way, Living Software will make the big step from artificial intelligence—using rule-based theory—to sentience. I just can't wait to start."

"When?"

"Realistically, probably not until May," Heintel said, and sighed.

"Of this year?"

"Yes. Yes, of course." The professor beamed, "As soon as we get the Globegrid work-around up for a while. Soon. So, can you help us with our funding shortfall?"

Susan Connor sat quietly in the rental car, forcing her own gray-matter processor to sift through what she had just been told. Living Software, an operating system itself written by software, would pretty soon offer to install itself on every network in the world. Most network operators would accept it. Even though the Globegrid computers were not now all linked in real time, they would still coordinate their files every five days, comparing and conforming the programs that Living Software had written and installed everywhere. There would no doubt be diagnostic applications left behind everywhere to monitor how the software was doing and report back to the LS master program on the Globegrid processors. And Living Software would, as its name implied, continue to live and grow, changing itself and its offspring to meet new security threats and problems.

Across the parking lot, Susan noticed that a surveillance camera on the streetlight had just turned in her direction. At least the fearsome NASA police had installed security cameras.

She had heard of Living Software for three or four years now, but this was the first time the implications were sinking in. It was more than just glitch-free programs, a lot more. And soon some human brains would be connected to a computer network on which Living Software was running. The human interface would be firewalled off, of course, on a sub-net. Right. Megs was right, there was a lot of technology that was about to be sprung on an unsuspecting world. And that was just what was in the open. What about the technology developments that were hidden? How ironic that the Chinese and others knew about the underground research and development, but Washington did not. She had to find the full extent of it, before it, too, was attacked and set back or destroyed. Megs had pointed her in the right direction, but now she needed more help to uncover the partially hidden new world of computer science and genomics, of nano and quantum computing, of reverse-engineering the human brain.

She thumbed through her notes on the PDA, went online to get the number for Jupiter Systems, and connected through to the main number in Menlo Park, five miles away. "Could you put me through to the office of Will Gaudium, please?" Mr. Gaudium, a founder of the information systems giant, was no longer full time in Menlo Park, Susan was told, but she could send an e-mail to his assistant who would consider her request for a meeting. Susan dashed off a message explaining not just that she was a Fed who wanted to interview him on a matter of national security, but also that she wanted his help understanding the security implications of Living Software and the Human Brain Reverse-Engineering Project.

As she drove away from SCAIF back to the main gate, she was distracted, her mind still in a fog, trying to understand what was spinning around her and why she had not seen it before. And why no one else on this case apparently got it yet. She needed to talk to

Jimmy, get his reaction. . . . And then it happened. In her peripheral vision, she caught a flash up ahead, then heard the sound of a
thud. At the end of the road, near the gate, over a half mile away,
a cloud of dust billowed up, and shooting out of the dust cloud came
a truck, a red eighteen-wheeler tractor-trailer, coming fast down the
road right toward her.

Suddenly she knew. No processing time was required. The situ-
ational understanding was instant. The gatehouse had just been attacked and now SCAIF was about to go the way of CAIN and the
beachheads. Where the hell were Jimmy and his guns when she
needed them? The truck was probably one giant bomb.

Without stopping for second thoughts, Susan threw the car into
park, pulled the belt off her bag, and strapped it around the steer-
ing wheel and the seat-belt hook. Then, aiming the car for where
the truck would be in a few seconds as it came around the curve,
she pushed open the driver's door, threw the gear into drive, set the
cruise control for seventy, and leapt from the car as it sped up.
Hitting the grass hard, she rolled, and then, her back facing the
road, she assumed the fetal position and waited.

And . . . nothing happened.

Nothing. If the car had missed colliding with the eighteen
wheeler, at least the truck should be roaring by her . . .

The ground shook below her as though a dinosaur had put its
foot down next to her. Then the concussive wave pounded her
everywhere on her body, like she was being punched by ten men.
As the sound overloaded her brain, she was simultaneously aware

of pieces of flaming metal landing all around her, setting the grass on fire. It had worked, she thought as the air rushed out of her lungs and she passed out.

The impact of the Nissan hitting the charging truck had set off the detonator. The truck bomb had gone off on the approach road, blowing out windows across the campus, sending a column of smoke and debris thousands of feet in the air, causing a crater thirty feet wide and eight feet deep, throwing the chassis of the truck cab over the fence and off the base. The person or people inside the truck cab would never be found, except for microscopic pieces of flesh that would be analyzed for their DNA signatures.

Inside the windowless SCAIF, the earthquake shock absorbers had adjusted instantly when the blast occurred. The rows of parallel processors did not miss a byte. They continued to hum and to glow blue.

2030 Greenwich Mean Time
The Cabinet Office
Whitehall, London

"Sol, I thought I would just check in before I go home," Sir Dennis Penning-Smith said into the secure telephone in his London office. "We've seen media reports of a terrorist attack near the Googleplex."

"You're working too late for a man of your age, Sir Dennis," Rubenstein teased his old friend.

"As I recall, Sol, you are four months older," Sir Dennis replied gravely.

"Yes, but it's five hours earlier here." Rubenstein got down to business. "Yes, we are still getting details on the explosion, but the most important thing is that one of our officers was there and was apparently responsible for preventing the attack from getting to Google or the university research center. That center was linked to Globegrid and was probably the target. Don't know yet who did it, of course."

The voice link was traveling over a military satellite channel, and during the brief pause in their conversation they could both hear the subtle sounds of its transmission and encryption. "So it continues," Sir Dennis intoned. "Sol, our Beijing station thinks that there is some sort of internal tension in the Chinese leadership. We have a source there who is in a position to know, has access. The source, however, won't give up his subsource, who we think is pretty highly placed. The subsource says he will only meet with a senior official of our Secret Intelligence Service."

"Could be a lure," Rubenstein cautioned.

"Funny, that's what Brian Douglas said."

"So let me guess. The Deputy Director of SIS decided to assign himself the task," Rubenstein replied.

"Of course. Brian lands in Beijing about now," Sir Dennis said, looking at the antique clock on the fireplace mantel. "He knows how to sense a setup, how to arrange a meet so he can get out."

"Indeed, he proved that in Tehran, but I doubt he speaks Mandarin and he is a few years older now than when he did the Iran mission."

"Aren't we all?" Sir Dennis said, standing up and looking out at the evening traffic coming down from Trafalgar Square and passing below his window on Whitehall toward Parliament. "Sol, the media is full of speculation and leaks that China might be behind the attacks. Senators talking about the need to respond. I hope your President is not feeling the need to—"

"The President is ensuring we are prepared, that we have a spectrum of options if the evidence goes where you and I think it will." Sol's view from his Executive Office Building suite looked south from the White House complex across the park toward Reagan National Airport. Aircraft taking off veered sharply to avoid the no fly zone over the White House. The huge spotlights were just coming on at the Washington Monument. "My job—no, Dennis, *our* job—is not just to come up with the evidence, but it is then to tell our political masters how to handle it without making a complete mess of things."

Sir Dennis reached for his battered Peterson pipe. "Or to help the Chinese to figure out how to undo what someone in their government may have done. So bloody minded of them about Taiwan, willing to sacrifice their own economic progress to reclaim something they haven't had in sixty years. The deal they struck with us on Hong Kong worked out nicely. It's still independent for all practical purposes, a Special Autonomous Region."

"I agree. What kind of capitalists are these Chinese, anyway?" Rubenstein joked.

"Indeed."

1830 EST

The Dugout

Watertown, Massachusetts

Soxster sat in a room lit by the light from seven flat screens. He was in the Dugout, a computer facility more capable than those run by most information technology companies. The Dugout, however, had been built with devices found in dumpsters in parking lots behind information technology companies—castoffs rebuilt and improved by Soxster, Greenmonsta, Yankeehater, Fenwayfranks, and the rest of the hacker gang that rented the space in the old shoe factory. They all had day jobs at universities and high-tech corporations in the Boston area. By night, they got to their passion, exploring cyberspace, its dark recesses, its faulty glitched-up networks, its unprotected systems around the world.

"When we find an app, a program, that has a glitch, we tell the right people," Soxster had assured Jimmy Foley. He hadn't said how fast they did the notification.

The first to arrive at the Dugout that afternoon, Soxster had tried to track down Susan and Jimmy. Now that he had succeeded in finding Susan, he was sending a text message to Jimmy.

Jimmy Foley had just pulled into a roadside rest stop in the California desert, to empty his bruised kidneys. When he had found out that he could rent a Harley Heritage Softail near LAX airport, he had leapt at the chance. The bike had a fat front fork like the classic 1949 Hydra Glide, and was made to look original right down to the Fat Bob fuel tank. Now, with most of southern California behind him, he was thinking maybe he should have gone for the car that the office had reserved for him. He felt his PDA vibrate and flipped it open to read the text messages.

SOXSTR: James, assume you know what Connor found up north and what happened?

JXF3: Hey, no, what's my boss up to?

SOXSTR: She is ok. No damage. Just read her chart off the Stanford Hospital net. Minor concussion and some scrapes. Supposed to be released in a few hours. So much for HIPAA, eh? ;)

JXF3: Not funny dude.

SOXSTR: No, for real. U been cut off from the net? The blast at SCAIF. Susan was there, man.

JXF3: Yeah, been on a bike driving across the desert from LA. What happened?

SOXSTR: The Globegrid node near Stanford where Susan was visiting. It's on Moffett Field, NASA-Ames. 18 wheeler smashed thru the gate, killed some guards, then went kaplooee on the campus. Knocked all the windows out at the Googleplex, right in the middle of their afternoon massages and Pilates.

JXF3: And Connor was there when it happened?

SOXSTR: Must have been somewhere nearby. Can't ask her cause they took all her toys off her in the ER.

JXF3: Jesus. Thanks. I'll find out more from IAC.

SOXSTR: Wait. I found TTeeLer again on the net. Got him into a one-on-one chat room and he gave it up that he was TTeeLer. He's been hiding out in an apartment near Twentynine Palms. He's AWOL from the mob that hired him. Afraid to move.

JXF3: Did he tell you anything more why he left them?

SOXSTR: Just that they had him doing the usual money crime stuff on the net, then hacking infrastructure, then he heard about some plan to kill people and he boogied.

JXF3: Get his street address and I'll go get him.

SOXSTR: He wants to meet you in a public place first. Check you out.

JXF3: I'm meeting a friend at a grille called Globe & Anchor. See if you can get him to go there.

SOXSTR: Will do. Jimmy, watch your 6. This shit ain't over. Whatever this shit is. EOT.

1610 PST

The Globe and Anchor Grille and Pool Hall

Twentynine Palms, California

A cue ball smashed against racked balls as Jimmy walked into the dingy poolroom side of the Marine hangout. He scanned the few people in the room, looking for someone who would fit the description Soxster had just sent him. There were no matches. "Gimme a Bud, will yah. I'll be right out. Gotta wash some road off me," Jimmy Foley called out to the young blond bartender. As he strode by her on his way to the men's room, he judged from the diamond on her finger that she was a Marine's wife. Despite the motorcycle helmet and gloves, the dust and grime from the highway had made it through to his hands, face, and short cropped hair. He made an attempt to clean up, although the word *clean* was not what came to mind in the smelly men's room. Nonetheless, the cold water felt bracing on his face. He put his face in the sink and let the water run over his head. He flashed back to too many nights as Lt. James X. Foley III in Marine bars around the world.

After he toweled dry with the coarse, brown paper towels, he walked into the toilet stall and withdrew the Sig from under his biker jacket. It had no safety. He cocked it to put a round into the chamber and then thumbed the decocking lever. As he reentered the poolroom, Jimmy noticed a young man standing at the bar with two poured glasses of beer. He matched the description of TTeeLer. "Hey, didn't you use to hang out at the Dugout?" Jimmy said as he walked up to the bar.

"Long time ago, in a galaxy, far, far away. Or at least until they kicked me out," TTeeLer shot back, turning to view the room behind him. He did not offer to shake hands.

Jimmy nodded to the bartender. "Bag of pretzels." Then he pointed to a table in the corner, away from the door. "Let's sit down."

Opening the pretzel bag onto the table, Jimmy did his ingratiating teenager look over at the bartender. As he did, he said softly to TTeeLer, "My name is Jimmy. I am an armed police officer here on federal business. I can get you out of here safely, but we'll want to talk with you once we get somewhere secure."

"We can talk here if you're not recording this. But if you're wearing a wire, forget it. I am not incriminating myself," TTeeLer insisted.

"Calm down. Talk quieter. No, I am not wearing a wire. I am here to get you out, safely."

TTeeLer shook his head, "Not tonight. In the morning. I have to spend the night with Naomi. She's this single mother in the apartment next to mine. I want her and the kid to follow me out of this shithole town. And I have a lot to explain to her tonight."

Jimmy watched two off-duty Marines playing pool. "It's not safe to go back there if someone has made you while you have been out of the building. This is a small town."

"No shit, Sherlock," TTeeLer said, hanging his head down. "But I think the goons probably stopped looking for me in town. Last thing they think I'd do is stay here."

"Okay, so let's talk. Who are they?" Jimmy asked.

"I don't know who the big guys are. I just see the local staff. Mainly Americans. Goons for security and some cyber-savvy crooks, who get instructions and ideas from some off-planet being, L.A., Moscow, I don't know where. A higher intelligence than them, anyway." TTeeLer was very stressed out and twitchy. His dark blond hair was stringy. Jimmy took him to be about twenty-two, maybe a few years older.

Jimmy put his head in his left hand, obscuring his mouth to anyone looking at him. With his right, he felt for the Sig on his waist and he kept an eye on the door. "So let's start with the money. What did they have you do to raise money?"

"Usual, at first. Phishing messages for bank accounts and credit cards. Then we forgot about the banks and hacked into the credit-card clearing companies, pick up a couple of hundred thousand names, card numbers, socials. Big bucks. Then we started dropping this app, Ethercap, onto cable TV and DSL systems in wealthy neighborhoods. Remotely, of course. Cable or DSL, they're nothing more than a local area ethernet. Then we'd pick up every e-mail, every web page anybody on the street saw or sent. Some kinky stuff, but also big online stock-trading accounts. Easy to pick off their passwords with a keystroke logger. Open a bank account in the Caribbean. Sell the stock, bank transfer the money out. Easy pickings."

Jimmy kept smiling.

"Then we hit on this sweet deal with the music sharing systems, peer-to-peer. Turns out in every company, some idiot has downloaded music sharing software. You just go online and instead of searching for 'Beatles Greatest Hits,' you type in 'Merger Plans' or 'New Product Plans' or 'Personnel Files' and you get the company's secrets right through their firewall." At that thought, TTeeLer smiled.

"All of which you then sell on the Net," Jimmy mumbled. "Soxster said something about infrastructure? What's that all about?"

"That's where it all started to get all weird. They were having us hack into the power company and shit. Map the network. Leave a trapdoor to get back in easy. SCADA systems. Railroads, pipeline companies, Army bases. I couldn't see the money in it, but hey, they still paid me the big bucks, some in cash and some in direct deposit. Deposits came from a bank in Kuwait."

Jimmy sipped slowly at the beer, not wanting to have to go back to the bar or ask the bartender to come to the table. "But that's not why you left, went AWOL."

"Not AWOL, I quit. I just didn't tell them I quit, because my guess is that it's the Hotel California, you can never leave." More off-duty Marines came into the room and got cue sticks and beers. "No, I left when I heard them talking about needing to hack in somewhere to change the formula on something. He said, 'It'll kill 'em all, hundreds, maybe thousands.' Listen, whatever your real name is, Jimmy, I will steal from you in cyberspace if you are stupid enough to let me, but I am no killer. Nobody's giving me the needle in some state pen. So I waited for the next cash disbursement and left the reservation a week later."

A Marine had started to hit on the bartender and was now getting yelled at by about three others, confirming Foley's suspicion that her husband was in the Corps. Things looked like they would settle down peacefully. "Where is the reservation?"

"Near town, not far, but outside. I got out by hopping in the back of a delivery van. Hopped out at his next stop about twenty minutes later and I was in town. They never let us go into town since the day we showed up out here. But the reservation is big. Lots of buildings, satellite dishes, runway. Shit, man, they even had little UAVs, RPVs, you know, planes without pilots. And a lotta guns."

Jimmy was using his detective training in interrogation. Just let the subject talk. Do not make a big deal out of what you want to know, pick it up in pieces, come back to it. "So the formula they're going to change so that a bunch of people die. Any idea—"

TTeeLer hit the table with his fist. "Man, I have racked my brain. I mean, the whole reason I hung around for a week after I got my cash was just to see if I could find out what shit they're planning, but I got nothing. And I think some of them were getting suspicious of me askin' about things."

"Ever see any Chinese? Russians? Arabs?" Jimmy queried.

"Russians, yeah, but only a few at our place. But I'm sure there are other places, doing other shit. We were just here because they were really interested in what was going on at the base, but they wouldn't let me in on that shit. Enough for tonight, man. I'll tell you more when I get the written deal, the no prosecution deal. Tomorrow. "

Jimmy tried to think if he had offered him that. "Sure. Tomorrow. When and where?"

TTeeLer looked around the pool hall. "There's a 7-Eleven near

Amboy and Adobe. Ten o'clock tomorrow morning. There'll be three of us, including a kid who's four. And bring some help, buddy, just in case." Jimmy Foley watched for any reactions in the room as TTeeLer walked toward the back of the hall, then ducked through the kitchen door. At least, Jimmy thought, the kid was smart enough not to walk out the front door, but not smart enough to stay out of trouble.

Almost a half hour later, Jimmy looked up from his PDA to see Dr. Mark Rathstein coming toward him. "Foley, sorry I'm late." He was trim, in a blue polo shirt and khakis, with graying hair and glasses. "Good to see you. Long time. You look great. Welcome to Twentynine stumps."

"Dr. Rathstein, didn't expect you would want to meet in a pool hall," Jimmy said, thrusting a hand out. Mark Rathstein, he knew from his Marine days, was a Navy doctor who also had a Ph.D. in electrical engineering.

"I come here to work when I want to get away from the office," the doctor said, and then yelled to the bartender, "Two Coors Lights."

"When I saw you were coming, I checked that it was you, then got myself assigned as your host," Rathstein said. "You left NYPD?"

"No, Doc, just got assigned down in D.C. to work with the spooks for a year, to learn how Feds think. Think of it as field research. Supposed to increase my chance for promotion. Great to see you, too, and thanks for volunteering to show me around. So, what is this place out here in the middle of nowhere?"

The doctor waited while the waitress deposited two cold mugs of Coors and a bowl of popcorn. "How's your dad doing? Great guy. Did he retire yet, or is he still doing law at seventy-plus?"

Jimmy winced. "Thanks for asking. Yeah, Dad retired. Had to. Fast-onset Alzheimer's. They can't do anything for him. He's in a home near my brother's on Long Island."

"Sorry, Jim. My mother went that way," Rathstein whispered. He took a small sip of froth and beer. "So you asked to see the base here? Marine desert training base. Amazing you never got stuck here before going to Iraq. What we're doing at the hospital is an extension of what we did a few years ago in Bethesda. Back then we were giving Marines from Iraq new arms and legs, lightweight, electronic, tied directly to the brain. Now we're giving them new arms and legs before they've lost the ones they were born with, so they don't get shot up in the first place."

Jimmy leaned across the table. "Doc, listen, as a jarhead, we all owe you guys a world of thanks. The body armor in Iraq saved lives by protecting our trunks, but not our limbs. We had more guys lose limbs and live than in any war before. Thousands. What you guys at Bethesda did with your gizmos was make those lives worth living." Jimmy toasted him, clinking his mug against the doctor's. "How's this new stuff work?"

Dr. Rathstein beamed, excited to share the story of his work. "Think spacesuit. Not just Kevlar plates here and there, but the entire body is inside a suit that is heated and air conditioned. The suit monitors body functions and reports problems, fixes some of them by itself with medication patches and injections. There's liquid nutrition supplied. And, of course, the whole thing is bullet- and flame-resistant and Netcentric, connected with an internet address."

"Bullet resistant ain't bulletproof," Jimmy said while dripping yellow mustard on a pretzel. "Sounds like a heavy load to be luggin' 'round on top of all the weapons and shit they have to carry."

"That's the whole point!" Rathstein chuckled. "All of their limbs are server motor–assisted. They can run faster than a sprinter, throw a ball farther than the best quarterback, jump higher than a track-and-field star. The exoskeleton suit lets them carry over a hundred and twenty pounds of additional equipment on outside hooks with little or no effect on speed or motion. A few battalions of them could beat any army in the world."

Foley put down his beer mug and stared at the doctor. "Shit. We're talking Imperial storm troopers, like in *Star Wars,* with the helmets and all?"

"Sort of. The suits come in green or desert camouflage, not bright white like in the movies. Yes, they have helmets, with air filtration and built-in radios, intranet connectivity that you can see using a visor that also does night vision and telescopic. The listening system has 'dog ear' parabolics. And you literally have eyes in the back of your head, because there's a camera in the rear of the helmet that allows you to see what's behind you." This time Rathstein took a gulp of beer. "Don't you want to ask if you can take a leak?"

Jimmy laughed. "I assumed you could do that. You probably recycle it into Gatorade so the gyrenes don't short circuit your space-suits. What I was puzzling out was how you could take a dump."

"That is still a problem, I admit," the doctor said in a more subdued manner. "But with liquid nutrition and certain medications, the intervals when that becomes necessary can be extended to seventy-two hours or so, for now."

Jimmy almost choked on his mouthful of beer. "That's great, Doc, now the Army guys will be right when they say us jarheads are all full of shit."

"No, no. The Army has a similar suit under test at Fort Irwin over by Barstow. Ours is better," Rathstein said, his finger jabbing at the air. "And we have two companies here wearing them in field conditions. They have only one company. We've been in full suit for weeklong operations, with several changes of batteries, of course. They've only gone three days at a time in the suit. Tonight we're going to prove ours is better in a head on test. We're playing them in baseball. And you have a seat on the first-base line."

1750 PST

U.S. Marine Desert Training Facility

Twentynine Palms, California

They drove onto the base in Dr. Rathstein's hydrogen-cell Chevy Suburban. He had a visitor's pass ready for Foley. A few minutes inside the sprawling base, they came to a halt before a sand dune and got out. The sun had just set and there was still pale orange light in the west, reflecting off the few clouds on the horizon. In the east the sky was already black and the stars were brightening. Jimmy remembered now how cold it could get in the desert on a winter's night. And how quiet it could be.

"What's here?" Jimmy asked as they walked toward the dune.

"The baseball game," Rathstein said, as though it were obvious. "The Marine Superskels against the Army Spacetroopers." He continued to walk up the dune.

At the top of the dune, Foley looked down into the shadows. He made out a few tables on the left with people sitting at them, and a single bench with four people on the right. They appeared to be watching something, but there was nothing to see. He blinked and stared out as far as possible. In the dusk, in the distance, he made out what might be a man standing in the sand. Then he heard a sharp ping, the sound of a ball hitting a metal baseball bat.

"Let's go get helmets so we can see the game," Rathstein said as he jogged down the slope.

Fitted with a sand-colored, oversized football helmet, Foley was given a quick tutorial in its use. The visor had a night-vision device. A projection that appeared to float in front of him showed statistics on the game, like a Fox Box. It also showed real-time statistics, how far the ball had been hit and where, how far the fielder had thrown it and how fast. The Army was up by three in the bottom of the fourth. The Marines' left fielder had just caught a ball and then thrown straight to the plate to get the third out by stopping the runner from first. He had thrown 2,408 feet, from somewhere out in the darkening desert. There were no lights on the field, but with the visor Jimmy could see players scattered over a great distance bounding across the sand the way Neil Armstrong had jump-walked on the moon. Each of their jumping strides took them almost eight feet into the air and landed them in sand almost twenty feet ahead.

As the flying teams changed sides for the top of the fifth inning, a man wearing a tan tracksuit came over to the bench. He was not wearing a helmet, sporting instead a set of dark, wraparound sunglasses. "Mark, I assume this is our guest, Detective Foley? I'm Bill Chin, DARPA project director at the Palms. We thought you'd like to see our project in action before you meet with the security guys in the morning. Enjoying the game?"

"I'm not sure Major League Baseball has anything to worry about yet. No city could build a park big enough for these guys," Jimmy joked. "There's definitely not enough open room in the Bronx."

"I don't think what our troops are wearing will be the style for the New York Yankees anytime soon. The game is just a way to let the guys get used to their combat suits. And a little PR for the Pentagon brass to show at the next appropriations hearing," Chin said, sitting down next to Foley on the bench. Chin held his right arm out and felt his own tracksuit with a gloved left hand. "This tracksuit will be all the rage in Manhattan in two years. The civilian suit. Doesn't stop bullets, but it does everything else the combat suit does. And it comes with a fly and back flap. Wall Street will love it. The glasses could give you a full Bloomberg board projected out front. You can wear a flexible keyboard or tabloid on your arm or just speak the computer instructions into your mouthpiece, or as I like to call it, your Chin piece."

He demonstrated unfolding a flexible tabloid computer screen from the tracksuit's right arm. "And when you're getting too excited about your day trading, your onboard cardiologist program calls to tell you that your vitals are elevated."

Jimmy played with the flexitab computer for a few seconds. "Why not just have the suit give you CPR?"

"Oh, it could. It could also give you a sedative and call for an ambulance, since it knows exactly where you are on the enhanced GPS grid," Dr. Rathstein added.

"The reality is, Mr. Foley, that everyone who will have one of these suits will be as close to Superman as we are going to become until we build some sort of comic-book antigravity device someday," Chin replied. "The standard medicine kit can keep you awake for seventy-two hours with no side effects. You could lift a small car with one arm. You don't have X-ray vision, but you do have telescopic and night vision. You're directly wired to the internet, so all the knowledge in the world is instantly available to you and you can talk, chat, text, or e-mail anyone anywhere. You are part of the connected consciousness."

Foley, who had taken off his helmet, looked at Chin in the dark. "So how much will it be at Macy's menswear?"

"I bet we could get it down to a little more than one hundred K a suit in two years," Chin said and smiled.

"If you're taking orders, I'm a forty-four long," Jimmy shot back, "but I think I'll need a pay raise. At that price, not many folks will be including that in their 2014 fall wardrobes."

"No, not many," Rathstein chimed in, "but then, in the comic books there was only one Superman and we're talking about there being tens of thousands of supermen."

"Sounds great." Jimmy got up to watch the game better. "Unless you're one of the other ten billion people on Earth."

"Why did the SCAIF attack fail?" The man they called "the General" sat in the chair by the fireplace. The lights in the room were off.

"They made it through the main gate at Moffet as planned. The two in the lead car took out the gatehouse and the police car with grenades, and then the truck pulled through. The truck got halfway down the road toward the computer lab, but then it blew up," the Asian man answered. "The guys in the lead car didn't stay around to find out why." He heard logs collapsing in the hearth as the fire burned through them. He heard the General exhale, a long breath, through his nose.

"It failed because we have to use these amateurs, because we recruit under false flags," the General said as he stood to tend to the fire, "because we seek to do this all with few casualties. Minimize collateral damage. Nonsense." He tamped down the crumbling logs with a poker. "Specifically, it failed because that black woman drove a car into the side of the trailer and that set off the bomb prematurely. I had an observer there." He placed another log on the embers.

The Asian man was disturbed that the General knew more than he did about why the attack had failed. There was something, however, that he was sure the general did not know yet. "The two in the lead car are safe. They changed cars and drove down the Pacific Coast Highway to Carmel. They're holed up in a cabin at a small hotel there. Waiting until things calm down. Waiting for their next assignment."

The General reseated himself. "At least the dog attacks worked. Maybe they'll realize now that those dogs had ears all this time. Such good stock tips. Well, the internet and cyberspace has been hit. Now we have gone after their robotics. Even this crowd in the White House will be able to figure out that their technology is under attack."

The Asian man stood silently, thinking about the failed truck bomb. Finally, he spoke: "If I may ask, who was the observer you had at SCAIF?"

"The observer? The observer is a man who eliminated two people in a cabin at a small hotel in Carmel a short while ago."

5 | *Thursday, March 12*

Chen Fei sat in the cockpit, listening to the briefing in his head-set as his aircraft idled on the taxiway in the early-morning light. He would lead the three-ship mission today, a great honor. Today the targets would be aircraft, remotely piloted. This would be the first day that they would test the airborne laser gun system, one air-craft against another. If it worked, and he knew it would, it would give Taiwan the technological edge over China. One aircraft equipped with a laser could engage a dozen or more enemy fight-ers. The laser could fire at distances greater than the longest Chinese air-to-air missile. It could switch from one target to an-other in nanoseconds. The Chinese on the mainland had nothing like it in development. Once they knew Taiwan had it, the main-land air force would be deterred.

Chen Fei knew the state of the Mainland's People's Liberation Army's air defense capabilities because he held the highest clearances of any of Taiwan's test pilots. He alone among the pilots was also in the special security clearance compartment that allowed him to read the progress of the American laser program. Every day, the computer warfare unit at the Lung Tan Air Force Base summarized what had happened in the development and testing of the American system by the Boltheed corporation at the secret facility in the Nevada desert. It had been that way for five years. Everything the Americans had done, the Taiwan engineers had copied, every mistake and failure, every technological breakthrough and engineering design. Only three times in those five years had the Boltheed computer network changed in ways that kept the Taiwan warriors out, and then only for a matter of days. The firmware implants in the firewall and intrusion-detection system that the Taiwan intelligence agents had inserted in the network were never detected.

Now Boltheed was ready to test the Advanced Tactical Laser Cannon with a squadron of the new F-35 Block 20 fighters over the Nevada and California deserts, and unknown to Boltheed and the Americans, Taiwan would also be testing a squadron of its aircraft over the Taiwan Straits.

"Gentlemen, this is a very big day for Taiwan." Chen Fei recognized the voice of the program commander, Colonel Zhang. "To review one final time, following takeoff to the north, you will proceed down the west coast over the Straits at altitudes between forty and forty-five thousand feet, depending on cloud formations. Somewhere after passing Penghu Islands on your left, you will detect two formations of drones made up to look like PLA fighters. They will be armed with air-to-air missiles and cannon. You will take out the lead fighter at maximum lethal range, before he can engage you with missiles. Then close and eliminate the remaining aircraft in dogfight maneuvers. Make sure you drop all the targets over water. If you see real PLA aircraft in the vicinity, abort the mission. We do not want them to know what we have yet. Not yet. Good flying."

With that, Chen Fei called the tower for permission to take off, received it, powered back on the single jet engine, and the aircraft bolted forward down the runway. He saw the runway markers pass by quickly, 1,000 feet, 2,000 feet, 3,000, and soon the aircraft was in flight. After two minutes, he called to his wingmen. Their aircraft were right behind him. "Jin dui, this is Jin tou zi. Let's get to altitude fast to save fuel. "

Fifteen minutes into the flight, the three ship went feet wet over the East China Sea and banked left to begin the run south, parallel to the coast. By choosing this route, Colonel Zhang, commander of the laser program, was simulating real-world conditions. He insisted on real missiles on the target aircraft. These were the skies where Taiwan's air force might one day have to defend the island against the far more numerous PLA air force. When the laser cannon shot down the target drones, they would fall in the water, not on Taiwanese villages. The Chinese would see the exercise on their radar and be impressed with the state of the Taiwan Air Force's training, but they would not know that the drones were downed with lasers. Not yet.

Following the success of the independence-minded Taiwan National Party in the December elections, Chen Fei knew that the prospects of a military confrontation were not just theoretical. Despite their mutual economic dependence, Beijing and Taipei had been hurling invective at each other for the last four months to a degree unseen in twenty years. Mainland officials talked publicly about invading the island if it formally declared its independence from China.

"Jin Two, drop to angles thirty-eight. Jin Three, go up to angles forty-five. When at altitude, flip on scanning radar at low power. Scan from two hundred eighty degrees to eighty degrees. Copy?" Chen Fei's two wingmen moved their aircraft above and below his and then both turned on the smaller of the aircrafts' two lasers. Together the two aircraft would scan over twenty five thousand cubic kilometers of airspace, using their lasers to look for the targets. These lasers acted as radar, but unlike radar they gave off no electronic signature, no radio frequency emission, that would allow other fighters to detect their presence. Some advanced American aircraft carried laser-detection systems, but the laser beam had to strike them at exactly the correct angle and stay there for two to three nanoseconds for the detector to register.

The Penghu Islands navy base was coming up on the left, the east, and the sun was high enough now to light the base against the coastal mountains behind it. There were scattered light clouds at about twenty thousand feet. They looked yellow in the morning light. Before his aircraft had even passed Penghu Islands, the lower wing man, Jin Two, called in: "Target identified. Two ship formation at angles thirty, sixty degrees off my nose, ninety klicks out. Tracking west to east-northeast."

Chen Fei acknowledged, "Roger, Jin two. Continue track." He quickly switched to his long range electro-optical system and visually acquired the target. They were made to look like PLA J-12s. Chen Fei called in to Control. "Jin touzi, acquired two target drones simulating J-12s at angles thirty, climbing and heading toward the coast at Penghu Islands. Moving in for long-range attack."

In his headset, Chen Fei heard the familiar voice of the one of his fellow pilots who today was guiding the exercise. "Jin touzi, this is Control. Acknowledge target acquired. Do not, repeat not, drop target over land, and remember, when you go to engage in dogfight mode, there will be more drones."

Chen Fei turned up the power on his idling laser and dove from forty thousand feet to thirty-five. The ocean below was moving by fast. He touched the toggle switch that locked the laser's pointing mechanism onto the target that he was tracking with the electro-optical system. Then he powered the laser up to tracking mode. The green numbers flashing on the bottom right of his screen indicated how close the target was: 65, 60, 55 kilometers out. Chen Fei hit the power level again, moving the laser into combat mode and setting the range. He had chosen the drone on the right from his perspective. At fifty kilometers, he flipped up the protective cover on his joystick and hit the attack button with his thumb. He paused and hit it again. Then he called out into his headset: "Fox Four, two bursts."

The laser gun on the underbelly of the aircraft, where the cannon had been originally, had emitted a 300 kW burst for almost a second. The beam had traveled at the speed of light and then, four seconds later, another had leaped from the aircraft. The heat from the beam had caused the target aircraft's missiles to heat to the point of exploding on the aircraft's own launch rail. Now the solid-state laser had to cool for up to thirty seconds before it was ready to fire again.

"Roger that. Jin Two here. I can see the target. It split in half. Splash one."

"Jin Three: I count four more targets at angles three eight. Eighty klicks out. Heading one seven five degrees and coming fast."

Chen Fei had felt the adrenaline building, but now it was a rush. Even though it was only an exercise, this would be the first dogfight in which one side used lasers instead of missiles. How quickly could they drop the remaining five drones as they maneuvered against them? He barked into his headset, "Jin Two engage the wingman. Jin Three, with me, let's get the four ship. Tally-ho!" He pulled back on the joystick to return to forty thousand feet, keeping Jin Three above him and to his right. "Let's swing around to heading two seven zero so we can come at them out of the sun. Then we fire our own little suns." He checked the laser control. It had returned quickly to full power after the two long-distance bursts. Now he dialed it down to close in combat mode.

He could hear Jin Two describing how he was engaging one-on-one with his target, but it was distracting. He dropped the volume on that frequency, and as he did he heard a loud pulsing in his ears. He knew what the noise meant before he heard the words from his radar warning receiver: "Alert. Alert. Radar lock on." Despite being blinded by the rising sun, the oncoming fighters had seen him on their radar. Chen Fei switched the laser to automatic antimissile fire and flipped his own radar from standby to scan. Almost as soon as he had, the laser control panel went from green READY to red FIRING.

Chen Fei noted four short bursts recorded on the panel as the laser shot out to where it thought an incoming missile would be. Immediately, he saw two small flashes in front of and below his aircraft. His laser had blown up the incoming missiles. With the laser now slaved to his target-acquisition radar, he fired back, hitting two bursts. The explosion below him was instant and much brighter than the destruction of the air-to-air missiles. He had destroyed another drone.

Jin Three had fired at almost the same time, causing another explosion, another aircraft destroyed. "Splash number three," his wingman called out. Chen Fei checked his radar to find the other two aircraft in front of him. They were climbing fast, probably on afterburners, trying to get above him for a look-down, shoot-down kill. He caught a yellow glow in his peripheral vision and quickly looked down at his laser control panel. The blinking yellow light showed the word CHARGING. He could not fire. The eight bursts he had fired had dropped the power level below the minimum. As Chen Fei thought for the first time how much trouble he would be in if his expensive laser-carrying aircraft were destroyed, he pulled back hard on the joystick and went to afterburners on the engine, standing his aircraft straight up for a 10G climb.

The dark of the cockpit was suddenly flooded with light as the door in the back of the room was thrown open. Colonel Zhang burst into the pilots' cockpit room. "Break off the attack and get those birds out of there now!" No one was supposed to enter when pilots were remotely flying their aircraft; they could lose control and crash their vehicles.

Chen Fei stood to attention, pulling off his headset. "Colonel Zhang, we are in the middle of the test."

"No, you are not! The target drones are still aloft, about fifty kilometers further south. You are shooting down real PLA fighter aircraft! And they have real pilots in their aircraft!"

An alarm sounded and Chen Fei looked back down at his cockpit. While he had been standing at attention, a PLA fighter had shot a radar-guided missile at his RPV. Chen Fei had not noticed or responded. The automatic antimissile laser had not enganged because it was still recharging. On the front screen of the wraparound cockpit windshield, words appeared in red on a black background: "Your aircraft has been destroyed." For the first time, Chen Fei was glad that he was not actually in his aircraft.

0630 PST

Marine Desert Training Facility

Twentynine Palms, California

Jimmy Foley had risen early at the visiting officer's quarters, donned his running gear, and set out to do five miles in the cold morning desert. He needed the exercise, but he also wanted a chance to think. As he stretched outside the VOQ, he realized that it was now four years since he had run the New York Marathon. He had finished in three hours and nine minutes. Not bad; it had qualified him for the Boston Marathon, which he had never gotten around to running. Now, four years on, he wondered if he could do it in under three-thirty. He headed out, thinking again about the idea that the rich would soon be able to buy spin-off technology from the Pentagon, exoskeleton suits, giving them great strength and tying their bodies into cyberspace for diagnostics. He laughed out loud as he ran, thinking about what his new friend Soxster could do with that.

He had woken up twice during the night, anxious about the meet with TTeeLer this morning. The FBI's L.A. field office had taken charge of the planning after Jimmy had reported in to the Intelligence Analysis Center and they had passed word to FBI headquarters. Already FBI personnel were working behind the counter at the 7-Eleven, the dry cleaners next door, the used-car lot across the street. He wondered whether the Feebs would get anything more out of TTeeLer than he had. Chances were he would just clam up until a U.S. Attorney gave him immunity in writing. The running was coming easier; he was moving smoothly down the road. The anxieties of the night were giving way to the rising endorphins from the run, but he realized that he was going to have to find his own way to geo-locate the ranch where TTeeLer had worked. Or maybe Soxster could do it.

As he turned a corner by a barracks, Jimmy saw a company of Marines jogging toward him, returning from their morning five-mile run. Despite the cold, they were in tan shorts and T-shirts, not spacesuits. As he approached them, he yelled out, "Hoo-rah!" Some gave a weaker "Hoo-rah" in return. He missed the camaraderie, the certainty of being a Marine. He did not miss Iraq. If he had had an exoskeleton suit in Iraq, he thought, he might never have been injured, might never have lost that year in hospitals in Haditha, in Ramstein, in Bethesda. He might still be in the Marines, be a major by now.

But he had found a good place in the NYPD. And he had found Janice. Never thought he'd marry an investment banker, but he had and it was working. She wasn't clingy or possessive. She gave him his space. They had their separate careers; some people thought they had their separate lives, but they were wrong. How many married couples could still have videophone sex like they had had last night? When they were actually together in the same place, it was even better, perfect. The two weeks on Mustique at Christmas had been heaven. As he thought about diving with Janice in that turquoise Caribbean undersea world, he realized he was approaching the giant baseball field where he had seen the game last night. As he ran up the sandy slope, he heard yelling from the other side.

Below him, as he hit the crest of the dune, he saw dozens, maybe scores of the black-spacesuited Marines spread out across the field. Regular Marines and civilians were scattered around, attending to the suited supermen. He spotted Dr. Rathstein talking to six men at a table at the bottom of the dune. They seemed agitated. He jogged up to them.

"Jimmy!" Rathstein seemed startled to see him. "You already heard what happened?"

Foley caught his breath, filling his lungs. "No, Doc, hadn't heard. What did happen?"

Dr. Rathstein signaled for the men with him to step away, to go about the mission he had given them. "It's awful, Jimmy," he said, running his fingers through his hair. "On this morning's exercise, we lost touch with Echo Company. All the telemetry from their suits shut down. We came out here looking for them and found them like that. . . ."

Jimmy looked at the troops in the spacesuits. Some were standing in the parade rest position, legs spread apart, left hand in the small of their backs. Some had both hands behind their necks. Others had their arms spread out behind them, as though they were about to take flight. A few had their arms up, as if surrendering. None were moving.

"We're trying to get them out of the suits now, but they're all asleep. Looks like the suits gave them a big dose of painkillers and sleeping agent, then the suits froze up, turned off. I think some kids have OD'd." Rathstein turned and looked out at the statue-like men of Echo Company. "It will be the end of the program," Rathstein continued. "The Marines will shut it down. I can hear the generals now: 'Can't have our boys attacked by your suits, Doctor. What if it had been war?' "

Foley thought that the man was actually about to cry. "How did it happen?"

Rathstein shook his head and said, "I have no fucking idea." A gust of wind blew sand onto his face.

0730 PST

Base Operations Center

Marine Desert Training Area

Twentynine Palms, California

"Soxster, this shit is not funny," Jimmy Foley said into his headset. "I got a hundred Marines in sick bay out here, drugged up like dopeheads." Foley was standing in the middle of Navy investigators and Marines who had set up a command post to figure out what had happened and prevent it from happening again. They were also contacting the families of the hospitalized Marines from Echo Company.

"No, Jim, really I know—it's just the dog bots, man. You gotta admit that was great. Thousands of silly-rich guys shitting their pants as their status symbols go nuts and attack them, after having posted their tax returns and medical records in chat rooms all over cyberspace." Soxster could barely get the words out between laughs. "Every hacker at Infocon Alpha in Vegas will be claiming credit."

"People got hurt, a couple died, dude," Jimmy intoned in his deep voice. "So who the hell did it?" He could hear Soxster tapping away on a keyboard. He waited.

"Okay. So the hack on the Marines was an RF signal to get around the firewall on the base network. Short distance. They called the server they used 'Mini-UAV3.' So maybe they bounced the signal down onto the troops from a mini-UAV flying above the base. Those things are so small, nobody woulda seen it," Soxster said, still clicking away on the other end of the call.

"Those things are like toy airplanes, they don't fly very far," Jimmy noted. Soxster didn't reply. He was onto a lead, doing a route trace-back, his mind running down digital corridors in cyberspace. He had called up the record of his first chat room meet with TTeeLer, when he was still at the ranch. TTeeLer had used an anonymizer, a server meant to hide his tracks and obscure his real online identity. Soxster was now into the anonymizer's billing record.

"This is all for national security, right?" Soxster asked as he sped ahead. "You got a Get Out of Jail Free card, Jim, right?"

"Yeah, yeah, sure, whaddya got?" Foley asked, wondering whether he could get an ex post facto waiver of a few laws, or whether they would even get caught in the first place.

"Okay. So when TTeeLer was chatting with me, he was originating on PacWest's network, in southern California, coming out of the telcoms hotel in downtown L.A., let's see, shooting out east to the giga-router in the San Bernardino hosting center, on to the Desertnet Internet Service Provider. . . ."

"Good, good, then what?" Jimmy urged him on.

"Hang on, hang on, dude, you think this shit is easy?" Soxster mumbled as his fingers flew across the keys. "Hold your pee."

Jimmy said nothing, but his breathing sounded heavy on the line. He began counting ceiling tiles and trying not to think of how many laws they were breaking.

"Desertnet's main router is on Ocotillo Ave. in Twentynine Palms. The packets came in from a smaller neighborhood router up Del Valle Drive and into them from a WiMax on Rainbow Canyon Road. It gets a relay from a WiMax transmitter that's named 'Bagdad Road.' You got a Bagdad out there? Isn't there a letter *h* in Baghdad?"

"You gotta be kidding me. A town called Bagdad?" Jimmy shook his head. "I had a bad enough time in the real Baghdad. What's with one here?"

On the other side of the country, in the Dugout, Soxster ran one more check. "Well, unless I am badly mistaken, the ranch that TTeeLer was operating out of with the other hackers is within about two miles of that town. And they have a really wideband satellite dish. Look for the dish."

"You're the man!" Jimmy yelled in the Marine base's operations center. "Sox, I love you, buddy." He realized that a Naval Investigative Services agent was looking at him oddly. "Not you, this guy in Cambridge. Never mind. Look, we need some helicopters."

1435 PST

Route 101

Santa Rosa, California

"I am perfectly fine. They released me," Susan insisted into her mouthpiece as she accelerated to pass an eighteen-wheeler. "Sam, I don't care. You can call the attending yourself. Her name is Isabel Moreno and she actually saw me. You are doing long-distance diagnosis, Dr. Benjamin."

"I don't need to call her. If you had a concussion, even a minor one, you should still be under observation and bed rest. Any first-year would know that," Sam Benjamin insisted from his office at Johns Hopkins Medical Center in Baltimore. "Besides, it doesn't sound from the press reports like anyone near that blast would have only a minor concussion."

Sam was the grounded one in the relationship, the practical one who did the planning and the worrying for both of them. He admitted that Susan was "more creative," but he thought it was the kind of creativity that most often emerged from chaos. As he stood by a nurses' station on the sprawling medical campus, he pictured his girlfriend about to pass out behind the wheel on some crowded

California freeway. And, as usual with Susan, there was nothing he could think to do about it.

Susan put the car on automatic freeway mode so that she could concentrate on the call. "Look, I'm going to take it easy. I'm driving up to wine country north of San Francisco. I've been invited by this famous computer scientist to visit him at his vineyard. It will be very restful, bubele, really. Besides, how many days has it been since you had eight hours' sleep, so look who's calling the kettle black." Susan knew how to counterpunch, how to get his hot buttons: using his grandmother's term of endearment for him, putting him on the defenses, playing on their racial difference.

She heard Sam exhale in exasperation at the other end of the call. "Okay, Suz, call me later today. And don't push yourself too hard. If you start getting dizzy, go lay down."

"Thank you, Dr. Benjamin. Would you recommend I pull over first?" she said, and chuckled. "Don't answer that. But there is a professional question I have for you. What do you think about connecting human brains to machines, to computers?"

"You don't need it," he joked. "Seriously? We've been doing it for over a decade. It's the only way to cure some forms of depression. You place a small battery behind the neckbone and run a wire deep into the central cortex. I do about one a month. There are lots of other applications, too—epilepsy, some forms of Alzheimer's. The guys over at the Marvin Center for the Brain here are doing all sorts of other experiments. If you pass out and end up with brain injury from a car crash, you can find out for yourself. So don't push your-self too hard today, for once."

"Yes, Doctor. No, seriously, I will, promise. Listen, I have to get off the highway now. I will call you later. Love you. Bye." She took control of the driving back from the autopilot program and put the car onto the exit ramp for River Road. It was her first time to Sonoma County and its Russian River region. As she drove down River Road to Westside Road, following the car's navigation sys-tem, she thought how different it was from the nearby Napa Valley she'd visited several years before. Where Napa was filled with tourist traps, buses, and wine-tasting rooms, one right next to the other, this area seemed more about growing the grapes. Field after field of vines stretched out alongside the narrow road.

When she'd told Soxster that Will Gaudium had agreed to see her and had suggested she come to his vineyard, the Cambridge hacker had insisted that she stop at the Kistler winery. "Kistler is the best American chardonnay, period. Remember I told you? You gotta stop there if you're in Russian River." Now she sat in the nearly empty parking lot, looking at the small, neat, stone building. She was glad for a chance to catch her breath. After a moment, she strolled down the beautiful stone walkway, past the little meditation pool and miniature waterfall, past the door to the tasting room, to the observation deck above the vineyard valley below. Spring was just beginning to bring green back to the valley's palette and to awaken the sleeping vines.

How would she explain to Sol Rubenstein why she was meeting with a retired corporate computer guru, when things were blowing up somewhere every day this week and the Pentagon was developing options to respond by doing something to China? Sol and Rusty had given her great flexibility. They had great confidence in her ability to think differently than the straitjacketed Washington bureaucracy. Indeed, Sol had stopped her from being part of the FBI-led investigation so that she would not be prejudiced by their assumptions. That had pissed her off initially, but now she was glad at what they had done.

Following her own instinct, with help from Margaret Myers, she had focused on what was being attacked, not who was attacking. That had brought her to SCAIF just in time. As disturbing as her partial memory was of the incident at SCAIF, it was what she had learned there before the attempted bombing that had really left her chilled. Sitting on the bench overlooking the valley, she called Professor Myers in Boston.

"Megs, before you say a word, let me just say I'm fine. Not even a scratch."

"I know, dear. Soxster pulled up your chart from the hospital. Oops, I'm not supposed to say that." Myers chuckled. "Where are you now?"

"In Russian River. I've got an appointment with the tech guy you told me about, Will Gaudium." Susan felt a calm coming over her from the beauty of the place.

"Well, if you're thinking you want to find out where some of the zero-publicity technology breakthroughs are, he'd be the man to know," Myers replied, looking out on the scullers on the river. She had never seen them this early in the year before.

"We have to find out where the leading-edge technologies you talked about are, some of the hidden ones without U.S. government funding, before they're set afire or blown up," Susan said, standing up and walking to the edge of the balcony over the vineyard valley.

"Well, Susan, if you can get Gaudium to talk to a Fed, you are going to the right source. He's so worked up about the risks of the new technologies that he's made it his business to know about them."

"I don't think it will be too hard for me to seem worked up about it too, Megs. Some of what I'm learning is . . . well, I was going to say scary, but let's be professional and just say that it raises many complex policy and ethical issues."

"Remember: facts, gaps, theories, then analysis," Myers chanted. "Problem is, we are short on everything but gaps. Off to class now. Call me if you need me. Be careful. Ciao."

Susan stared out at the beautiful, manicured valley below, thinking about the questions the technology breakthrough raised. Then, realizing where she was, she snapped out of her trance and headed for the tasting room, trying to remember Soxster's definition of malolactic. Twenty minutes later, frustrated by the tasting room's refusal to pour any chardonnay and having decided that she did not really care for their semillon blanc, she drove up to Gaudium's winery, Bacchanalia. She arrived twenty minutes early for her appointment and sat in the car in the tasting room parking lot. The tasting room seemed modeled on its famous neighbor, Kistler: small, with extensive fieldstone work, granite outcroppings, and small ponds. There seemed, however, to be a Japanese or Zen touch to the flora and garden architecture. It also offered an even more breathtaking view of the broad valley below.

Susan noticed that there were only two other vehicles in the parking lot, both Cadillacs, a DTS sedan and a hydrogen-cell Escalade SUV. Before she could get out of her rental car, a small gaggle bustled out of the Bacchanalia tasting room. Susan recognized the appearance of the group, the way the men and women looked, neat in their blue blazers and ties, the way they placed themselves relative to one another, the way they moved. It looked like a small Secret Service detachment doing an OTR, an Off the Record event, a private activity by a protectee. Now she saw who that protectee was, presidential candidate Senator Alexander George, the man in the center of the half dozen agents. He looked less coiffed than he had at the Kennedy School forum. He was wearing a windbreaker and jeans. So I'm not the only one who wants Gaudium's advice, she thought as she waited for the three-vehicle convoy to pull out.

Once inside, she was politely ushered into a special tasting room. Wood-paneled and appointed with modern leather couches, the room was all about the view. Its two picture windows showed the vine-filled valley below with a crispness and clarity that almost made them seem unreal, like an image on the new Very-High-Definition screens. "May I offer you some of our 2010 pinot?"

Gaudium said as he entered the room holding a bottle in one hand and offering the other to shake. He was taller than she had expected for some reason, with a thick crop of unruly brown hair and a weathered face. In an old checkered shirt and worn jeans, he might have been mistaken for the viniculturist just in from his fields. "Thank you for coming up here to see me. I almost never get down to Menlo Park anymore."

"No, no. Thank you for seeing me, especially on such short notice," Susan said, shaking his hand. His grip was strong and the skin felt callused, coarse. "I hope my coming didn't drive the senator away. I know how little he cares for those of us in the federal bureaucracy, except perhaps his Secret Service detail."

Gaudium motioned toward two chairs by the window. He waited until he was opening the bottle of pinot noir to respond. "Actually, Senator George is a very thoughtful man. We've been talking on and off for almost six years. I'm supporting him for President. I paid for some of the March on Washington last year." He poured some of the dark ruby-colored wine into two wide, stemless crystal glasses. "But you're right about him not wanting to have too many federal employees. Those guards were private. He doesn't think the taxpayers should have to pay for the protection of candidates at this stage in the campaign."

He spun the wine in the glass, sniffing its aromas. Susan copied his hand motion and breathed in a surprisingly strong but pleasant nose of fruit flavors. "Very nice," she offered after tasting a sip. "Light and smooth, but with so much flavor, and in waves."

"Rain came late that year. I'm so glad we delayed the crush. Everybody up here did. Best pinot since the 2004." Gaudium beamed. "Westside Road is its own little microclimate, and its been producing the best pinot for almost forty years now."

He closed his eyes as he sipped and held the wine in his mouth a moment, then swallowed and opened his eyes again to look at his guest. "But it's not the wine you came to talk about, if I understood your message correctly."

Susan put down her glass. "No. It's information science, computer technology. We're trying to understand why there've been these attacks on the internet beachheads and the Globegrid labs, on CAIN and SCAIF, and why now." Gaudium spread some cheese and fig on a plain cracker as Susan spoke.

"And you have a theory and you want me to react to it, right?"

"I do. Very good," she said, regretting her tone as she did. "I'm beginning to realize that computer science is about to make a major leap, at least in some countries." Gaudium nodded and sipped again at his wine. Susan continued, "Living Software that is close to flawless, massively parallel processors linked together, direct brain-machine interfaces. Put it all together and it's a big change, one that has somehow escaped Washington's collective consciousness."

Gaudium smiled knowingly. "Information technology is a tremendous addition to our planet. I know—I was there at the beginning of the internet explosion in the early nineties. That's how I can afford to be a winemaker with some of the most expensive patches of grapes in the country. But like anything else, it can be taken to an illogical conclusion, if you'll excuse the pun." Susan hadn't noticed a pun and Gaudium kept going.

"So, we are at an inflection point, a vector point with IT. And most people have not noticed. Living Software will never be flawless, but it will be close enough to make it difficult for us to regain control of it. And don't doubt for a minute that we have lost control of it. Humans did not write that software and we really do not know what's in it. All the operating systems and major applications have gotten so complex now.

"Then there came the 2009 Cyber Crash, and the government funded this Living Software monstrosity in response. It keeps changing, improving—and when it's combined with Globegrid, it'll be in most of the networks and systems in the U.S., Europe, and Japan." Gaudium's mood had changed as he spoke, growing more serious and agitated.

"Is it a threat to China, or to other nations not in the consortium?" Susan asked casually as she reached for a wafer.

"Of course. So, they say that the consortium will open up to the entire world at some point, but they don't say when. Naturally, China, Russia, and the others feel left out. But they may eventually be glad they are. Who knows what LS will decide to do once it examines the major networks and systems in this country? It could shut some of them off or create new ones. What if its efficiency criteria eventually decide humans aren't efficient? I know, I know, it sounds like some film you saw as a kid, but we really are moving in that direction. Machines are better at most things than people. Most people you see all day long are doing jobs that machines could do, and do better. How long will it take LS to figure that out and start acting on it by creating programs to do those jobs?

"And once people start buying BEPs, brain-enhancement packages, that connect them to cyberspace, LS will be inside human brains, too. So who wouldn't want a BEP that prevents Alzheimer's and other diseases of the brain, speeds up memory and thinking, provides direct linkage to all the public databases, makes it possible for all sensory experiences to be heightened? You'd pay the hundred thousand for that, wouldn't you, if you had that kind of money?" Gaudium paused, looking at Susan's expression. "No, I'm sensing that maybe you wouldn't. But most people would."

Susan looked out at the valley. "No, I wouldn't. But I am not a purist, I do take memory-enhancement pills now. The Center pays for them. It's just that I think that if you have a brain-computer connection, it runs a risk of blurring what it means to be human."

"Precisely!" Gaudium almost screamed in the tasting room. "What people should be focused on first, the greatest threat, is what the genomics and biological sciences are doing to what it means to be human. Bio Fabs are creating life to do the work of machines. Human Machine implants are silicon doing the work of carbon-based life." Gaudium jabbed his finger at the tabletop.

"I'm confused. I thought we were talking about the growing influence of computer science, not biology," Susan responded, feigning naïveté.

"Both are problems, and they're linked. But it is all about humans changing what it means to be human, creating a new species, splitting off a race that will soon enough look no more like we do today than we look like Neanderthals. That's what has already started with genomics moving beyond fixing to enhancing. Fixing was all right, because it meant raising people up to the norm by repairing genetic mistakes, like Tay-Sachs syndrome, diabetes, the rest. But enhancement? What enhancements do we order? Who is to decide? And who gets them? We know the gene that gives superior IQ by thickening the prefrontal cerebral cortex. Let's make it even bigger, see what that does."

As Gaudium's speed and volume rose, he did, too, leaving his chair and standing with his back to the picture window above the valley, focused on Susan. He had gone from mellow winemaker to furious evangelist. "Sure, replacing defective organs by having your own good stem cells grow a new bladder or liver is fine, but turning off the aging process in cells? Pretty soon the rich will never die, except by accident or violence. As if we didn't already have a population problem.

"And now they want superchildren! Believe me, it's further along than you think. They've gone underground because of the states that have passed laws against genomic engineering. But my investigators have found them. They're creating superkids, with all the flaws taken out and all the genetic enhancements designed in. Tall, blond or red haired, brilliant, everlasting. Our own little gods and goddesses. That's what people should be really worried about. That's what this election will be about!" He turned his head toward the valley, then back at her. "I'm sorry if I get excited . . ."

Susan stood up to reduce the physical distance between them, but even when she was standing, Gaudium towered over her. "No, it's okay. I think I understand, or at least I'm beginning to. I'm supposed to uncover secret activity by other governments, and I think what I'm uncovering is activity here in the U.S. that has been kept secret from most of us, maybe because we just don't understand it."

"No, Susan, it's more than the fact that it's just written up in technical journals that only scientists read. After the fights about abortion and then stem cells and evolution, the Transhumanist science community stopped revealing their research at conferences and in journals, as scientists normally would. They pretended it was to protect patents and intellectual property, but it was really because they feared the public's reaction would nip their science in the bud before they had a chance to develop it into marketable products. Once they get treatments that prevent cellular degeneration, boost IQ, replace eyes and ears with enhanced sensors, tie humans directly into the grid . . . *then* they will market their inventions to the rich and famous. Then everything will change. . . ." Gaudium took a deep breath to calm himself and then sipped the last of the wine in his glass.

She followed suit, then added: "That's what Senator George was talking about at Harvard. The rich will actually *be* smarter, instead of just thinking they are." Susan sat down on one of the tasting room's oak-backed chairs. "And if they turn off cellular degeneration, combine that with organ regeneration . . . those motherfuckers will live forever." She blushed. "Oh, I'm so sorry, I didn't mean to—"

"No, no, I love your passion. And you're right. Death, for the Enhanced, will only result from violence and accidents." Gaudium poured more pinot. "But they'd still be human. Except that when they add electronics into the body, nanobots roaming our bodies fixing things, when they allow the brain to connect to the grid to access data and to automatically report malfunctions, the way OnStar automatically tells the police when you have an accident in your car . . . Then they'd begin to become parts, just parts, of a larger network."

"A larger network whose software will have been written by . . . by software?" she added.

"Right. You see it, too." Gaudium opened another wooden panel on the wall, revealing a whiteboard. He began drawing. "So, here is a farm growing Frankenfood, some genetically enhanced fruit or vegetable. Humans act as the pickers, because in most cases we don't yet have machines that can do that well. Then the machines take over. They wash, destem, package it into cartons with bar codes or RFID tags. The machines decide what trucks the packages go on, what rail cars, or planes. They decide what stores they go to, based on what other machines have told them about inventories and sales. They decide on the price based on a sales intelligence software. You buy the box of tomatoes and the RFID tag tells the checkout system, and deducts funds from your account when you wave your debit card near the reader. When you get home, if you have one of those new intelligent fridges, your refrigerator reads the RFID tag so that it can tell you when the tomatoes are about to go bad. Perhaps it also tells a marketing intelligence system that Susan buys tomatoes twice a week. . . ."

"It's a good thing I can't afford one of those fridges then. Do most people know when they're using something connected to the internet?" she asked.

"All new devices are connected to your home wireless system, which is connected to the internet," he said in a dismissive tone, as if stating the obvious. "But don't you see the important thing here? Look at the flow of this system," he yelled, and moved the red marker across the whiteboard. "In that entire process with the tomatoes, the human is reduced to doing manual labor, the things requiring the least intelligence. I can show you hundreds of examples where the humans are reduced to being beasts of burden and the computer-controlled systems do the work requiring higher cognition. The Enhanced won't be doing the beast of burden jobs, of course. No, they will be interacting with machines at higher levels. Gold men. Silver men. Bronze."

Susan smiled. "I've heard that argument before. Plato's *Republic*. The classes cannot mix and order is preserved by the Magnificent Myth that keeps the bronze men under control."

"Absolutely right. End of democracy as we know it. End of humanity as we know it. Yes! That is the problem in a nutshell," Gaudium said, shaking his head in quick little moves. "The

Magnificent Myth or Noble Lie that Plato had in mind was telling the bronze men that the gods intended this three-tiered system and that the gold men were made better, even though they may not be. But with this neo-eugenics, these Enhanced humans will actually be better than any normal human. And so, eventually, the Enhanced humans will rule the lesser life-forms like us."

He stood there, still shaking his head. "Look, I'm going to Infocon Alpha in Vegas tomorrow morning in my VLJ. I'm giving the keynote. Why don't you come with me?"

Now she was going to have to explain to Sol and Rusty why she was flying off to Vegas with a man she had just met, in his personal Very Lite Jet, a man who seemed to be the prototype for the brilliant mad scientist. But she'd bet anything Gaudium knew where some of these underground labs were, and if she could find them, warn them about the attacks. . . . "I'd be glad to," she told him.

"You can spend the night in the guesthouse, then. And will you join me for dinner at seven?"

1730 PST

Twentynine Palms, California

"You'd better be right about this, Foley," Major Mike Zerbrowski was saying into his mouthpiece as the helicopter lifted off from the Marine base. "It's goin' to be hard to explain why I used Marines to go after a civilian complex."

Yes, I had better be right, Jimmy Foley thought. It had been a bad day so far. TTeeLer had missed the meet at the 7-Eleven and the FBI had eventually given up and most of them were lying around a pool at the Red Roof Inn.

Foley and the Marines watched the videotape from their Remotely Piloted Vehicle again. Flying out toward Bagdad, as Soxster had suggested, it had come across a fenced-off area with a security gate up a dirt road. It was a big ranch spread out on the way to the copper concentrate leach facility, at about forty-one hundred feet above sea level. It was at the seam of the Mohave and Sonoran Deserts. There were both Joshua trees and yucca, a private airstrip, three large satellite dishes, four large buildings, and maybe twenty cabins. Over two dozen vehicles were parked, but there were few people outside. It was listed on the county tax rolls as "American Energy & Mineral Research Corporation," with a corporate head-quarters in the nation of St. Kitts. Folks at the nearby Miner's Diner said they never met anyone from the place.

Jimmy had spent the day convincing the colonel commanding the 7th Marines that he had discovered the location of the culprits who had attached Echo Company by drugging them and taking control of their exoskeleton suits. Foley was convinced this was the place where the Chinese were using American hackers to monitor and subvert the military's work, maybe also the place from which they had sent the signals that sent the Pacific satellites off.

It had been harder to persuade the colonel to put Marines back in exoskeletons after what had happened to Echo Company, but Dr.

Rathstein had been persuasive. "If we shut off the Netcentric functions, then there will be no data entering or leaving the suits. No one can hack in again. The guys will just have tactical radio links, voice, like in the old days." He also produced over two dozen exoskeleton-experienced volunteers from Bravo Company. What got the colonel to say yes was Jimmy's argument that the 7th had been attacked and the colonel had inherent authority to act in self-defense; if he waited for Washington to approve a plan, the bad guys would be gone.

With the sun starting to go down, Jimmy watched the two other UH-85 Arapahos lift up, one on either side of the bird he was in. Each of those two helicopters carried four Marines in exoskeleton suits with the new M-912 combined individual weapon. The M-912 was a double-stack multiple-grenade launcher, an electronically initiated, very-high-rate-of-fire 9mm Lugar parabellum automatic rifle and Taser-style stun gun in one weapon. It would have been too heavy for troops without the lifting strength provided by the exoskels. Jimmy and the major in the lead Arapaho wore standard body armor and carried only side arms. Three Marine criminal investigators and two counterintelligence officers were sitting in the back of Jimmy's chopper. "Military forces can act in their own protection, even in the states. It's in the rules of engagement. And you can act without warrants and higher-level approvals when you think there is an imminent national security threat. Trust me, I know this *posse comitatus* stuff," Foley bluffed.

The three-bird formation of Arapahos was coming toward the

ranch low out of the dark eastern sky. Suddenly, ahead of them, red streaks jumped up from the ground.

"Missiles, missiles!" the pilot yelled over the radio. "Break formation, dive!"

The Arapaho seemed almost to tip upside down as it banked and dove for the surface. The pilot righted the aircraft a few feet above the desert floor. Twisting his head to see through the window to the sky behind them, Jimmy saw four fireballs slowly descending. The pilot had had the presence of mind to release diversion flares as he maneuvered out of the path of the incoming Stinger-like missiles.

"Talon Two, Three, you still wi' me?" the Arapaho pilot asked, calling on the other two helicopters.

"Roger that, Talon One, Talon Three is on your tail," came the response. Then: "And Talon Two, who are these guys got Stingers out here?"

"Break formation. Talon Two, approach your target low from the east-northeast, heading zero eight zero. Talon Three, from the northwest at heading two eight zero. Do not break ceiling above three zero zero feet." The lead pilot then began a long turn, giving the other aircraft time to get into position for a simultaneous assault on the site.

"I don't see anybody down there where the Stingers came from," Talon Two called in.

"Talon Three in position," Foley heard over his headset. Then the other helicopter confirmed its readiness.

"All Talons, go, go, go." The Arapaho lurched forward. "Remember, no touchdowns, drop, discharge, and pull out."

The desert turned into dust devils as the choppers descended. The exoskeleton Marines leaping from the Arapahos reminded Foley of Heinlein's *Starship Troopers,* giants totally encased in their own individual ecosystems, impervious to attack. The exoskel Marines jumped into swirling sand and fanned out by bounding across the ground. Also dropping from the helicopters were several four foot long vehicles with miniature tank treads, Bombots. They carried multimode cameras and sensors designed to find booby traps and bombs. Another model carried a high-rate-of-fire electronic gun system.

Jimmy Foley and Major Zerbrowksi came up behind the squad moving in from the east. He heard a small thud up ahead and realized that the lead unit had made it to the large warehouse-like building. The thud was probably the sound of the Marines using a light explosive charge to blow the lock off the main door. Foley realized he had not yet switched his headset from the aircraft band to the ground frequency. As he switched over to the chatter of the Bravo Company 'skels, he heard, "Sending the Bombots into building one."

Normally, the exoskeleton troops would have the visuals in their helmets of what the Bombots were seeing as they drove around inside the buildings. However, with the Netcentric connections turned off to prevent another hacker attack, only their voice radios connected the exoskels to the tactical communications system. Only Jimmy, the major, and two gunnies had the Bombot's visuals on their portable monitors. The vehicles scanned the rooms with their electro-optical and infrared cameras, but they were also equipped with self-sensing microcantilevers that detected the smallest particles that could be explosive residue. They tested by creating faint popping noises, actually detonating particles in the air.

"Bombot reports building one secure," he heard on the ground freq. "We're going in."

"Building two secure." That meant both the warehouse and the residence had been taken and checked for booby traps.

He was getting close enough and the sand was settling, so he could make out the shape of the thirty-foot-high warehouse. "Building three secure." That was the multibay garage building. Foley headed for the warehouse.

On the ground outside the building were what looked like two large toy aircraft, maybe the unmanned aerial vehicles that Soxster thought had been used to beam signals down directly to the exoskeleton-suited Marines? Zabrowski bent over one of the little planes. "Writing's in English and Chinese."

"Yeah, well, ever found a toy that's not made in China?" Foley asked, and kept going.

Foley heard the chattering back and forth on the tactical channel. None of them had found anyone. There were lots of computers, but no people. Signs of recent occupancy, but no one home. "Got a video-monitoring studio here," one of the Marines announced on the radionet. Foley joined him and found six flat screens, flipping among various video feeds. They had not shut the system off. But the feeds were not coming from the ranch. They seemed to be from industrial facilities, parking lots. Then the White House appeared on one screen. They had been hacking into surveillance cameras all over the country. Foley hit the computer console in front of him and a GUI appeared with a search box. On a hunch, he typed in "SCAIF." A long list of dates came back. Jimmy typed again. "SCAIF, bombing." It came back with three listings. He hit the third. On the center flat screen above him, a tape began to run. The image was grainy, maybe on telescopic. A cloud like a small explosion appeared in the distance, then a large truck came roaring down the road. A car crashed into the truck from the side and the screen was immediately filled with a flash. There was no sound. Then the camera panned back and to the right. There was someone on the ground. The image zoomed in. "Jesus, Susan!" Jimmy said. He reminded himself that he knew she was all right. That scene had taken place yesterday. He tapped his mike: "We got a bunch of evidence over here."

As he reached down to the console again, he heard in his headset, "Major, we got a stiff in the warehouse. Big bullet hole in his forehead."

Foley accompanied Major Zabrowski inside the large structure that he guessed was forty feet by a hundred. The front part was divided up into vehicle bays, some of which had dusty jeeps and trucks. The rest of the space was office cubicles, many with flat screens and headsets. Following the voice of a gunny sergeant directing them, they made their way back to a cubicle near the far side of the building. The body was still on a gurney. An IV drip stand was on its right and some sort of brain scanner on the left, with its wires still connected to pads on the skull. There was also a large, bloody hole in the middle of his forehead.

They had tried to learn what he knew through drug inducement and lie-detector brain scans, which Jimmy Foley knew from his own experience worked well, unlike the medieval hocus-pocus of polygraphs. Jimmy wondered what had happened to Naomi, the single mom, and her kid. He swallowed hard.

"You know this guy?" the major asked. "Who is he?"

"This is TTeeLer," Jimmy said with an overwhelming sense of guilt.

"What kind of a fuckin' name is that, Major?" the gunny asked. Zabrowski shook his head.

"It's geek," Foley volunteered.

"Greek? I heard of Stavos and Dimitri, no TeeTee," the Gunny said, and laughed.

"Geek, computer talk," Foley corrected, remembering what Soxster had told him. "TTL. It's part of a computer packet, how long it's good for, how long it lasts. It means Time To Live."

"Well, in his case, I'd say it meant time to die," the gunny said, bending down to examine the body.

Jimmy looked up and saw, on the other side of the room, the surveillance camera inside the glass globe. It was moving slowly. When it was pointed at Foley and the major standing over TTeeLer, the lens zoomed in. It could just be an intelligent video program that was directing it, Foley thought, but it had an erratic pattern that made it seem driven by hand. He turned his back on the camera, flipped his frequency to the All Mission Personnel channel, and said softly, "Do not run, but quickly withdraw from all buildings, withdraw now."

The noise was from above, sharp and loud, THWACK, and with it came an instant rain of metal shards everywhere. They hadn't checked the roof, Foley thought as he looked up. The ragged metal roof fragment hit his right eye and angled into and through his nose. Foley felt no pain, but through his left eye he could see his blood gushing out. Then he fell over onto the corpse.

2008 PST

Will Gaudium's Home at the Bacchanalia Winery

"I wasn't sure at first whether you were only pretending to agree with me," Will Gaudium admitted as he poured the Late Harvest Laborscum, "but the expression *in vino veritas* hasn't lasted two thousand years without reason."

"Well, here is the truth: I hate dessert wines," Susan protested, convinced that she had already had enough wine for two nights.

"At least try it," Gaudium pleaded. "My wife loved it." He tended to the dwindling fire, stirring the embers and adding a log.

Sipping the liqueur-like wine, Susan had to admit, "I can see why. Like honey, but not syrupy or oversweet."

"Just like you," Gaudium let slip. "I'm sorry, that was inappropriate, Susan."

"No, Will, don't be upset. It was fine. *In vino veritas.* I love getting compliments," she said. "But, if you don't mind, tell me about your wife."

Gaudium inhaled. "Breast cancer. Three years ago. Happened fast. Tried everything, but it was aggressive and we caught it late." He swallowed and, Susan thought, his eyes teared up. "You see I have no problem whatsoever with genetic alteration to fix mistakes in our cells. If I could have spent all my money to save her that way, I would not have hesitated. But instead of doing research into that our scientists were doing Viagra and Botox."

"Will, I'm so sorry," Susan offered. "And then, with her gone, you threw yourself into this work?"

"Yeah, basically. I was approached by some venture capitalists from Sand Hill Road. They were raising a new fund to invest exclusively in nanotech, human-machine interfaces, life extending pharma, all that. That's when I really looked closely into these fields, and came away shocked that we were so close—so close to fundamentally and irrevocably altering humanity."

For the first time, Susan saw the man sitting next to her by the fire not as a part of her investigation but as a warm, honorable, principled human being. Older than her, but still strong and fit and caring. He had built a big company on the basis of his technical brilliance, retired to be with his wife and make wine, and then lost her. Instead of any of the grief-driven things others would have done, he had put his money to use trying to educate the public and the government on a threat that only someone with his background and expertise could have seen holistically.

Susan reached out her hand and took his. She said, "I think I can help you."

1920 EST

Cleveland Park Neighborhood

Washington, D.C.

"Drop me off opposite the fire station," Sol Rubenstein told the cabbie. The blue and white taxi pulled in at the corner of Connecticut Avenue and Porter Street. The Director of National Intelligence had not been in a taxi for several years and fumbled about trying to determine how much of a tip was appropriate to program into his RFID credit card. Wearing a Washington Nationals baseball hat and a windbreaker, he assumed that the likelihood of his being identified was small. His picture had seldom been in the media and he made no television appearances.

The light changed to stop the end-of-rush-hour traffic still moving north on Connecticut Avenue toward Maryland. In a small group of pedestrians, Rubenstein crossed the street toward the firehouse. His fellow travelers looked to be mainly twentysomethings on their way to the new laser holograph movie at the Uptown Cinema.

Rubenstein broke off from the group shortly after crossing Connecticut and moved quickly into the Yin Ching Palace restaurant. Personally, he preferred dim sum from one of the more authentic Chinese establishments in Washington's miniature Chinatown near the convention center. The chief of the Chinese intelligence service's Washington station had been fairly insistent that they meet at the old Woodley Park restaurant. Perhaps there were too many Taiwan sympathizers in the Cantonese establishments downtown. Maybe the Chinese intelligence service, the Guoanbu, owned the Yin Ching, though that seemed unlikely.

As requested, Rubenstein moved quickly to the last of the bright orange booths, on the right-hand side in the corner. There, pouring a Sam Adams beer, was a young Chinese professional who could have been in his late thirties or perhaps early forties, Shen Ruikai. He wore a gray polo shirt that bore the red letters MIT. On the seat next to him was a faded blue Red Sox hat. "Sol, thanks for putting up with all the cloak and dagger. Not my idea. How you been?"

"I thought you ran everything for the Guoanbu in D.C.—hell, throughout the U.S.—Shen. What's the matter, you been demoted?" Rubenstein joked. He had known Shen Ruikai for three years. They had exchanged lunches and dinners. Both Rubenstein and Ruikai were loyal to their governments, but they also both knew the value of informal channels and officially off-the-record discussions. It was Rubenstein who had initiated the discussions, but Ruikai had warmed to them once he understood that he was not the target of a heavy-handed recruitment. Rubenstein also knew that Ruikai told the Guoanbu about the meetings, lest anyone think he had become a U.S. double agent.

"Sol, you know I don't bullshit. I got this instruction from Director of Second Bureau in a personal message," Ruikai explained with some chagrin.

"How is Wu Zhan?" Rubenstein asked. Wu had been the Washington station chief before Ruikai and now ran the Foreign Intelligence Division of the Ministry of State Security, the Guoanbu's formal name. Rubenstein had gotten to know him during the interagency effort Sol had run to uncover the scope of Chinese intelligence activity on American companies. Although his team had found massive economic espionage, including widespread electronic spying through computer-network penetration and implants in products assembled in China, the American government had kept the results of the investigation quiet, plugged some of the holes, deported several Chinese graduate students, and demarched the Chinese government. Rubenstein had also put a 24×7 tail, rather overtly, on the Chinese station chief. As a result, Wu Zhan had been withdrawn back to Beijing. Rubenstein later learned that his friendly adversary had been promoted to run all of Chinese intelligence's foreign operations.

"He misses Washington," Ruikai joked. "Misses you."

"Doesn't trust his successor is doing as good a job of stealing from us?" Sol shot back, only half in jest.

Shen Ruikai hesitated and Sol sensed that his joking remark had hit home. "Apparently, he does not trust me for something, Sol. I was directed to give you this message in writing. As you will see, I am not instructed to give you a substantive message. Instead, he invites you to visit him as soon as possible."

Rubenstein took the text, which had been translated into English. Ruikai continued, "The backstory, Sol, which I got on the secure phone, is that Taiwan shooting down our fighter aircraft has really embarrassed the big generals of the People's Liberation Army. They want to do something. And this comes at a time when some in the Pentagon think that maybe China is responsible for the terrorist attacks in the U.S. The Guoanbu in Beijing thinks the tensions between us are too high. Dangerously high."

"That must be because that is what Guoanbu's Washington station is reporting to Beijing," Sol observed. "Is that what you are telling them?"

The Peking duck arrived and both men halted the conversation until the waiter distributed the pancakes, spring onions, skin, sauce, and duck meat. Even when the waiter departed, Ruikai did not answer. He carefully stuffed a pancake and then looked up at Rubenstein. "Without revealing my sources and methods, Sol, I might have reported that many senior officials of your government have the belief that China is somehow involved in the bombings this week. They are, of course, wrong. Perhaps I have told Beijing that the Pentagon has been tasked to develop retaliation options. And that POTUS will ask the television networks for time on Monday night."

Now it was Rubenstein who took his time carefully assembling his duck package. Then he smiled across the table. "Without commenting on the accuracy of what you might have reported, tell me why Wu thinks that in the middle of all of this, I should spend a week dragging my raggedy ass to Beijing?"

Ruikai sat back in the booth and took a large gulp of the Sam Adams. "Here is where I can only speculate. You know that Wu is very close personally to our President. He may or may not be speaking for him. There may be a deal, which Wu cannot put in writing yet. Our President may not want to seek approval for a plan only to have your side reject it. But, Sol, I am guessing. All I do know is that my instructions were, first, to tell you that you could leave tomorrow and be back on Sunday on the nonstop to Hong Kong. Wu will meet you there. You will be the only one in the first-class cabin on the flight out of Dulles. Second, I was to meet you here, at the Yin Ching Palace. I don't know why this place—it's not very trendy."

Sol Rubenstein did not reply. Ruikai saw Sol's eyes focus in the middle distance. Then he said slowly, "I don't think Wu has a flair for the melodramatic, Shen, do you?" Shen Ruikai shook his head.

Rubenstein signaled for a waiter. "Menu, please." Ruikai looked puzzled. Sol accepted the menu, turned it over, and handed it to Ruikai, his finger pointing to a box on the back cover. It read:

The Yin Ching Palace was the location of secret talks that led to the peaceful conclusion of the Cuban Missile Crisis in October 1962. A KGB officer met with ABC News television reporter John Scali and passed along a back-channel message from Soviet Chairman Khrushchev. Nuclear war between the United states and the Soviet Union was averted.

Rubenstein stood up to leave and placed his Nationals cap back on. "Tell Wu I will see him in Hong Kong on Saturday. Call my assistant with the travel details, but I must be back Sunday."

6 | *Friday, March 13*

He was aware of a humming and then of that feeling in his left arm that meant he had an intravenous feed. He tried to open his eyes and succeeded only in raising his left eyelid. The light coming in through the window was too bright, forcing him to quickly shut the lid.

"You've always been a very good patient, Jimmy, and there you are waking on cue from the stimulant."

He recognized the deep tones of Dr. Mark Rathstein. Without again attempting to open his eyes, Foley tried to talk. His mouth and throat were bone dry. He whispered, "Update me, Doc. What happened?" He felt a plastic straw on his lips and sucked in some water from the bottle Rathstein was holding. "Thanks."

"It's been a long night. We got you in here about twelve hours ago. Slight concussion, cuts, but your Mark II personal optic had been shattered by a piece of the metal roof, like a little dagger. Thank the gods it stopped at the back of the optic orb and didn't keep going into the brain." Rathstein spoke slowly, calmly. "I replaced the optic with a Mark V. It's much more capable, but you will have to get used to it once the swelling goes down and you take the dressing off in a few days."

Foley struggled to speak, coughing and clearing his throat. "Guess if I was goin' to be stabbed in my superman eye, this was the best place in the world for that to happen. Thank you for . . ." He coughed again. He remembered now how much he hated the struggle to get rid of anesthesia in his body. It took days last time.

"This time we will have to tell your civilian employer about the eye. There is little chance now that they will seek to disqualify you from your job. The enhanced personal optics have an established track record and you now have the state-of-the-art model. Would have cost you a bundle in the civilian world. I'm writing it off as research here. You're the first case of an upgrade from the mark two to the mark five." Rathstein was keeping the discussion to the implant. "You will notice that it has greater telescopic range and clarity, better low-light vision and infrared. The interaction with the brain is the same, through the optic nerve. You can also link directly to a helmet and a visor to do split screen, including from the camera on the back of the helmet, so you literally have eyes in the back of your head. And you can feed what you see through the visor to the Net so that you can let other guys in your squad or back at headquarters see what you see."

"No X-ray vision yet, Doc?" Jimmy asked, half joking, as he slowly opened his left eye, his human eye, again. "No way to use stem cells to grow me a new eye?"

"Not yet, but we will use stem cells to grow you back a tooth for the one you lost. No X-ray vision yet, either. Haven't been able to deal with the power problems, although there is a millimeter wave experiment that is interesting," Rathstein said, offering the water bottle again. "The primary power source for the Mark V is solar. There are nano-photovoltaic cells on the surface of the unit. A secondary power pack for low light conditions is in the same place as the old one, behind your collarbone."

Foley raised his right hand and felt the bandaging below his neck. "How often does it need to be changed?"

"It doesn't," Rathenstein said. "The biomotors program finally produced the results we were looking for. It runs off of ATP, a nucleotide produced naturally by your body for intracellular energy transfer. Welcome to the molecular future."

"Better living through chemistry, I guess," Jimmy said with a weak smile. "Jess?"

"I spoke with your wife. She took it all quite well, considering. I told her you would call her around noon and then we would be getting you on your own personal VLJ home," Rathstein continued.

"I shouldn't put her through . . ." Foley could not finish the sentence and began to cough again. He thought of what time it must have been in New York when Rathstein had called. His job kept interfering with hers. As an investment banker, she made more than ten times his police salary. "I need to call her. And Susan, see what trouble she's up to."

"By the way, Jimmy, speaking of your family, I think I may have some possibly good news about your dad. I called his doctor on Long Island after you sent the doctor the e-mail authorizing me to consult." Foley had almost forgotten their conversation about his father's Alzheimer's. Rathstein was sounding almost excited, which was unusual for the normally cautious doctor. "They have tried all the drugs and they've cleared some of the plaque, but they have not tried the continuous deep electrical stimulation or, of course, the experimental nano. So I persuaded my colleague at Cornell Medical Center to take him on as part of their test program. It may not work, but it's definitely worth a try."

"Mark, I can't begin to thank . . . I mean . . ." Foley struggled for words. He held up his arm, reaching toward the doctor. Rathstein moved closer and let Foley grab his arm. Jimmy's grip was still strong.

Rathstein noticed Foley swallow hard. "The others, Doc," Jimmy rasped. "What happened at the raid?"

"You will have to talk to the naval investigators. They want to see you, but I told them you were being medevaced to your civilian medical system in New York. A buddy of mine at the Hospital for Special Surgery in Manhattan is taking you. He has worked with the new optic. "

Foley grabbed the bedsheet tightly with his right hand. "What happened?"

"The buildings were booby-trapped. Somehow the Bombot

sweeps didn't catch them. They all went up. We had about ten guys in emergency. Lot of surgery last night. I did two other eyes. Altogether, we installed an enhanced leg and two arms, three eyes."

He paused. Jimmy opened his left eye and stared at him. Then Rathstein admitted, "We lost two Marines. They were not in the exoskeletons."

To the doctor it looked like the news had put his patient in physical pain, clutching harder at the bedsheets.

"If they had been in the suits, none of them would have expired. I have to get the suits recertified for use. Maybe now that you have found the guys that were hacking into our net…" The doctor grimaced and looked out the window at morning sun, now beaming directly into the hospital room. "How can we do Netcentric warfare if…"

"We didn't get them," Foley whispered. "But I will, Doc. I will. I will find out who the fuck they are. And we will get those superman suits back on our Marines. You guys gotta be able to secure the link. No more wards filled with gyrenes without limbs. Not again. Not next time."

1005 PST

The Café at The Hotel, Mandalay Bay

Las Vegas, Nevada

Susan heard Soxster behind her. "Jimmy's offline, flying back to New York, and you jet off to Vegas with Gaudium. Is the threat from China over and you didn't tell me?" She was sitting in the up-scale snack bar of the hip hotel in the Mandalay Bay complex. Unlike the theme-park hotels on the strip, The Hotel had no ubiquitous slot machines or other gambling paraphernalia. It could have been in Tribeca or on the Sunset Strip: quiet and elegantly *cool*. "How is The Breakfast and The Coffee?"

Susan smiled at Soxster's lack of opening small talk as he appeared from behind her. Then she smiled at his red T-shirt, which read "Infocon Alpha 2012" and "I am not a Fed." Below the words was a drawing of a cartoon figure in a trench coat, wearing a stethoscope and listening to a box connected to several telephones.

"You like it? All the federal law-enforcement and spy agencies come to Infocon to learn our latest techniques. I thought of getting you a Not Fed T-shirt, too, but . . . don't you just hate people who lie with their T-shirts?" He rustled in a plastic bag and produced a folded blue T-shirt, which he passed across the table. "Instead, I got you this one."

Susan unfolded the shirt. It read "I am not a terrorist" and had a drawing of Osama bin Laden with a red *X* across it.

"Good morning to you, too. And thanks, I guess, for the T-shirt." Susan leaned across the small table. "Jimmy is doing fine. I just talked with him and he'll be back to duty next week. Although my bosses want me to crack this case by Sunday for some reason. Fat chance.

"And, yes, we still have a real problem with the Chinese. I'm trying to find out what's driving them crazy and get to their next targets *before* they do, instead of at the exact same time, like at SCAIF. It's just possible that the hidden technology Gaudium knows about is that target." She paused. "I can see what he's talking about, you know. If we move ahead with Living Software, with Enhanced people, we'll leave much of the world in the dust. We could also leave humanity in the dust."

"Whoa, humanity in the dust?" Soxster mimicked. "Did Gaudium get you to drink some of his Kool-Aid? Talk about sleeping with the enemy."

"Will is not the enemy," Susan shot back, and then regretted it. "Fuck you. Look, mind your own business."

"Wow, just a figure of speech," Soxster said, backing away. "And what makes you think the Chinese aren't doing this technology stuff, too?"

"They aren't. I checked. The Chinese are good at large-scale implementation, but not big on innovation. And because the rate of technology acceleration is itself constantly increasing, once you get ahead, you stay there. Unless someone goes around blowing your shit up." She had said all of that very quickly and then took a deep breath and slowed down. "No Kool-Aid, either. I just think that some of the issues Will raises are important. But for now, I'm just trying to get him to tell me where some of this technology is. Besides, *you* told me to go to Infocon."

"Yeah, it's a good place to learn what's going on. Every cracker and hacker is here somewhere. Remember the difference?"

Susan sighed. "Yes, Sox, hackers are people who can take systems apart to learn how they work and break. Crackers are criminals who do the same thing with illegal intent. Do I get a star? More to the point, do you get one? Have you learned anything so far?"

Soxster put his right hand up to cover his mouth and spoke softly. "TTeeLer was hired by whoever was looking for hackers last year, around the same time as seven other top skill guys. They were all given tickets to L.A. Then they disappeared. Aside from TTeeLer, none of them has surfaced on the Net or in the so-called real world since . . ."

"Since what? Come on," Susan insisted.

"Easy, easy," Soxster countered. "Okay, so one of the other guys in the group with TTeeLer was Packetman. He'd been saying what a great hack it would be to take control of all the stupid robot canines just to show how bad their security is and how ridiculous an idea it is to have a dog as an automated personal assistant. He'd been working on the code."

Susan saw from Soxster's smile that there was more. "And . . . ?"

Soxster rubbed his hands together gleefully and got that evil smile on his face again. "So I thought I would just look for Packetman, the way I found TTeeLer. I know his PGP key, so I thought I would put out some Netbots to see if I could find it anywhere and, eureka! He was in a secure chat room, but I got in, never mind how. And he's talking about he got a big reward for penetrating the Man-O-War project. What's that, some super-secret plan for a stealth destroyer or something? Apparently, they're going to do something to stop it."

"Got me. It means nothing to me." She could see how disappointed Soxster was that his research had not been useful. "But I suppose what you found out does maybe tell us that the attack of the killer robot dogs was designed as a message about how bad our security is—how they can get through it, listen in to our offices, mess with our systems. It doesn't make sense as anything else. But it doesn't sound like a shot across the bow by China. . . ."

"Maybe it does," Soxster replied. "The robot dogs were all assembled in Guangzho, probably with a little extra programming in their firmware so they could be accessed and controlled later on. You guys ought to look at the pieces. Guess what else is assembled in places like Guangzho? Sytho routers and firewalls."

"Sox, everything is made in China."

"Yeah, but when that specific everything can connect to the internet, it gets worth their while to slip in a little extra on the motherboard, some little circuit we didn't ask for that acts like software, opens up a hole in any firewall, responds to coded packets by opening up the control plane in a way that only they can issue it instructions." Soxster sketched a circuit design on the back on a napkin. "Next thing, they can copy any packet moving on our systems, or replace them, or black-hole them."

Susan frowned in confusion. "So you're saying that the Chinese may have placed back doors in some electronics sold by some American companies?"

Soxster shook his head. "No. Not some. Most, if not all, the computer systems running our internet, our phones, our power grid, our trains and planes. Remember, Sooz, 'everything is made in China.' "

"Touché," she conceded.

"Infocon Alpha is starting up 'bout now. Let's go hear your new buddy. Will? Was that what you called him?"

"Piss off," Susan said, smiling.

Amid the crowd of T-shirt- and jeans-clad guys in the Mandalay convention center, Susan stood out because of her sex and her business suit. Soxster stood out because he was with her. They passed booths and tables set up by people who ten or twenty years earlier had been showing off their science fair projects in high school. Now they had freeware, shareware, and some special programs available for a price. The vendors and the attendees were the strangest set of conventioneers she had ever seen or could imagine. She suddenly had a sense of déjà vu. Sam Benjamin loved the old *Star Wars* movies and had made her watch them with him too many times. This was the cantina scene on Tatooine come to life!

Gaudium had just been introduced as they walked into the hall. He was walking up a set of stairs that rose up from the back of a very deep stage. An aging heavy-metal band was crashing out its noise, and there were literally smoke and mirrors. Blue smoke wafted up from below stage and ancient disco balls were spinning. The scene was replayed on two giant screens, one on either side of the stage and, also on the screens, streams of greenish numbers and symbols scrolled down and a sentence blinked on and off at the bottom. "Is he The One?" The crowd roared. When they quieted down, the band stopped and the disco balls ascended out of sight. The last whiffs of blue smoke floated out into the hall.

Will Gaudium began. "It's time for humanity to take the red pill!"

The crowd roared again. Susan yelled in Soxster's ear, "What does that mean?"

He looked incredulously at her and yelled back over the crowd noise, "*The Matrix*, sister. The pill that lets you see reality? Seriously, Susan, you gotta get out more!"

Gaudium continued. "We have seen a revolution in our time. The IT Revolution. It has made the world a better place. It has allowed us to share knowledge, strengthen free speech and human rights. But now it is going too far.

"The hardware and software I and others invented was for human use. But now we are giving control of IT over to the machines. Machines that write software humans can't read or understand. Machines that run everything we rely on all day, every day. Machines that spy on what we say, what we write, what we eat, what we buy, what we do.

"Now IT is busy creating nanobots to enter our bodies and probes that will connect our brains to cyberspace. Science fiction? No! As a result of the Human Brain Reverse-Engineering Project, hundreds of humans have *already* downloaded much of their memories and thought patterns onto computers."

The crowd buzzed.

"Now IT is joining up with genomics to create Enhanced humans—if we can even use the word 'human' to describe creatures with forty-eight chromosomes instead of forty-six. Science fiction? No! I know for a fact one laboratory has been generating just such creatures ever since last year!"

The buzz grew to a roar. "What's he talking about?" Soxster asked Susan.

"Beats the shit out of me," she replied, "but this is certainly not him in his mellow winemaker mood."

"My friends, this is all no longer theoretical. The technology is accelerating every day. Most of the breakthroughs the public does not fully understand, and many they do not know about at all. If they even know about Living Software, they think of it as some benign way to make our programs run smoothly—but I am telling you: When a machine is as smart as a human, it will not be long before no human is as smart as a machine. If we allow Living Software loose in cyberspace, it will take over like kudzu in Carolina, like zebra mussels in a pond. The machines will no longer be our servants—they will be our masters. *The Matrix?* Science fiction? Not anymore!

"Four years ago, when we crossed over from eliminating genetic defects to creating Enhanced humans, science went over the line. Bio Fab and Synthetic Biology, which should be an oxymoron, is over the line. When they link up Globegrid and let Living Software run loose on it, we will cross the final barrier. We will have reached the Breakpoint!"

The crowd was quiet now, trying to absorb his words.

"We face a Hobson's choice. As every new advance fundamentally alters what it means to be human, we will either destroy ourselves . . . or somewhere along that path, something will go very, very wrong. The only thing that might save us from destroying ourselves completely could be an event so terrible that it shocked us out of our complacency. Without Hiroshima, the Cold War might not have stayed cold. We do not wish disaster upon ourselves—we cannot—but in the world that we are creating, would it be the lesser of two evils if it wakes up and saves humanity from its own enslavement?"

"This is starting to creep me out," said Soxster. "Can we go?" Reluctantly, Susan agreed. In the corridor, she said, "Sounds like your fellow hackers aren't as willing as you to let Living Software put them out of business."

"Yeah, well . . ." Soxster looked puzzled. "I have no idea what half of that stuff was. His Breakpoint sounds like Kurzweil's Singularity, but downloading human brains onto computers? Forty-eight-chromosome people? Got me. I'd say he's let the alcohol content of his pinot get too high."

"Maybe we'll find out at the Hilton," Susan said absently. Seeing that she had only added to Soxster's befuddlement, she continued "Oh, I forgot to tell you. He's invited us both to lunch at the Hilton. Something to do with some theme park ride."

Soxster rolled his eyes. "Will we have to kill what we eat?"

2332 Local Time

The Spa, Lower Level of the Mandarin Oriental Hotel

Beijing

"You know who I am?" Brian Douglas asked the man on the other side of the steam room.

"Of course, Mr. Douglas. You arrived here on your diplomatic passport using your true name," Wi Lin-wei replied in American-accented English. "I am sorry for the venue, but I have established a pattern. Patterns do not raise suspicion. I have a late-night massage and steam here two nights a week. You happen to be staying at the same hotel, using the same health club after your long flight. And meeting here, I can see that you are not carrying a weapon or a recording device."

"Perhaps you have seen too many American gangster films, Mr. . . ."

"I love movies, American, British. My name is Wi Lin-wei. I work in the office of President Huang." He walked through the steam and dripping moisture toward Brian. "Your talent spotters would call me a midlevel functionary in a high level office."

Brian Douglas was surprised at how high level the office was that this source worked in. "Your cousin, Hui, whom you have used as a cutout with us until now, said you had something so sensitive that I should fly my carcass all the way from London to hear it," Brian said, continuing his tactic of placing the source on the defensive. "Are you here on your own or has somebody sent you?"

Wi looked at the low ceiling, where water droplets were hanging. "Let us say that there are a few who would be glad that I am providing you with this information, but if I am found out they could deny me three times, as Peter did to our Lord. And like our Lord, I would be crucified. I have placed my life in play here tonight, Mr. Douglas. You know what would happen if we were found together. My sources would not be able to save me. But they are high level, the highest."

Brian Douglas considered his source. Perhaps he was just a very good actor. "And what is your motivation, Lin-wei, if I may be so direct?"

Wi Lin-wei used both hands to do a minor push up on the ledge and then swung his body back against the wall. Adjusting his large white towel, he began slowly: "I believe in what President Huang is building, a nation that is not only prosperous and has modern technology in the cities, but one that cares for the less successful, one that gradually allows more self-expression and institutions other than the Party." He paused. Brian let the silence hang in the steam. Wi continued, "Mr. Douglas, I have spent some time on trade delegations. In Helsinki, in Stockholm, and even a little time in Edinburgh. No one there wants to overthrow the system, but they are allowed to worship as they choose and to join civil society organizations, to say and write what they want. Also, the governments provide for the less successful, even those in the countryside. I drove for a week throughout the countryside of Scotland with two colleagues. It is so green."

When it was clear that there was no more coming, Brian asked, "So you love China and just want to see it better? And who does not, eh?"

"The PLA. The military leaders want order. They want the big companies they own to make money, not to share their profits with the poor and the villagers. More important to them even than money is the honor of China. They will sacrifice economic growth for that honor. And Taiwan is an offense to that honor, especially when it shoots down the PLA's jets."

It had all poured out of Wi so quickly and with such a tone of bitterness that Brian's confidence in him increased. "The money we are paying you—that is not a factor in our meeting?" Brian queried.

Wi jerked this head around to face Brian. "Hui keeps all the money you give him. I told him I do not want your money. I do this for China."

"You are a patriot, then, sir," Brian responded, trying to offset any implied insult he may have made. "We cannot stay here much longer. They close the gym at midnight. What is the sensitive information that you want us to have?"

Wi leaned forward. "It is for the Americans, but I do not trust their people to get it to the top there. They lose important information and they leak it. Can't connect the dots. You, I believe, can, your Sir Dennis and what *The Economist* called his English-speaking network of intellocrats."

Brian could not suppress the smile that Wi's observation produced.

Wi continued. "President Huang cannot always keep the PLA in line. He has let them go on an alert, moving the fleet out into the Pacific, arming missiles."

"We've noticed," Brian deadpanned, hoping that was not what Wi thought was sensitive.

"A dozen years ago, President Bill Clinton sent two aircraft carrier battle groups to waters off Taiwan when the PLA threatened. The American Navy claims publicly that it forced our fleet to turn around in the Indian Ocean during the Islamyah crisis a few years ago. If the U.S. Navy comes to Taiwan now, the PLA will not back down or run away, not without bloodying the Americans. And that could get out of control."

"And the PLA thinks the American Navy is coming to defend Taiwan?" Brian asked.

"You tell me, Mr. Douglas."

Was this all a ruse to get the answer to that question or to urge the U.S. to keep the 7th Fleet away? Brian wondered. "They don't tell me their sailing plans. And if they did, of course, I wouldn't tell you."

"The PLA thinks that they will come—not just to defend Taiwan, but to retaliate for the bombings in America," Wi replied, the tension rising in his voice.

"So the PLA did the bombings in America?" Brian said, almost casually.

"I don't know. Neither does President Huang," Wi insisted, "and if I did, I *would* tell you."

If it was true about Huang, that was an interesting fact, Brian thought. "So what should I tell my cousins in America, Lin-wei?" As he spoke, the miniature device inside his ear canal beeped three times, stopped, and beeped three times more. Then he heard three clear code phrases. "Trouble," Brian said, and moved quickly to the steam room door. He turned and looked at Wi, who was standing up, looking frightened. "Come with me now. Move!" Brian yelled at him.

"What? What is happening?" Wi asked in the locker area outside the steam room.

"There's a police sweep, checking IDs in the lobby. Special Security police. Some are on their way down the stairs that lead to this spa, now. Grab your shoes, wrap them in your clothes," Brian ordered. Grabbing his own things from his locker, Brian moved quickly to the rear of the room and jumped up on a bench. Wi followed quickly. Brian reached up and swung open a grate over a large air-conditioning panel. A flexible plastic ladder fell out. "Climb up as fast as you can," he said to Wi. When Wi disappeared into the ceiling, Brian followed him and pulled the grate back up behind him. "Keep climbing," he urged Wi. "Push on the grille up there on the left. Don't let it bang. Let yourself down into the room."

Brian heard voices, calling out in Chinese, from the spa locker room below him. He leaped down into the baggage storage room and saw Wi hurriedly hiding amid the suitcases. "The woman at the spa desk will have told them that there were still two people inside," Brian said to Wi.

"No, I doubt it," Wi said, shaking his head. "I pay her much money, twice a week." Douglas looked skeptical. "I get happy ending after massage," Wi admitted.

Brian chuckled, not only at Wi's admission but at the sight of himself standing half-naked off the lobby of a five-star Beijing hotel. "All right, then we stay here for a while. You were saying . . . what I was to tell Washington's pooh-bahs?"

The Chinese man dropped his towel and stood there in his briefs. "President Huang has some people in the Ministry of State Security that he trusts. He has them investigating the PLA's role in the bombings in America. But he doesn't know what to do when he gets the answers, doesn't know how to stop the PLA and their supporters in the Politburo from doing something to Taiwan and its Independence Party. He needs help, Mr. Douglas."

"The Special Security police don't normally check IDs in a five-star hotel at midnight, Lin-wei. I would be very cautious, were I you." Brian noticed that Wi was literally trembling. Then he noticed a yellow stain on Wi's briefs. Apparently, he was a genuine source, or a truly excellent actor.

Noon PST

Quark's Space Station Bar, the Hilton Hotel

Las Vegas, Nevada

"I ordered you their blue Romulan ale. They don't have pinot noir," Will Gaudium said as Susan Connor and Soxster joined him. They were seated in a restaurant that looked like a movie set for some space-travel saga.

"Interesting choice of cuisine. Hi, call me Soxster."

"It's not the best place to dine in Vegas, but if we stayed at the Mandalay, I'd get hounded by the people at Infocon Alpha," Gaudium said. "Besides, I want you to take the ride here, if you haven't already. You get chased by the Borg."

That figures, Susan thought. The Borg was a *Star Trek* creation: creatures that used to be human but had machine implants and were now part of a greater computer consciousness called The Collective. Gaudium was riding his hobbyhorse again.

"Do they catch any tourists?" Soxster asked. Susan scowled at him.

"It's not fiction anymore," Gaudium insisted to Soxster. "Did you hear my speech? Combine the Human Brain Reverse-Engineering Project with this Living Software monster, and then tell me how that's different."

Soxster looked at Susan. "May I?"

"Have at it," Susan said, folding her arms across her chest and leaning back in the chair to watch.

"Look, Mr. Gaudium, I have enormous respect for what you did at Jupiter Systems, but I think you're really overreacting. We've had human-machine interface for a while now. Cochlear implants that connect to the auditory nerve that connects to the brain—those are twenty years old. Artificial-vision devices connected to the optical nerve have been around for five years. Brain stimulating electrical systems for depression and other diseases for a decade or more."

"But they weren't connected to the internet," Gaudium countered. "They weren't memory boards to increase retention or processing, like with the nanotech they are fooling around with now . . ."

Soxster shook his head, disagreeing. "The human brain's access to memory and knowledge made a quantum leap when we got the internet and then Google's search engine. What difference does it make if I have to use my hands and fingers to access that 'collective' or if I just have to will the access with my brain? People who can't move their arms were able to move a mouse around on a computer in 2004. If I wear a visor that lets me see the internet projected holographically in front of me, that's fine, but if I see it in my mind's eye, that's not?" Soxster was on a roll. "And as far as Living Software being a monster, would you rather have the wild cybercrime and hacker penetrations we have now? Punctuated periodically by cyber disasters like in 2009? Living Software is nothing but a program that knows how to spot errors in computer language and then rewrite the language to fix them. And like Linux and the Open Source Movement, which you used to support, Living Software kernels communicate with each other about what they have seen and done so that they don't have to reinvent the wheel every time. It's cool shit. Awesome. Something like the young Will Gaudium would have come up with."

"I can refute everything you just said, but say you're right—which you're not, by the way." Gaudium turned to look at Susan. "There is still the problem of nano and—let me finish, I listened to you—of genetic engineering. It's one thing to write out the defects in human biological code, but another to add new capabilities and new chromosomes! How the hell does anyone know what they will do?"

"Okay," Soxster said, "nanotech has to be regulated so we don't all inhale tiny computers into our lungs every time we take a breath, I agree. But I'm no expert on DNA and genetics—are you saying that human evolution is over?" Soxster pointed his finger at Gaudium. "Please don't tell me that you don't believe in evolution, like your pal, Senator Bloviater. If he gets elected president, this country will become a theocracy, and then we can all act out Heinlein's *Revolt in 2300.*"

"Of course, I believe in evolution, and no, I don't think it's over," Gaudium agreed. "I'm a scientist. Senator George is just the only person willing to make the regulation of scientific and engineering advances a big issue, to promise that he will stop this unthinking leap into a posthuman future."

"He can slow it, but he can't stop it—no one can," Soxster insisted. "Come on, you know that. Science and technology advance, that's what they do. Your pinot noir grapes are highly cultivated hybrid clones that wouldn't occur in nature. How do you know that humans altering their genetics isn't the next step in evolution—a life-form becoming sentient and deciding how to adapt itself? That's what Teilhard de Chardin thought: Technology leads to the ultimate evolution. And *he* was a Jesuit. Not your Breakpoint, but his Omega Point. If Neanderthals could talk, they might have sat around their caves jerking off worrying about the post-Neanderthal future. You talk about the Borg and space travel. How the hell do you think this sentient life-form is going to do deep-space travel without downloading brain function or doing significant genetic alteration? Maybe this is the beginning of the evolutionary step that permits deep-space travel? Maybe orthogenics is right and this is where evolution has been pointed all along."

Sensing a pause in the oral combat, Susan jumped in. "Will, you said something in your speech about a lab that was already generating people with extra chromosomes. Is that really true?"

"Of course. Why would I make it up? I pay people to go out and track down these things. There's a lab in the Bahamas where at least several hundred children have already been born with the additional chromosomes. The parents pay one hundred thousand dollars for it. The additional chromosomes are what their inventor called a 'universal delivery vehicle for gene modules.' Once the structure is in place, the parents can pick any number of attributes and input them into the embryo like options on a car. Don't want to pass on your hairline? They have a modification for that. Mother die of breast cancer? They can help. Don't like the weight you put on after college? They have a metabolic enhancement. ADD, dyslexia, almost anything predetermined by genetics, they can fix now or will be able to later. Do you think democracy will last long once we have a wealthy elite like that?"

"Can you prove it?" Susan asked.

"Want to see for yourself? I'll have my pilot fly you there, Marsh Harbor. One of my men will meet you there and take you over to Man-O-War Cay, that's the island where the lab is. You asked me to help you find underground technology that the Chinese might want to eliminate. Well, that's certainly a candidate, don't you think? They'll want to eliminate an American super race. And maybe we should let them!"

"It's a deal," Susan replied quickly, "I'll go."

"I'll set it up," Gaudium said, getting up from the table. "I'll call you with the details, but now I have to run to a press conference. Don't leave here, however, without taking the ride."

Susan and Soxster sat quietly until Gaudium had left the restaurant. Soxster took a drink of the blue ale and spat it back into the glass. He looked up at Susan. "How are your Memzax pills doing?"

"I remember. Will just said Man-O-War. Packetman knew about it, too. Something to do with penetrating their network. Stopping something." Susan closed her eyes and repeated.

Soxster was quiet for a moment. Susan kept her eyes shut. "While I'm testing the strength of your biochemical memory enhancement," Soxster said, looking at his watch, "Tell me this. What's today's date?"

She opened her eyes. "Friday the thirteenth. Why? Are you superstitious?"

Soxster shook his head no and smiled smugly. "Do you know *why* Friday the thirteenth is supposed to be bad luck? It's the day in 1307 that the King of France lured the head of the Knights Templar, Jacques DeMolay, to his palace in Paris to capture him while simultaneously rounding up hundreds of Knights throughout Europe. Didn't you read all that DaVinci crap a few years ago?"

"I had better things to do," Susan said, and sipped the ale. With a pained look on her face as she swallowed, she asked, "So is there some moral to that story?"

"Yeah. Don't do like DeMolay and get lured someplace where the other side has all the weapons." Soxster put his hand on Susan's. "Don't go."

"Are you kidding? I have to. If Will's right about the place, it's a prime candidate for whoever's taking down our technology. The President thinks it's China, and Sol and Rusty think he's going to decide on retaliation in a matter of days. If we can uncover an attack before it happens, maybe we can find out who's doing the attacks."

"Then take Jimmy, or me—don't go alone," Soxster urged.

"Jimmy is convalescing with his wife in Manhattan. You need to get back to the Dugout and see what you can find in cyberspace about all this. I'll be fine."

Soxster looked unconvinced, but said nothing more. As they stood up to leave, a group of tourists came running into the restaurant, the kids screaming, being chased by actors dressed up like a cross between men and machines.

Soxster looked at Susan. "Let's skip the ride."

7 | *Saturday, March 14*

1130 EST

Brighton Beach

Brooklyn, New York

"I'm coming in with you," Jessica Foley said as she parked the car at a meter under the old metal of the elevated train tracks.

"The hell you are," Jimmy Foley told his wife. "I don't want them to know who you are, that you even exist."

"My existence is not really a state secret, Jimmy. This is not negotiable. Dr. Rathstein said you shouldn't even leave the apartment this weekend. Remember, hotshot, you were in a hospital in California when you woke up yesterday. I don't want you passing out by yourself in the middle of some Russian mafia lair in Little Odessa," she said, grabbing and squeezing his hand.

"I knew I shoulda taken a cab," he said, and then laughed and leaned over and kissed her. Despite the residual anesthetics in his system, he had had no difficulty doing that and a lot more during the night before. "All right. Take your ring off. Your name is Susan Connor and you are my partner at the Intelligence Analysis Center and you will let me do all the talking."

"I thought you said Susan was African-American?" Jessica asked.

"It will confuse them, if they even know that much," Jimmy said, getting out of the car. He had woken up early and waited until 0730 before calling his old NYPD partner. Detective Vin DeCarlo was up, making pancakes for his three kids and letting his wife sleep in, as he did every Saturday. Unfortunately, he was also going to take the kids to the Rangers game and could not join Jimmy on his outing to Brighton Beach. His information about what was going on in the Ismailovskaya, the Russian mob, was priceless. He had stayed on the Russian crime beat when Jimmy had left for his year in Washington.

With the bandages over his left eye, Detective Jimmy Foley knew he did not look as formidable as he wanted to. He had, however, worn his best suit. He just hoped that Jessica did not look too much like his wife. They crossed the busy street, dodging cars, to the Pushkin restaurant, where Gregori Belov had agreed to meet for an early lunch. The Russian sat alone on the banquette in the semi-circular corner booth, among the overstuffed pillows. He had a thick head of silver-white hair, broad shoulders, and a florid face. He wore a black suit and white shirt with no tie. Jessica guessed he was in his early fifties. "For a mobster's lair, it has a lot of lace and tassels, and red," Jessica said *sotto voce* as they moved through the nearly empty room.

"*Dobriy den!* James, James, back from Washington so soon, and with a new partner? Much nicer," Belov bellowed as they approached his throne. "*Rada tebya videt.* They don't have good Palmeni or Sacivi in Washington?" He took Jessica's hand and kissed it delicately. "Gregori Belov. *Ochinprivatna.*"

"Delighted," Jessica said, blushing. "Susan Connor, Foley's partner." It was only half a lie, she thought.

"Foley and Connor—sounds like the NYPD union," Belov said as they both settled in on his left.

"Mr. Belov, thank you for meeting on such short notice. *Spasiba*," Jimmy started.

"Mr. Belov. Mr.?" the Russian said, opening the bottle of vodka on the table. "*Pyatizvyozdnaya*, my favorite—it means 'with five stars.' The honey in it is good for my throat. *Pazhaltsa!*" He poured them each a four-finger shot.

"*Choot-choot*," Jimmy said, trying in vain to get less in his glass.

"*Na zdarOv'ye*," Belov toasted, and then, looking at Jessica, "*Za vas.*"

"It means 'to you,'" Jimmy explained.

"You do not speak Russian, lovely lady? Oh, please forgive my rudeness," Belov said, bowing his head. "English only from now on." He downed the vodka. Jessica sipped some, but Jimmy emptied his painted shot glass. "Miss Connor, do you know that Jimmy learned his Russian in the Marines? He was supposed to learn Arabic, but the class was full and they had all of these Russian instructors left over. Monterey, yes, James?"

"Monterey, yes, Gregori. Defense Language Institute. Again, thank you for the meeting," Jimmy tried again.

"Vinny DeCarlo calls me at eight-thirty in the morning and says you must see me or the world will end. Of course, I see you. The understanding that you helped to broker here in Brooklyn is holding. Street crime is down. The Bratva, if there were a Bratva, is not selling drugs here and has provided useful leads on others who do, the Mexicans, Colombians." A waiter had been standing quietly, holding menus and a wine list. "Jimmy, if I recall, wants the borscht and then the Palmeni. So do I," Belov told the waiter. "And caviar, of course."

"Well, then, make it three," Jessica added quickly.

"And the *mukuzani*," he said, rejecting the wine list and turning again to Jessica. "Georgian wine, but dry, velvety, almost smoky." He looked back at Jimmy and his bandages. "So I know you want to get right down to business, but I have been good and have not asked—so first, who poked you in the eye?"

"That's what I'm here to find out, Gregori."

"Ah, so this is personal. Well, then, I will be even more helpful." Belov smiled at Jessica, then at Jimmy. "How can I help? Who can I kill? Just kidding, of course."

"The word is that with Dimitri Yellin missing, you have, shall we say, adopted the Ukrainian chapter?" Jimmy asked.

"They came to me. They knew I am not responsible for Dimitri's disappearance. My daughter married his son, Sergei. We do not compete. We had different sales districts, different product lines. We watch each other's backs. Sergei asked me for help keeping his group from splitting up. The Georgian, Karinshasvili, tried to recruit some of them." Belov spoke quickly, in bursts, like a Kalashnikov on full automatic.

"I know it wasn't you, Gregori, but what did happen to Dimitri?" Jimmy asked.

"I have tried to find out from Sergei, of course," Belov said, spreading the caviar on a pancake. "Dimitri had a contract with someone, a *shishka*. He never knew who it was, but the man paid handsomely and in gold and cash. To do the job, Dimitri had to buy things and get some people from back home. Sergei says the money left over has disappeared. The gold transferred out of their account. The vehicle carrying the cash vanished." Belov consumed the pancake in one piece and washed it down with a vodka. "Jimmy, you said this is personal. Whatever Dimitri did for this man . . . Sergei is now my son, under my protection. Tell me you are not here investigating Sergei or his men."

Jimmy Foley reached his hand across the table to Gregori Belov. "I am not here investigating Sergei or his men." The two men shook on it. "I want the man who contracted with Dimitri Yellin, and I need him very soon, this weekend."

The borscht arrived. "I understand what you want now, Jimmy, and how much you want it, but this weekend?"

"It is not only personal, Gregori," Jimmy added. "A great deal depends upon it."

Families had been drifting in, filling up the Pushkin, but none had interrupted Belov's lunch to wish him well or pay tribute. They respected his space. Looking around at the Saturday luncheon crowd, Jessica wondered where Belov's security was. She had lost the thread of the conversation and knew that Jimmy would never explain it to her afterward. At times it almost sounded like one of her midtown lunches trying to convince a client to do an initial public offering.

As the main course was being cleared, Belov dabbed his lips almost daintily with the linen napkin. "For me to find out what you want, I may need to spend some money, and I will certainly be running some risk," he suggested.

"The government will be very appreciative," Jimmy replied.

"The government? The federal government?" Belov asked. "At a high level?"

"At a very high level," Jimmy said confidently.

"Jimmy, there is a company upstate that has been trying to sell things, food and the like, to Fort Drum, the mountain troops there. They need a long-term contract with decent margins so they can give our troops the very best."

"I'm sure the Pentagon can be persuaded to want the very best for Fort Drum, Gregori."

Belov signaled that he was going to push back the table. The meal was over. Four men came out from behind the red curtains, two on either side of the table. They were not waiters. Standing, Belov again kissed Jessica's hand. "You are lucky to be with Jimmy—

he will make a good father." He then turned to the bandaged detective. "Also, Jimmy, I have a nephew in Massachusetts. He wants to resettle in Nevada. Not Novosibirsk. *Da?*"

Jimmy looked at the Russian mobster. "I need the information fast, Gregori. Very fast." The men shook hands, and as the Foleys left the restaurant, their host began circulating among the tables, like the mayor of Little Odessa.

0855 PST

Las Vegas, Nevada

"I wish we hadn't abandoned the ranch so quickly," Packetman complained.

"We had a compromise of site security. We had no choice," the General spit out. "Let's get on with it. You have everything here that you had there. Explain to me how it will work. How do we unplug the electrical system?"

Above them in the darkened room were three seventy-two-inch screens, one showing a map of the western United States and Canada, the other two with a maze of lines and color-coded boxes. "So, there are three electric power zones in the country—East, West, and Texas," Packetman explained.

"I always knew Texas was different," the General said, staring at the diagrams.

"The Western Interconnect includes everything west of the Mississippi in Canada and the U.S., plus Baja in Mexico. It's divided into five subzones. We are going to attack each of the five differently. Watch." Packetman threw a Keynote briefing slide up on the middle screen. "In CBRC, California basically, we are going to cause the voltage levels to drop on the north-south bulk electrical system by giving instructions to their SCADA control system, but we will play 'man in the middle' and catch the signals that are sent back up to the reliability coordinator command center in Riverside. The signals we send to the center will make it look like everything is fine. Then, when the voltage gets low enough, bang, a cascading failure of the grid."

"How did you get into the control system, if that is not a trade secret?" the General asked.

"It is, but you pay me well. Hacked the firewall between their consumer billing system and the transmission reporting. Took a while, but I've been inside for over a year, programmed their intrusion-detection system not to notice me," Packetman said, and beamed.

"So California goes out. That trips everything else?" the General queried.

"Might, but just to be sure, I got into the RMRC area—that's around here, Nevada—by putting a radio out in the desert. The power company broadcasts control instructions to some of their unmanned sites in the clear on radio frequencies, not by landline.

Easy to get in by overpowering the real radio signal. And once you're in the network, you can go anywhere. No encryption, no access authorization, no internal firewalls. They have all their generators' turbines spinning synchronized at exactly the same speed all over the country, sixty cycles. If I change that by twenty percent, it knocks up the power fourfold. We applied a binary patch to the firmware of all the generators to override the governors that limit their speed."

"I don't understand a word you just said," the General complained, towering above the seated hacker.

"We're going to send so much power down the lines from the plants that it will fry the big transformers just outside the plants and the high-tension wires will get so hot they will droop and then melt. With one five hundred thousand–volt line disabled, two other five hundred thousand–volt lines will become overloaded and shut down. This, in turn, causes the main power artery between geographic regions to shut down. Safety systems will automatically shed load in an attempt to keep the system in balance. However, the increased demand on the generators at other electric utilities causes a ripple effect.

"Every generator on the entire grid has to be spinning at exactly the same rate, sixty hertz, before it can be connected to the grid. They have software that minimizes frequency error, and software turbine governors that prevent the spin rate from going too high. We hacked that software so some of the generators will spin so fast that they will jump right off their moorings and go crashing around the floor, damaging all their turbine blades. It will take months to repair some of them. And Siemens and GE don't have huge warehouses of extras sitting around. It's all Build When Bought."

The General smiled. "That I understand. All of these little programs will start at the same moment?"

"All the executables are keyed to the power grid's atomic clock time. It all happens at nine o'clock, in ninety seconds." Packetman hit a stroke on his keyboard. "And we can watch it all live on their reporting system. The Saturday shift guys, they'll freak. Let's hope our emergency generators here work so we can watch."

"We could have made it much worse," the General observed. "Could have been a Monday-night rush hour in July. Could have been the entire country."

"Yeah," Packetman smirked, "but they're not gonna get it back for a while. The nuclear plants especially take a long time to come back up. The blackout will go on for days, into the workweek. And if we want, it could be weeks."

0859 PST

Electrical Reliability Coordination Center

Riverside, California

"It's so hot for March that they'll be turning on the air-conditioning in L.A., Phoenix, and Vegas before noon. You watch," Danny Hubbard told his supervisor, Fran Cella, as the two sat below a fifty-foot-long wall of large computer screens. In front of them were smaller screens and a bank of switches and lights. The indicators were all in the green. The voltage level on the transmission lines showed well above the critical minimums. The indicators had been reprogrammed by Packetman never to dip, never to alarm, no matter what the incoming data actually was. The same code change had been made systemwide by one cyberbot inserted into the control network.

"Yeah, but at least it's Saturday, so the load is light," she said, carefully dipping her Chinese herbal chai in the dragon-covered pot of piping-hot water.

Then, at substations and transformers throughout the California and Baja electric grid, an instruction message was received in the computer code language of the supervisory control and data acquisition system: drop voltage. Each programmable box obeyed. Monitoring systems scattered throughout the state instantly noticed the entire grid's voltage drop below safe minimums. The monitoring systems sent alarm messages to control centers: "High loading, low voltage without electrical faults on unprotected lines." Slightly over a minute later, three different sensors in the field sent in priority messages: "Potential for cascading failures." Packetman's handiwork sent the messages into cyber black holes. No needles moved. No lights flashed. No Klaxons sounded.

"How much are we buying today from Pacific Northwest?" Fran asked, blowing on the cup to cool the black tea. As she spoke, the large screens abruptly went dark and the room plunged into blackness. Fran Cella leaped out of her chair, reaching for a telephone. "Son of a bitch!" she screamed as the scalding water spilled down her chest. Slowly, a few dim yellow lights came on from battery pack emergency boxes mounted on the walls. "We lost power? *We* did? We're supposed to be running the grid, for Christ sakes! Danny, how's the grid?"

The big boards had failed to come back on. Danny Hubbard was glaring at a small monitor in front of his position and rebooting his desktop computer. "I thought the center had its own backup emergency generator?" he asked as his system spun up. "We're only on batteries."

"We do have a generator. Supposed to test it again next month," Fran said, hanging up the telephone. "Lines are dead. What's your screen say?"

"It says, 'System was improperly shut down. Data loss may have occurred.' No fucking shit!"

At the nuclear power plants in the desert, generators went into automatic shutdown mode because of the absence of external electrical power to support their emergency systems. Regional air traffic control at Los Angeles Center, running on its emergency generator, queried aircraft whether they had enough fuel to return to Honolulu or make it to Dallas. At LAX, the tower slowed landings and began stacking aircraft in the skies over the Pacific. Under the streets in Los Angeles, San Francisco, Oakland, and Berkeley, subway trains stopped dead in darkened tunnels.

Elevators in high-rise apartment buildings and office towers froze between floors. In casinos in Las Vegas, Reno, Laughlin, and Tahoe, gamblers fought over chips in dimly lit halls. At the ports in Long Beach and Oakland, giant cranes halted with shipping containers hanging in midair. At hospitals in twenty states, staff struggled with emergency generators, as nurses began shutting off patient monitors to shed load on the backup power and started trying to pry open windows for ventilation. Police moved patrol cars with lights flashing into intersections to direct traffic on surface streets, as the traffic control lights sat unresponsive.

At gas stations throughout the region, pumps stopped working. Quarter-mile-long trains with food, cars, and coal halted on tracks throughout the West as the railroad's control system went dark. At the prisons in Soledad, Folsom, and San Quentin, inmates clashed with guards attempting to put the institutions in lockdown. Pharmacies in Phoenix, Denver, and South Central Los Angeles were looted. At windowless high-rises filled with telephone switches and internet routers, batteries failed and switches crashed due to inadequate loads from backup power systems. Burglar alarms went off across the region.

Military bases in California and Colorado went on alert and rolled armored vehicles to the gates. The watch commander at LAPD headquarters ordered all off-duty officers to report in and issued the coded radio message that meant "don riot gear."

On the beaches of Venice and Malibu, no one noticed. The volleyball continued uninterrupted.

Basement Conference Room 3

The West Wing, the White House

"Rusty MacIntyre will be sitting in for Sol today," National Security Advisor Wallace Reynolds announced to the Secretaries of Defense and State. "You all know Russell, of course." Reynolds was in jeans and a Princeton sweatshirt.

"Why does he gets Saturdays off?" Secretary of State Brenda Neyers asked, only half kiddingly. "He's not Orthodox."

"He's out of town," Reynolds said testily. "He cleared it with the President. I just wanted to get a briefing today on what we could do in cyberspace, so we understand things better when we get the briefing on all the various options Monday from the Pentagon. I don't know about you, but I don't get how all this stuff works. And I thought if China or someone is messing with our computer things, well, maybe we could do that kind of thing too. Tit for tat. What was it you said, Bill—bytes not bombs, or something?"

Secretary of Defense William Chesterfield nodded at a general, who pointed his finger at a colonel, who turned on the projector. A slide appeared on the wall with two words written in white on a black background: Information Warfare. The General, Major General Chuck Mann, United States Air Force, spoke: "We define Information Warfare to be those actions which we take to affect the information available to the enemy, to include leaflet drops, radio and television programming, e-mail messages, and other media.

Whenever possible, our doctrine holds that the information used shall be truthful, although it can obviously be tailored to stress those things which we want the enemy to believe.

"In the 2003 liberation of Iraq, we successfully employed all of those media to send a message to Iraqi Army officers that they should not oppose us, that we were only after Saddam and his sons, they could stay in the Army, and that they should send their troops home for a while and should park their tanks and other vehicles in non-threatening formations. Many did what we asked and American lives were saved."

Brenda Neyers coughed. "Only to be lost later because we double-crossed the Iraqi Army, fired the Iraqi Army's officer corps, and failed to seize their weapons. We paid for that little lie for years, with the blood of our troops."

"Brenda, please," Wallace Reynolds chided. "There's no need to get into all of that again. It was almost a decade ago that all of that started. Not on our watch. But, General, if I may, I thought we were going to talk about computers?"

The General looked at the Secretary of Defense, who nodded for him to answer. "Sir, I was asked to prepare a briefing on Information Warfare. Computers do play a role. We did send the Iraqi officers e-mails."

Rusty MacIntyre saw the conversation was going nowhere fast. "Wallace, the military use the term 'Information Warfare' inter-changeably with the phrase 'Psychological Warfare.' What you are interested in, they call Computer Network Attack."

"Yes, right, Rusty. General, what can we do in this Computer Network Attack business?" Reynolds asked.

The General, still holding a small laser pointing device aimed at the screen, shifted on his feet and looked again at the SecDef, who sat poker faced. "Well, sir, that's all restricted, but I guess I can tell you, huh? We have developed some ability, especially after the Cyber Crash of 2009, to do some offensive work. Although frankly, sir, most of our attention is on information collection, not disruption. But we could, if ordered, do some things to some countries' air defense radar and some of their communication systems. I mean, if we had enough lead time and support from CIA, NSA, and the others."

Wallace Reynolds sat staring at the general.

There was a brief knock on the door and a member of the Situation Room watch team entered the room and passed a folded note to MacIntyre. He realized, as he read it, that all eyes in the room were on him. He folded the paper back up and turned to Wallace Reynolds. "Other nations apparently have the ability to do more, like turn out the electrical power in half our country," Rusty said dryly.

"What do you mean?" Secretary Neyers asked.

"All electrical power grids are down west of the Mississippi, except in Texas. That does not happen by accident," Rusty asserted. "The attack on our cyberspace and technology that started on Sunday, by disconnecting our cyberspace from the rest of the world, and continued with attacks on some of our major labs and commercial communications satellites, probably including the assassination of the heads of our federal science agencies, has now involved the largest power blackout in American history, one hundred million Americans thrown into chaos."

"If this is supposed to convince us to back off from the China-Taiwan dispute, I think it's having the opposite effect on me," the Secretary of Defense asserted.

"You don't know that China did this," Neyers replied.

"It wasn't Botswana, Brenda," Chesterfield shot back. His answer hung in the air.

Finally, Wallace Reynolds looked at Rusty MacIntyre. "How long will they be out?"

"Don't know."

Reynolds looked at Neyers and Chesterfield, who said nothing, then back at MacIntyre. "Can you go find out, Rusty? And while you're out there, ask the folks on the Situation Room watch team if we have an emergency generator. Have them check it."

1230 EST

Finneran's Boatyard

Marsh Harbor, Abaco Island

The Bahamas

"Are you lookin' to go to Hopetown?" the old man said from the boat. His aging face was brown, creased deeply, with white stubble sprouting here and there. "You Miss Connor? I'm Mr. Waters, Charles Waters. "

"Yes—are you here to take me across?" Susan asked, evoking a broad smile in the man. Several of his front teeth were missing. The thirty-two-foot Boston Whaler had twin battery-powered outboard motors, and the old man handled the new-looking boat as if it had been his for decades, a part of his body. He kept the speed down until he had maneuvered around the sailboats and docks in the harbor. Then, clear of Abaco Island, he opened it up for the short run across to Elbow Cay and its harbor at Hopetown. It was still winter in Washington, but in the Bahamas the temperature was in the low seventies, and Susan Connor felt the warmth of the sun as the boat bounced across the perfectly flat sea between the islands.

"Been to our 'Islands in the Stream' before, miss?" Waters asked.

"No, but I read the book," she replied, trying not to show her surprise at the boatman's Hemingway reference. "Is this the place?"

He nodded his head. "These cays. But they say the Stream is beginning to shift now because of the ice meltin' up north."

At the northern end of the Bahamas, Abaco and its smaller barrier islands of Elbow Cay, Guana Cay, and Man-O-War lie to the east of the Gulf Stream, in line with Fort Lauderdale. Although largely unknown in the United States, the island cluster has always been affected by the large neighboring nation. The victory of the American revolutionaries in the 1780s created the first settlers, refugee colonial Loyalists from the Carolinas. The Prohibition era brought a different kind of American, one willing to chance a run across the powerful Gulf Stream to Florida, carrying rum and Scotch. In the second decade of the twenty-first century, state and federal

laws and regulations against certain types of stem-cell organ generation and genetic engineering caused some Americans to quietly
convert some large villa complexes into high-tech labs and clinics.

"Still pretty shallow here," Susan noted. She sat in the seat by the
windshield to the left of the old man, looking over the side and
through the clear water at the rocks and sea grasses below.

"Doesn't get anything but shallow in these islands, not till you go
out into Atlantic, other side of Elbow Cay beyond the reef," Mr.
Waters said as he drove with one hand and sipped a Red Stripe with
the other. "We don't get many sisters goin' to Elbow or Man-O-
War. They still white man's islands."

"Really. I didn't know there were a lot of whites outside of
Nassau," Susan yelled back.

"They been here since they ran out the Carolinas when Georgie
Wash done won the war. Inbred and all. Talk funny." He cut the engine as they approached the mouth of a waterway leading into the
interior of Elbow Cay. "Now they're a few little hotels and cabins
on Elbow Cay for tourists, but Man-O-War's still just them original families. They make good boats out on Man-O-War and there's
a coupla big villas, but mainly its them same white-folk families that
come in the seventeen hundreds." The boat turned a corner to re-
veal a little crescent-shaped harbor, dominated on the right by a
candy-cane-styled lighthouse and on the left by a series of short
docks attached to open air bars. Even though the temperature was
in the high sixties, women in tank tops and shirtless men sat at tables in the sun. They were the white tourists who had found a place

off the beaten path. Rock music from one bar's speakers bounced across the water toward the lighthouse.

"This here's Captain Jack's," Mr. Waters explained as he threw a line onto the dock, "where you s'pose to be. I got your bag. Pleasure to take you across."

Susan now saw the man who caught the rope. He was tall, broad, in a short-sleeved blue Oxford button-down and white slacks. He was black and, Susan thought immediately, handsome. "Miss Connor, Mr. Gaudium sent me. I'm Arnold Scott." He helped her out of the boat and led her to a table under an umbrella. "I assumed you wouldn't have eaten, so I took the liberty of ordering you some lunch. Grouper and conch fritters, fresh and locally caught."

Over lunch, Scott kept to small talk about the islands and about himself. He said he had been told not to ask any details about Susan. She wondered what he knew. He was a graduate of Morehouse, class of 2003 ROTC. He had been out of the Army, Special Forces, almost two years. And he really enjoyed working for Dominion Commonwealth Services.

"Let's take a walk so we can talk more about what we're going to be doing," Arnie Scott suggested. They left the dock bar and wandered down the dirt road lined with small, pastel-colored cottages, an old London red telephone booth and a red British Royal Mail box. There were no cars on the island and little foot traffic. Susan noticed a golf cart beside a small grocery store. Scott suggested he show her the Atlantic side and the reef. They walked through the courtyard of a small hotel, the Hopetown Lodge, past its outdoor bar, to the beach. The bright white-sand beach seemed to stretch endlessly off to the right, entirely unoccupied by bathers. An almost unnaturally fluorescent turquoise water spread out from the beach to a line of foam a few hundred yards offshore. There, the Atlantic hit the long coral reef protecting the cay.

"Kind of ironic. Ponce de Leon landed here almost exactly five hundred years ago looking for the fountain of youth. Now these guys come here seeking life-extension genes," Scott said, shaking his head in disgust. "The lab is at the far end of Man-O-War Cay, which is the next island over in the chain. It's a big villa, walled off, with its own dock. They usually fly the patients directly to the dock on a seaplane from Fort Lauderdale. They spend a night, maybe two. Get tested and then do the procedure."

The March sea kept up a constant roar as it crashed on the reef a few hundred feet away.

"Arnie, exactly what do we know about the procedure?" she asked while looking out to sea.

"Only the basics. We think they add the new chromosomes to the embryo, probably *in vitro*. We're hoping you find out more. However they do it, they have a high rate of success, a money-back guarantee, and no complaints that we could find." He shook his head in disgust, "Its like that movie *Gattica*, where you could order up whatever added features you want in your kid. You just pay more for each addition."

Susan stopped and sat on the sand near the water's edge. "The ruling elite, the first wave of an entirely new genus."

"Let's hope they're the first and the last," Scott said bitterly. He continued to stand, towering above Susan.

Susan looked up at her escort. "Are you, like, a foot taller than me or what?" she asked, trying to get him to loosen up.

"Only eight inches," Scott said, and chuckled. She thought he had a pleasant face when he was smiling, not trying to be Army guy.

"And seven years younger, and we are supposed to be married and wealthy?" Susan rattled off what she knew of their cover story from reading the folder Gaudium had left for her on his plane. "Would you believe that shit?"

"I made three hundred thousand a year for three years in Iraq. You are a partner in a major consulting firm in Boston. You got yourself a smart, rich, young stud," Scott said as though he were only reciting the lines he had been given. "The height thing . . . I don't know about that."

"Did you make three hundred thousand a year in Iraq?" she asked.

"Hell no," he said definitively. "I did the same thing as guys getting three hundred K working for those private firms, but I was still in the Army, ma'am—I got one-tenth of that amount."

They walked along the empty beach away from the town. "Let's go over how this is supposed to work and what I'm supposed to find out," Susan asked.

"My orders are to let you satisfy yourself that there is an offshore facility creating designer babies with extra chromosomes," Scott explained. "They bring in nine women at a time, by the way, three times a week, and they have been doing that for almost a year and a half. If you can, find out exact numbers, ideally their addresses."

"Can't you steal their database?" She thought she'd push a little further. "Hackers?"

"These guys are smart. Their computers aren't connected to the internet. They don't use wireless." Scott stopped in the sand. "If you can, if you are alone in a room with a terminal or printer, there's a tiny bug I'll give you. It transmits out far enough for us to pick it up with an antenna and relay hidden in a rock we'll place on the beach. That could set up a path to get us into their LAN."

Susan listened and then started walking down the beach again. "And we didn't fly in on their seaplane because . . ."

"They only fly in the mothers, and our story is that you wanted me to come along, wanted to relax first with a few days on the beach," he answered, catching up with her. "They won't let me in, but I'll take you over to Man-O-War in the morning and walk you up the Queen's Highway to the gate by seven-thirty tomorrow morning."

"Queen's Highway?" she repeated.

"It's another sand-and-dirt path that runs from one end of the cay to the other. Their idea of a joke over on Man-O-War," Scott said, and flashed a toothy smile. Susan was thinking what was he doing working for some private security company and what was it doing working with Gaudium? Then Susan heard herself asking Arnie a question her subconscious generated: "Does Will manage the company now or just own it?"

"Oh, I think he's just the owner," Scott replied. "He's so busy with everything else he does."

"Yes, I know. Senator George came by the winery while I was there with Will. Have you met him yet? Dynamic speaker."

"Yes, yes, he is," Scott enthused. "I was on his protective detail for a week and then this assignment came up."

Susan lifted her sunglasses onto her head. "And where are the two rooms, might I ask, where the Scott couple are supposed to be spending the night?"

"Dominion has a house on Man-O-War we've been using for the surveillance, but I assumed you might want to stay in a hotel, so I got you a room here in the Hopetown Lodge. The boatman brought your bag there. Unless you want me to hang around, I'll bring the boat over from Man-O-War and pick you up at seven tomorrow."

"See you then," Susan replied, thanking her instinct or subconscious or wherever that question about Will and the security firm had come from.

After Arnold Scott left on his boat back to Man-O-War, she walked slowly down to the water's edge. She felt alone, out on a limb. What was she doing on an out of the way little island no one had ever heard of, by herself? She had signed up to be an analyst. But she had wanted more, to be involved, on the edge with the most important issues, crises. Now, as Rusty had done in the Islamyah crisis, she was playing it solo in the field, like an agent. She was not trained for this. She had almost been killed at Moffett Field. Even Jimmy had almost been killed at Twentynine Palms. And where had it got them? Sol had to fly off to Hong Kong, grasping at straws, trying to avoid a showdown with China. What had she done? She looked out at the surf on the reef.

Gaudium. She had found him and come to understand him, really sympathize with and appreciate him. Nonetheless, putting aside emotion, although she could not prove it yet, the analytical side of her brain was telling her there was a connection between him and the attacks. There had to be. He actually owned the security company that was protecting Senator George and had ex–Special Forces guys like Arnie Scott doing surveillance on *in vitro* fertilization labs. Gaudium was aware of the Man-O-War lab and, if Soxster was right, the hacker Packetman was, too. Packetman had said they were going to eliminate something. And Packetman had worked at the ranch that Jimmy had raided, the ranch from where somebody had attacked the Marines and probably the satellites, the people who were planning to kill hundreds. Shit! Was that the Hiroshima event Will had in mind?

Susan felt for her BlackBerry. Its battery still had juice. She needed to call Jimmy. She hit his speed-dial number. Nothing happened. There was no cell service on this side of Elbow Cay! She ran up the beach to the hotel. At the outdoor bar, the bartender was laughing with an American couple, handing them drinks with little umbrellas. There was a phone on the bar. It would be better to use it; her room phone might be bugged. "I'm staying here," she gasped. "Can I use this phone to call the States?" She called Jimmy's mobile number.

"How's the patient?" she asked.

"Great. I just took the bandages off and I can see fine, better than before," Jimmy said as he stared out of his apartment window in Battery Park City, zooming in on the Jersey shore. "You heard about California and the west, the blackout? Almost a hundred million people without power. They're saying it could not have been an accident."

"Shit, that will put even more pressure on the President to do something to somebody," she said, walking with the cordless phone to a table near the bar.

"Find anything yet in the Bahamas?" Jimmy asked.

"Yeah, yeah, I think so. Remember Soxster said a hacker knew about Man-O-War and how the hackers were going to penetrate something, stop something?"

"Sure, that was Packetman. I just talked to Soxster about that, because he also said Packetman wanted to attack the power grid," Jimmy said, looking at his notes.

"Will Gaudium knew about Man-O-War, too, and it turns out that Gaudium owns a security firm that is surveilling the place here. The firm is called Dominion Commonwealth something. Can you check it out?"

"You got it," he said, sitting down at his computer terminal. "You liking Gaudium in the attacks?" The landline phone rang and Jessica Foley answered it in the next room. Now she was waving at him, signaling that the call was for him.

"No, well, maybe, could be somehow connected." Susan put her hand up to the mouthpiece and spoke softly. "Jimmy, remember what

TTeeLer said, how they were going to kill hundreds sometime in March? Packetman says they're going to destroy something related to Man-O-War? Jimmy," Susan stopped and exhaled, "Jimmy, what if the hundreds they're going to kill are the *in vitro* children conceived at the Man-O-War lab? They don't have their addresses yet, but ..."

Jimmy said nothing. Then: "That's like the Bible, Suz, the Pharaoh ordering the children be slain. Passover."

Jessica was walking the phone over to Jimmy. "It's him," she said, holding up a phone. "It's Belov."

"I'll know tomorrow," Susan replied. "See what Soxster can dig up and keep getting a good rest. We need you recovered." Susan terminated the call and walked the phone back to the bar and said to the bartender, "Thanks for the phone. Do you have any Balvenie?"

In New York's Battery Park, Jimmy Foley traded phones with his wife.

"James," the voice on the phone began, "It's your lunch date. I may have some answers. Can you come to the Teterboro Airport? Now?"

2030 Local Time

Hong Kong

Sol Rubenstein marveled at the city-state. It had been years since he had been to Hong Kong. Its magnificent Kai Tak island airport, connected to Central by a maze of tunnels and suspension bridges, and its skyline of architecturally stunning eighty- and hundred-story office towers were startling. Every square inch, even on the steep hills, was covered with apartment towers that Rubenstein belatedly realized were routinely fifty stories high.

The economic success of the mainland had created, in effect, two river states. Guangzhou and Hong Kong and a series of smaller cities were the Pearl River state. Shanghai and a series of lesser-known, several-million-population cities on the Yangtze made up the other river state. The upriver cities each specialized in a different product, and in many cases they accounted for half to seventy-five percent of the world's output in the categories of things they manufactured. The coastal metroplexes were the ports, economic hubs, and increasingly international centers for the two river states. Why did they need Taiwan? Why were they even thinking about risking this magnificent economic machine that they had built?

The flex-fuel BMW 785 had been waiting curbside after he was whisked through Customs and Immigration by an expediter. China was now growing more whip grass than the United States and fueling more cars with flex-fuel or ethanol blends. Rubenstein had been the only passenger in first class on the Cathay Pacific 787ER that had flown him nonstop from Washington. The flight attendants had been amazed. First class was almost always full. So far, the Chinese were making it painless to go halfway around the world for a mysterious meeting. He had, however, not experienced the day that somehow disappeared as he crossed the international date line.

Arriving at the Grand Hyatt on the waterfront, Rubenstein was escorted through the lobby to the twelfth floor, where there appeared to be a special reception desk. The floor, he was informed, was a special Asian spa area. His room had blond wood paneling, a raised floor, its own steam room, and a deep tub with a picture window. From his balcony, he looked down on a frenzy of ferries and passenger ships zipping back and forth to Kowloon, Macau, and up the Pearl River. The high-rise towers all along the waterfront were engaged in some sort of synchronized light show. Inside on the desk was the traditional welcome letter from the manager, but next to it was a business card. It read: "Simon Manley, Purveyor of Fruits and Nuts, Durban, South Africa." Sol almost laughed out loud. The card's sender had used the same alias during the Islamyah crisis a few years before. Sol surpressed the laugh, assuming the room was bugged and not wanting to attract attention to his discovery. He flipped the card over and saw the handwritten scrawl: "Welcome. I will be in the spa garden at 9pm."

The spa garden was a series of outdoor rooms, meditation pools, and decks. He found "Simon Manley"—Brian Douglas—in the spa's bar and then followed him out to the lap pool. "This place still has a British flavor, Queens Road, Lower Albert Road, where the Foreign Correspondence Club still feels very colonial. I'm not so sure that we actually gave it up," Brian mused as they looked out at the harbor traffic.

"In some ways, you Brits gave up Hong Kong, but China didn't get it. It's a Special Autonomous Region for fifty years," Sol recalled. "Right?"

"With its own little army of twenty-five thousand police and a navy of over one hundred vessels," Brian added. "The way they operate reminds me very much of England, of Scotland Yard."

"The only part of Britain this reminds me of is the Docklands, with all its clusters of high-rises," Sol replied, walking up next to Brian at the edge of the balcony. "Was your previous stop productive? Find a lot of nuts?"

Brian placed a small digital camera on the railing and pressed its power button. A green light appeared. It had not detected a laser or other technical audio collection, and it was now sending out ultrasonic sound waves to break up any remote collection. "I'm not sure whether the man I met was a sincere source or someone the Guoanbu was running at me. Basically, he said President Huang did not authorize any attacks in or on America, has some loyal Guoanbu types checking into it, and is having a hard time reining in the leaders of the People's Liberation Army. Seems the PLA boys took the shoot-down by Taiwan personally and are looking to teach Taiwan a lesson if they push independence, even though it will cost the PLA and China a lot economically."

"Hmmph," Sol replied.

"I know, I know. It sounds like what the Chinese would want us to believe, but they did at least make a good show of chasing me and the source into the air-conditioning ducts," Brian added, sniffing at his single-malt. "But maybe Huang does need help, and it's certainly true that sailing the Seventh Fleet up close won't help things right now."

"My President needs help, too. We've sustained a lot more damage than the PLA's air force," Sol countered, turning his back on the harbor.

"They still haven't gotten most of California's power grid back online," Brian observed. "And if it wasn't China that did that attack and the internet beachheads, who did? I'm still betting on Beijing."

Sol Rubenstein shook his head in agreement. "Apparently the Pentagon has cleared Botswana as a suspect."

1530 EST

George Washington Bridge

New York City

"Don't you think it's dangerous, meeting him at a private airport? What if he plans to snatch you, kidnap you, take you to Russia, for God's sake?" Jessica Foley was looking at her husband as much as the traffic as she drove him to the executive jetport a few miles away on the New Jersey side. "Can't you call for backup or something?"

"Jess, you watch too many cop shows. I don't want backup. It may be better that I'm the only one, I mean, we're the only ones that know about this, whatever Belov has in mind." Jimmy had thought about calling his old partner, Vinny DeCarlo. "Why would Belov kidnap me? He's trying to help me."

"The mafia don, or czar, or whatever you call a Russian godfather, is trying to help you? Give me a break!" Jessica looked away from the traffic for a second and at her husband. "Jimmy, you arrested his nephew in Boston, you're sending him to Siberia."

"Petersburg, probably, but not if Belov comes through for me. I shouldn't have brought you along this morning. I think he might have made you for my wife. He calls on our landline." Jimmy gently pulled out his Sig and chambered a round. He felt his left calf for the holster with the concealed carry Walther P99. Jessica just looked at him. "Stay in the car," he said as he walked into the executive jet terminal.

He looked out at the apron. There were scores of private jets, from VLJs to the near supersonic-cruise Gulfstream VIIs, that could get to the coast in under three hours. "Gregori wants to see you in his plane," a deep voice said behind him. Jimmy flashed his credentials to the security guards and walked around the screening post onto the tarmac and out to a Yak-188 halfway down the flight line. Belov stood by the foot of the stairs to the plane.

Jimmy looked at the odd Russian aircraft. "This is not a Boeing, Gregori," he began. "When you're flying, you always want the plane to be American."

"Somebody owed me some money, so I got a plane instead. It's a nice plane, flies to Petersburg nonstop." Belov shooed his guard away. "Jimmy, before we go inside, I need another promise."

"Your nephew and Fort Drum. What else?"

"You wanted information, Jimmy. You wanted it fast. I got some of it, fast. You can forget how I got it, yes?" Belov waited for an answer.

"Within limits. You guys didn't shoot the Pope again, did you?"

Belov climbed into the Yak, and Jimmy followed. "Jimmy, this is Sergei Yellin, Dimitri's son. He will tell you what he learned today."

Sergei looked to be in his early thirties. He sat in one of the large flight seats that could recline into a bed. There were small stains on his shirt, darkened blood. His right hand was red and swollen. Jimmy was beginning to understand Belov's concern about methods.

"As you know, Detective, the day that my father disappeared, his body guards did, too. I have been paying their families survivors' benefits, with Gregori's help." He nodded respectfully to his new protector. "Usually on a meet with someone, Papa would take his car and the Escalade for the men. Then there would be a backup car trailing, something simple like a Chevy, sort of undercover. That day there was no backup car, because Papa told Igor Tumanek to run an errand over to Queens. That's what Igor told me." He exhaled. He was nervous, anxious, irate. "But when Gregori called me today after he met with you . . . I checked the E-ZPass bill for the Chevy. It went over the GW bridge thirty-two minutes after Papa's Caddy."

Belov picked up the story. "Igor was simply running late, like a half hour late. He was not involved, I'm convinced. If he had been doing his job, he would have been outside the alarm company up the street here where the meet took place. He would have heard or seen something. Dimitri would be alive today."

Jimmy sat next to Belov on the couch and asked him, "So how does this help me?"

"Igor realized something was up when he got to the alarm company and there was nobody there, no cars. He's a bright boy, lazy but bright, so he thinks 'Why meet in Teterboro unless you're using the Executive Jet airport?' He drives over to the airport, to here, where we are now. Let him tell you what he did then. Come with me."

Jimmy followed Belov through the cabin door into the rear compartment. A man sat bound and beaten, strapped in a flight seat, with a goon on either side of him. One of the men ripped off the duct tape over Igor's mouth, and with it some flesh. Igor moaned and gasped for air. Jimmy noticed a large bloody bandage totally covering Igor's right ear and wondered if there was anything left underneath it.

"Igor, tell this man in English about the planes," Belov instructed.

He gasped again and nodded toward a bottle of water. They let him have a short drink and then poured the rest over his head. He was shaking, but he spoke. "When I got to the airport, I saw the man. Dimitri call him Spetsnaz, but he call himself Coming Ham. It was the man I had seen at the other meet, the time before. I was supposed to follow him after the first meet, get his license plate, but it didn't work."

Belov shook his head at the incompetence. "Never do business with someone you do not know. Greed! Igor, go on."

"Mr. Spetsnaz was getting into a Gulfstream, but first he talk to his men at their Boeing. They were loading big bags onto the

Boeing." Belov struck him hard across the face. "What did you think were in those bags, Igor, you idiot?"

Surprisingly, Igor Tumanek continued with his story. "I write down the plane numbers and give some money to the girl inside the terminal, check out who owns them. I thought if I tell Sergei I was so late, he'd be mad, so I didn't give him the names. Until today."

Belov stood and walked back to the forward cabin. Jimmy went, too, leaving Igor Tumanek with his mob associates. "The names come back to shell companies in Vienna and McLean, Virginia," Belov said, reseating himself next to Sergei Yellin. "You know what that means, Jimmy. You guys."

For a moment, Jimmy wondered if he was going to be strapped into a chair, too. "It means somebody wants it to look like CIA. Please give me the names and I will personally find out."

"And you will tell us," Sergei added.

"I will."

Belov stood. "Let's get off the plane. Sergei is taking Mr. Tumanek to Petersburg tonight. Or maybe Igor won't make it all the way."

Back in the terminal, Belov wanted to cash in. "Good enough?"

"If that lead gets me where I want to . . . Wait a minute. Hold on," Jimmy said, looking over Belov's head. There was a surveillance camera on the wall. He turned and looked out the window at the ramp. There were cameras all the way down the flight line. He walked over to the TSA screeners and pulled aside the supervisor, flashed his credentials again. "The cameras, they're digital? You keep back files?"

"Sure they're digital. Intelligent surveillance software does the looking for us, then it's all fed to D.C. in real time and stored at headquarters. I think they keep it ninety days. But you'll need a warrant."

Jimmy walked away, then hit his headset and then hit the touchpad inside his jacket. "Sox, my man. TSA headquarters. How's their firewalls and shit?"

"Piece a cake, James. Whaddaya need? How's the eye thing working? They give you an upgrade?" Soxster was already typing in the IP address of TSA's internal network.

When he was done talking to the Dugout, Jimmy walked back to Belov. Then he hit another speed dial. "Tommy, how are ya? How's my aunt doin'? Listen, Tom, remember that Russkie from up in Lynn there? The one I wanted to send to Novosibirsk? Yeah, that's the slimeball. Listen, Tommy, turns out he was an innocent bystander. No, really. So you're the charging officer on it, right? No, don't let him walk, we need him on a federal case. May hafta put him in the Wipp somewheres. I'll work out the details with ya tomorra. Great, Tommy. Hey, and remember the Yanks are gonna clobber them Red Sox down in Florida Monday. Right, Tom. 'Night."

"I assume that was Gaelic." Belov looked up at the tall, young Irish-American. "Thank you."

"Fort Drum may take a while," Jimmy said, shaking hands, "but it'll happen."

Belov began to walk off and then turned. "And thank your partner, Susan Connor. She looks so much like your wife, Jessica."

1830 EST

The Dugout

Watertown, Massachusetts

As usual, Soxster was the first to show up at the Dugout. Saturday night usually meant pizza, beer, and the liveliest activity in the private hacker chat rooms where passwords and credit-card numbers were traded for newly discovered flaws in websites and source code. He punched in his security code and then pushed the ten-foot-long warehouse door back on its wheels. The shards of glass by the door were the first things he noticed. Then he saw that the shelves, which had held every imaginable type of server, PC, and storage device, were empty. At their workstations, the monitors had been smashed.

Realizing that the men responsible might still be around, or have left a couple of thugs nearby, Soxster reached inside his parka to its zippered inside pocket and withdrew the P232 and its clip. It was a SIG-Sauer, but not the law-enforcement kind like Jimmy's. It was a knockoff of the famous Walther PPK, a .380 designed to fit in a pocket or an ankle holster. Jimmy had reluctantly talked

Tommy McDonough into giving Soxster a concealed carry permit, which was practically impossible to get out of the Mass. State Police. Soxster slipped in the clip and chambered a round. He wished he had spent more time at the Rod and Gun Club range in Acton.

Crouching down, Soxster moved into the Dugout, holding the gun with both hands. He moved behind Greenmonsta's workstation. It had been trashed and, he noticed, the hard drive had been ripped out of the Mac G8. All the hard drives were probably gone. He hoped there were fingerprints as he sat quietly on the floor, listening for any sound in the cavernous space. Quietly, he slipped out his PDA and tapped out a text message to the Dugout group list: "Dugout raided. Stay away."

Then he thought about calling Jimmy and remembered the urgency of the task Foley had given him. He carefully stepped back out of the Dugout into the corridor and hit the speed dial for Jimmy Foley. "The Russians, the Chinese, whoever, they've been here. Trashed everything, ripped off the hard drives. What do I do?"

The Foleys had just arrived back at their little Battery Park City apartment overlooking the Hudson. "Okay. Don't panic." Jimmy could hear the tension in Soxster's voice. "Clear the zone, but with your eyes open. Be careful of places somebody could be hiding. Then get in the car and drive over toward Boston University, 1010 Comm. Ave. It's Tommy McDonough's office. Don't take your weapon in with you. Stay there. Maybe he'll let you use his computer, but at any rate you'll be safe there. Tommy will send a forensics team over to the Dugout." Jimmy paused a moment and added, "There's nothing in there that shouldn't be in there, right, like—"

"Drugs? Hell no," Soxster said into his earpiece. "Shit! I bet those bastards took my Kistler chard." Soxster took the fire escape out of the building, hopped a fence, and hailed a cab to near BU. McDonough arrived while Soxster was still trying to explain things to the uniformed trooper in the State Police lobby.

"Jimmy said this was damn important," Tommy McDonough explained. "Better be, cuz I was comped Celtics tickets. Had ta give 'em to the neighbor kid." He showed Soxster into a room filled with computers.

"Wow, antediluvian," Soxster let slip.

"This is just stuff we've seized. Keep it for parts. Good stuff's back there. You set up in there, while I get the forensics boys in from their Saturday-night beans and franks with the family." On his way out of the door, McDonough turned back to Soxster, "They ain't gonna find no drugs in there, right?"

Soxster felt a little odd using one government agency's computer crime lab to hack another government agency's network, but moving fast was important and it would be late Monday by the time TSA agreed to give them what they needed. He was glad that he kept some key tools on his 100-gigabyte PDA. He was quickly on to an anonymity-providing server in Canada, then out to a university system in Texas, then the public library in New York City, on to a system located somewhere at an internet exchange point. He began capturing all of the digital conversations to find any traffic having an IP address that fell within the network ranges assigned to TSA. There were plenty to choose from.

The communication stream he chose was a file sharing app that tunneled over port 80, designed to let users access the internet with a web browser and not be blocked by the firewall. It was running as a TSA employee downloaded a pirated copy of a movie still playing in theaters. Taking that path in, Soxster scanned the network. There were no internal firewalls or file-encryption system. They also had not instituted identity-based access-control lists. He looked for big network storage devices where video logs would reside. Bingo!

It was huge, terabytes of files. He searched on "Teterboro" and "03.10.12." There were four cameras. He began with the file "Internal/terminal/magnetometer" and sent it sailing to the music file-sharing application on his new State Police desktop. As he started to load "flight line—north," the connection was broken and an image of a red stop sign popped up with the words. "You are engaged in an unauthorized transmission of government files out of the TSA network. This may be a criminal act punishable by a million-dollar fine or twenty years in jail, or both. TSA/CISO."

"Shit!" Soxster said in the empty room, and broke the connection. They must have had some egress-control system looking for large file transfers. Well, at least he got one big file out. Jimmy had said to begin looking at people arriving about three in the afternoon and freeze-frame the faces of all the adults. That would take a while, even using the intelligent video and facial recognition software he had acquired. And then there was the little problem that they had no database of faces with which to compare the images, no facial-recognition equivalent of mug sheets. Or at least, not yet. But he was inside a State Police computer room.

While the first desktop machine sorted through the file from Teterboro, Soxster moved to another workstation and logged in as "McDonough, T." He hit the "forgot password" link and the system was soon asking him to supply "favorite sports team." McDonough had said he had Celtics tickets, but his favorite team could have been the Patriots, Sox, or Bruins. Then Soxster thought: I bet McDonough went to Boston College. The Eagles. Soxster went with it and was quickly inside the State Police network. Not only did they have mug shots, they had access to FBI mug shots. Soxster got to work.

A few hours later, as the clogged local area network that he had strung together was churning away comparing faces at Teterboro Airport with known criminals, he checked in with Jimmy Foley in New York. "You know, James, already I can tell you an awful lot of these guys at the Executive Jet terminal have had serious trouble with the Securities and Exchange Commission."

"Not surprising. But no one who was mobbed up, no Russkies?" Jimmy asked.

"Nope, not using this database."

"Any Asians, Chinese-looking?" Jimmy asked.

"Sure, but I don't know who they are," Soxster said, starring at the faces zooming by on the screen.

"Can you believe there were one hundred and eight takeoffs out of that airport after three o'clock that afternoon? I got the printout from the FAA. That place makes LaGuardia look sleepy," Jimmy mused while poring through a spreadsheet. "No one went anywhere suspicious, unless you count West Palm, and they were all aircraft owned by big corporations or chartered by them: Mousenet, Google, Nanotech, Pharmagen." He scrolled down the list. "Then alphabet soup. GE, GD, SAIC, BAH, DCS, EMC, CNN . . ."

"We need Susan," Soxter admitted. "How's she doing down in the Bahamas by herself? Kind of scary, her soloing. I don't trust Gaudium, and I think she's fallen for his whole line of crap about how we shouldn't 'change what it means to be human.' "

"I talked to her this afternoon," Jimmy replied while cross-referencing company names. "I think she's getting suspicious of Gaudium, too. She wanted you to check out the private security firm he owns, Dominion Commonwealth Services—sounds pretty vague."

"That would be DCS? Didn't you just—" Soxster hoped he had heard correctly.

"Shit, yeah," Jimmy said, pulling up the flight list. "Gulfstream VII registered to DCS, Dover, Delware. Took off at 1705 headed for Santa Rosa. Where's that?"

"California. It's about twenty minutes south of Napa, and, guess what, it's even closer to Russian River," Soxster said, snapping his fingers.

"Could still be innocent. Gaudium owns a security firm, which undoubtedly does some business in Manhattan. Execs from the firm fly out to see the owner. Nonetheless . . . ," Jimmy said as he was hunting for the Dominion Commonwealth Services website. There wasn't one.

"Who doesn't have a website?" Soxster asked.

"It's incorporated in Delaware," Jimmy noted.

"They all are. I think Delaware gives out coupons for free upgrades at Marriott when you register three or more companies," Soxster joked as he surfed to the Delaware Secretary of Corporations site. "Okay, here it is. Their offices is a P.O. box in Sperryville, Virginia. Gaudium is not listed as an officer. There is an Elizabeth Eloh, who is the CEO, and an R. Nayk is the secretary and treasurer of the corporation. They are not publicly traded."

"Let's Google them," Jimmy said, looking for any reference to the company, anywhere in cyberspace. "Oh, here's something. They must be pretty legitimate. They ran a recruiting ad in *Army Times* and in *Christian Soldiers*. And here's a story about the guy who used to run SOCOM, Special Forces Command—General Bowdin, retiring to go be the COO at Dominion Commonwealth."

"Bowdin? Francis X. Bowdin?" Soxster asked. "Isn't he the guy that got forced out for giving fundamentalist evangelical speeches to the troops? Yeah, and he was mentioned in Professor Myers's article. He was a leading crusader against Transhumanism. Saw it leading to the 'End of Days.' "

"What the fuck is Transhumanism?" Jimmy asked.

"It's a movement that supports improving humanity through genetic engineering, enhancements of all kinds, including human-machine interface, brain downloads, nano implacements, things like your eye . . . ," Soxster sputtered.

"How do you know about my eye? Never mind, keep that fact to yourself," Jimmy muttered as he pulled up a Google image of Francis X. Bowdin in his Special Forces green beret. "Try an image of Bowdin on the facial-recognition software."

"Already did." Soxster sat looking at an image of Bowdin in civilian clothes, walking through the Teterboro security check at 1621 on March 10. "It still may not prove anything."

"Wait a minute. Jesus Christ!" Jimmy screamed into his headset. "It does prove something. The guy who hired the Russians who blew up the beachheads, the guy who probably them killed them. Dimitri Yellin called him Mr. Spetsnaz because he reminded him of a Russian soldier. Spetsnaz . . ."

". . . means Special Forces!" Soxster finished the sentence. "Once you look like an SF general, you always look like an SF general. It's been him that China has been using to fuck us over, bomb shit."

"I'll bet my wife's paycheck that it's been him." There was elation in Jimmy's voice. "But probably not working for China, but for Gaudium. Look at it. Bowdin's a religious fanatic all worked up about this Transhumanism, just like Senator Bloviator. He teams up with a rich, mad scientist who shares the same fears. Motive, means, opportunity."

"Wait, Jimmy. Susan is down on some atoll alone with Bowdin's guys, who are probably about to blow up some baby clinic."

"And she's probably about to be blown up in some baby clinic. I got to get a message to her without letting them know that we're onto them." Jimmy zoomed his right eye in on Ellis Island as his mind raced. "And I have to prove all of this to Rusty before the Pentagon bops China. It's been us, Americans, all along. Shit!"

8 | *Sunday, March 15*

"I didn't think you would come," Wu Zhan said, walking across the room to greet Sol Rubenstein.

"It's been a while," Sol offered, shaking hands.

"Since you rounded up my network and ran me out of Washington, you mean?"

"You left of your own volition, as I recall, before we declared you *persona non grata,*" Sol recalled.

"Yes, after the FBI accidentally ran my car off the road into Rock Creek."

"Was it the FBI that did that?" Sol asked. "No hard feelings?"

"The best thing you could have done for me. As you know, I now run the foreign intelligence service of the Ministry, but I report directly to the President on certain matters. Come, let us have breakfast—your flight is in a few hours and we have much to talk about."

As they sat by the window in the private dining room, Sol gazed again at the skyline, the busy traffic in the harbor. "Beautiful city, but why here? Why not in Beijing?"

"Too many people to see us in Beijing, including your embassy. Hong Kong is neutral ground," Wu explained.

"It's part of the PRC," Sol asserted.

"Yes, but it is a Special Autonomous Region. It has its own elected government, own charter of rights, own flag, own police. Beijing exercises little control." The waiter wheeled in a table with plates of scrambled eggs, bacon, pancakes, pastries, and fruit. "I developed many bad habits living in the States. High-cholesterol breakfasts were one of them." After piling his plate, Wu Zhan got down to business. "President Huang asked me to run operations to determine who was behind the attacks in the U.S., the internet bombings, the hackings. He did not know if it was the PLA or some arm of the Ministry. He asked me to spy on his government, my government."

"And, let me guess, it wasn't the PLA or the Ministry," Sol said flatly.

"You won't believe me, but I will offer you proofs. No, it was neither the Ministry of State Security, nor the military. But that is not to say that we do not monitor your cyberspace. As you yourself uncovered, we are well placed to see what is going on.

"The only connections to China were some hacks that were

routed through Dilan University. They originated in California. Is there a Bagdad in California? Also, the hacks into the commercial satellites came from near there, within fifty kilometers. I have had all the files translated into English and placed on this thumb drive," Wu said, placing a jump drive on Sol's side of the table.

"I am afraid that isn't proof enough. Somebody hired people in the U.S. to do these attacks. Who else would? You are threatening the new Taiwan government, placing your military on alert, running exercises along the coast and in the straits. You want us to back off, not to help Taiwan. So you send us a message. You're also worried about the technological gap we have blown open again and you had a plan on the shelf to redress it. You implement that plan as the way of sending us a message. In New York, we call it a two-fer." Sol spoke forcefully, staring at Wu.

"Sol, why would we do that? Our economy is tied to yours. We have lost billions already because of the attacks on the cyber connections and satellites. There are some who think a temporary economic dislocation is acceptable to get Taiwan back, but who is to say it would be temporary? And how do we control the provinces during an economic downturn? We are already having unrest in the villages." Wu paused to see if he was persuading his old foe.

"We're about to leave you in the dust technologically again," Sol countered. "To borrow from the late, lamented Chairman Mao, there will be a Great Leap Forward, but this time it will be ours. Of course, you want to slow us down."

"Yes, we have noticed the tech gap opening up again. We aren't as good at genomics, nanotech. Living Software will set us back, at least until you let us be part of Globegrid. But we have plans to catch up. We are spending billions of yuan on research and training." Wu reached into his idiomatic English: "Why kill the goose that lays the golden egg?"

"Wu Zhan, you know as well as I do that there are those in the PLA who think you have become too economically tied to the U.S., who would gladly sacrifice for a while to disentangled our two economies. We have our sources, too," Sol asserted.

"The PLA is a problem. They took the election of the Independence Party in Taiwan very badly. And to rub salt in the wounds, the idiots on the island then shoot down PLA fighter planes. Their apology and offer of money was offensive. They shoot us down using a new laser gun, no less. Something we don't have. That's the tech gap they worry about. PLA studies say that if they don't retake Taiwan soon, the defensive technology on the island may get to the point where it cannot be invaded successfully," Wu explained.

"So they want to invade it now?" Sol asked.

"Yes. And some of them even believe that the Pentagon has staged these attacks in America to blame them on China, so that the President and Congress will want to fight us. They think the Pentagon is planning something for later this year, for your election. That's why they want to go first and take Taiwan."

Sol looked out the window and shook his head. Then, looking back at Wu, he asked, "How can they possibly believe that the Pentagon would kill Americans?"

"They mirror-image, Sol. The PLA would murder Chinese; they have. The PLA also knows there is a big U.S. exercise coming, strategic bombers in Guam and Australia. Atlantic Ocean–based aircraft carriers coming into the Pacific. What other conclusion could they come to?"

Sol pushed away his plate and stretched his long frame out, with his legs extending away from the table. He briefly closed his eyes. The jet lag was hitting him. He sighed. "How do you suggest we back our two sides down?"

"Give us something on Taiwan, have them say they will accept a Special Autonomous Region status, like Hong Kong," Wu pressed.

"That's what this is all about, isn't it? You'd love that, have us abandon the Taiwan Relations Act?" Sol asked sarcastically. "Ain't going to happen."

"Without that, President Huang may not be able to control events."

Sol stood up. "Thank you for breakfast. I have a flight to catch."

0715 EST

Hopetown, Elbow Cay

The Bahamas

Susan had risen early and run three miles of the six-mile-long is-land, on the hard-packed sand below the high-tide line. She had run in college, but now her sport was tennis and she was getting pretty good at it. She had beaten Sam during their end-of-year getaway in Boca Raton. As she stood at the top of the stairs at the lodge, high above the quaint harbor with its 1863 candy-cane lighthouse, she spotted Arnold Scott at the helm of the whaler, just entering the harbor. Then she felt her BlackBerry vibrate, finally getting a signal now that she was higher up and facing Marsh Harbor. She checked her messages. There was an encrypted signal marked urgent from JXF3, Jimmy.

Scott waved up to her and began to maneuver the whaler into the lodge's dock at the bottom of the stairs. "Be right down," she yelled. She stepped back into the lodge and read the message. "DSC is run by a retired general named Bowdin. We think he recruited and ran the hackers, killed the Russian mobsters. We think he and Gaudium are in league. You may be right about them planning to kill the children, but we haven't figured out how. The kids are probably all over the U.S. You may just want to pull out now and we will send people in to find out. We can get the Bahamas police to sail over and get you."

She thought for a moment and then sent a message back. "May not be time to organize others to go in. I have to save the children, no matter how many chromosomes they have." She waved good-bye to the lodge owner as he sat down to an old PBX call router. All the phone lines in the little hotel were routed through the ancient switch to the one outgoing line.

"I see you're wearing your Sunday go-to-meeting clothes. Very nice," Scott said as Susan stepped down in to the whaler in a pink pantsuit.

"There weren't very many choices. I've been on the road for almost a week." Susan realized how big it had been as she said it. "But I wore sneaks for the boat."

"Well, it's very appropriate for an expectant mother, or one who hopes to be one," he replied. Scott expertly handled the boat through the crowded little cove, into the channel, and then almost stood the boat up in the water as he sped toward the next cay, Man-O-War. "No buoys around here. You really have to know where you're going, because it's so shallow and there are lots of sandbars," he yelled over the gas-driven outboards. The boat bounced across the clear water.

"If it's not too personal, have you thought about actually having kids?" Scott asked. "I don't mean these freak kids, but your own, natural ones?"

"You sound like my mother." Susan spoke over the engine noise. "Here's what I tell her: If my husband and I decide to, we'll let you know."

"It's fun playing your husband, but what does the real guy do?" Scott asked.

"Boyfriend. He's a doctor."

"I'll bet he's a white guy," Scott replied.

Susan gave him a look. "Well, as it turns out, this one happens to be. Why?"

"Tough for the brothers to succeed in America. Schools, drugs, gangs. A bright woman like you wants to be with successful men, and unless you go in the Army or are a super athlete . . . ," he explained.

"I know lots of successful black men, most of whom were never in the Army or the NBA," Susan countered. "You got to get out more, Arnie."

He cut the engine as the whaler moved into the harbor channel at Man-O-War. Susan could see a cute village of cottages and a few larger buildings. "Where's the clinic?"

"Isolated, all by itself on the northern edge of the island, about a mile and a half," he said, pointing. He brought the whaler into the large, wooden public dock and tied up. At the edge of the dock, Susan looked up and down the path at the few stores. They were closed for Sunday. "Before I walk you up there, we should go back to our safe house first," Scott declared.

"Why? I'm supposed to be at the gate by half past." Susan checked her watch. It was 7:20 A.M.

"Well, there are some guys there from DCS, came in last night, who you should meet first," he said, hesitating.

"No," Susan said, beginning to walk down the path, "No, Arnie, I think I'd better get moving."

"It's not a request," Scott barked. He reached out a long arm to grab her. She saw his hand move toward her in slow motion. Her synapses fired. They know. They know we're onto their plot to kill the children. The damn hotel phone. She bolted and sprinted up the path between two cottages. She saw his face, charging behind her, mean and focused. She ran hard, putting distance between them. There were clothes out on a line drying, and she dodged quickly behind them. No one was out on the pathways; they were in church. She saw a wooden stairway that led back to the water and she leaped down the steps. A dog went wild inside a cottage on her left. A rooster was crowing. She turned at the bottom of the stairs to look back, just as he arrived at the top. He was closing the distance between them.

She heard laughing from nearby and saw a large shop on a pier, opening up. A large white woman was putting a stick under a shutter window to prop it open and let in the air. Susan ran for her, down the pier toward the store. A sign said "Sail and canvas makers since 1793." She burst inside the store. It was filled with brightly colored canvas bags. "Susan! Stop!" she heard from too close behind her. She turned and pushed over a table piled high with red, orange, and yellow canvas tote bags, then ran into the interior of the factory and outlet. "What's going on out there?" someone yelled from inside. Susan turned a corner and saw three big women sitting at some sort of large cutting and sewing machines. Bolts of the bright canvas hung overhead.

"He's after me. He's trying to rape me," Susan heard herself scream as she ran toward the women.

She heard the nearest woman say, "Ain't none a our affair what you black people do." The white woman had arms bigger than Susan's legs and a look on her face like she had just seen an ugly bug. Arnold Scott exploded into the room, panting, "You can't escape us."

Susan saw an open doorway that led out onto the pier in the back. There was a small motorboat tied up. She ran between the machines toward the door and tripped over a pile of bags on the floor. She turned to get up, and Scott was over her. She kicked away, but he grabbed her ankle with a hand that felt like hot steel.

"I won't let you kill the children!" she screamed.

He reached down and put a hand under her, raising her whole body in the air, as she tried to kick his face with her one free leg. He was yelling, "You have to come with . . . ARRR, oh, oh." He dropped her hard on the wooden floor. She opened her eyes, but saw only lights and whirls, flashing. Arnold Scott was stretched out on top of one of the machines, with three large women standing around him holding blood-covered knives and giant scissors. One of them came over and stood above Susan. Susan watched blood drip onto her suit and saw that there was already a spray of fresh red blood on her side.

"Come on up, darlin'. Ain't gonna be no gang rapes or child killed on our island. Haven't been in over two hund' years," the large woman said as she pulled Susan up. "You get out of here now, fast, and we'll keep him 'til our men come."

Susan did not hesitate. She ran to the front door.

"You folks stay off our island!" she heard the first woman say as Susan made it onto the pathway outside. She was turned around. The clinic was on the north end; that would be to the left. She looked to see if Scott's associates were about and then ran again up to the main path. There was a hand-painted wooden sign where the paths met: "Queen's Highway." She turned left on the white sand path and began running again. The sand here was loose and she slipped. It was 7:30 by her watch. There was thick vegetation and palm trees on both sides of the path, but no more cottages. She began power-walking, inhaling deeply. She started to think. They would be waiting for her at the gate, the men from Scott's team. Her BlackBerry was still in her pocket. Again, there was no signal.

The path bent and then there was a long straightaway ahead. She could see a gate and a wall at the end. Then she noticed a golf cart and two men in blue blazers. Maybe they hadn't seen her. She began to cut through the underbrush toward the beach. Maybe she could approach the clinic-villa from the beach side and avoid the men at the gate. Prickly vines scratched her and tore tiny rips in her suit jacket. She was afraid the pink suit could be seen through the trees.

Finally she made it to the beach. Unlike the southern part of the island, the beach here was rocky, coral. She pulled off the pink jacket and felt the cold ocean breeze on her back, drying the sweat. Stumbling over the coral and rock, she kept close to the edge of the trees in case someone was watching the beach. As she approached the place where the villa's wall met the beach, she moved down toward the water's edge. The sand was hard. Then she ran. Her calves were hardening up, her legs heavy to lift. She did not slow to look along the wall toward the gate, but kept running to the stairs she saw ahead. They were carved in the coral and went up to the lawn in front of the villa.

At the top of the stairs, the lawn looked like a broad green putting field. She caught her breath, ran her fingers through her hair, and walked to the first door she could find. "Oh my God!" a woman called out as Susan walked into a lounge.

"Honey, what happened to you?" a woman in a flowered dress asked as she got out of her chair and approached Susan. "You look like you just ran through a windmill. Oh dear, is this blood? Are you bleeding?" The woman backed away.

Susan stood looking at six very well dressed white women in their thirties, who had identical expressions of surprise, horror, and distaste. "I fell on the path. I—I'm late for my appointment," Susan managed to get out. "Where is the doctor, the director?"

"Oh, you must be one of the new class, arriving today? We're the group that's flying back this morning. They all went in for the welcome lecture." The flowered-dress woman pointed up a corridor leading off the lounge. "But you'll want to freshen up first, I'm sure. . . ."

"No, no. I need to tell them—tell them I'm here," Susan said, brushing past the group and moving into the corridor. Halfway up the hall on the right was a door labeled "Pharmacy." She tried the doorknob and moved inside. No one was there. The cabinets were padlocked, but there, on the counter, was a telephone. She hit nine, hoping for an outside line, and then punched in Jimmy Foley's cell phone number.

It clicked into voice mail. "I'm at the clinic and I need to be extracted, and by guys with guns." She hung up and started to punch in the IAC Watch Office when she heard male voices, arguing, ap-

proaching. "You can't go in there," one man said. "She's having a sui-
cidal incident, a breakdown. We need to get her out of here," came
the reply. The rest was drowned out by an engine roar outside.
Susan peeled back part of the blinds to see out of the window, as a
large white seaplane pulled toward the coast-side dock. She saw an
awning-covered doorway on the outside a few windows down to the
left. If she could get to that door on the inside, it would be a straight
run to the seaplane.

She tried a connecting door to the next room. It opened into a
storage room filled with blue boxes. Something on the boxes at-
tracted her. "First Year" it said in large yellow letters. Under that,
she read: "Special Baby Formula, not to be used by children for
whom it is not prescribed. This formula has been created to enhance
your baby's special condition. It will be FedEx-ed to you every two
weeks. If for any reason a shipment is late, call 888-800-BABY." It
meant something. She tried to bring back the memory.

It was Jimmy's notes of his first and only meeting with TTeeLer
in the pool hall, in California. What was it? TTeeLer had said formula. She opened her BlackBerry and scrolled to the notes and the
recording Jimmy had made during the meet. She advanced through
the conversation, listening on her earpiece. Then TTeeLer's voice,
from the grave: "No, I left when I heard the talking about needing
to hack in somewhere to change the formula on something. He said
'It'll kill 'em all, hundreds, maybe thousands.' Listen, whatever your
real name is, Jimmy, I will steal from you in cyberspace if you are

stupid enough to let me, but I am no killer. Nobody's giving me the needle in some state pen. So I waited for the next cash disbursement and left the reservation."

They didn't know the addresses of the families with the extra-chromosome children, Susan thought, but somebody did, somebody who shipped the formula every two weeks. You don't need to get their addresses if you hack in and alter the formula in a lethal way during its manufacturing, inserting some gradual poisoning. The clinic will ship the children the poison without knowing it. When had the altered formula started being shipped? She couldn't just bolt for the seaplane; she had to tell the doctors immediately.

Susan opened the door to the corridor and found a man in a white medical lab coat slumped on the floor. She turned a corner. Two men in blue blazers were holding another man against a wall.

"It's her!"

"Stop!"

She ran for the door to the dock. The seaplane's engines over-rode any other sound. She charged toward the plane. Over the roar, she thought she heard a gunshot. Turning, she saw a man in a blazer point a gun at her from the steps of the clinic. She rolled onto the dock. Maybe she could get to the water before . . . *FWHACKKK!*

Another shot. But it also missed her. She lifted her head up to look toward the clinic. The man in the blazer was sitting on the ground, up against the door, blood pouring from his head. Susan rolled onto her back and looked straight up at the sky. Set against the deep blue was an incongruously red-orange helicopter, with a man sitting outside while the helicopter flew, sitting on a landing sled, holding a rifle.

The noise of the helicopter merged with the roar of the seaplane surrounding her and piercing through to her bones, but through it she could make out a few words: "United States Coast Guard . . . Royal Bahamian Police . . . shut down . . . do not attempt . . ." The helicopter hovered in front and above the seaplane until the larger aircraft shut down its engines. Susan stayed flat on the dock. The helicopter landed on the lawn. And then it was quiet.

0800 EST

Washington, Virginia

General Bowdin's Hummer H3H, powered by its hydrogen cell, turned off the state highway and onto the road into the town. "I didn't know there was a Washington in Virginia, except the real one, the big one. I guess it's kind of in Virginia," the driver said, taking advantage of being alone with the big boss, chatting him up.

"This is the real one, Todd, not that swamp up north. George Washington himself surveyed all around here before he joined the Army. Folks here named the town after him long before the Feds set up camp on the mosquito-ridden shores of the Potomac."

As they entered the town, the driver pulled to the side of the road. "Sir, my orders don't say where to go in the town. And they just say to take you to the inn. No name for the inn."

"Hell, Todd, it's not a big town. Just drive around—it ain't enemy territory."

The H3H got some stares as it slowly moved down Gay Street, past quaint shops, past tiny brick cottages that housed the county government, past two theaters, including one that had been a church. At the corner, the General spotted a building with both French and American flags. "That's got to be it," he told the driver.

"Gee, sir, the street name, what they did to that church, and now a frog flag—what kind of town is this? You sure this ain't enemy territory?"

A uniformed doorman had appeared and was trying to open the Hummer's door for the General. "Park in that lot over there," the General spat out to Todd, "and don't get out of your vehicle."

Striding into the foyer, the General was quickly met by a greeter. "Good morning, sir. I'm sorry to inform you that we do not serve breakfast to the public. Only dinner."

Bowdin looked around at the elaborate decor. "Looks like a damn New Orleans whorehouse."

"I wouldn't know, sir."

"I bet you wouldn't," General Bowdin sneered. "I am not the public. I am joining Mr. Gaudium for breakfast, if that's all right with you."

"Oh yes, very good, sir. He's expecting you in our Mayor's House suite, across the street. Please follow me, and if you like, we can go through the kitchen." They walked through a small bar, where a member of the staff was playing with two Dalmatian dogs. In the large, sunny kitchen, Gregorian chants played. The kitchen staff wore white pants with a Dalmatian pattern of black splotches. The General passed other Dalmatian-patterned staff doing Chinese stretching exercises in the herb garden. Across the street, they came to a two-story red house. "Let us know if there's anything you need, sir."

"General, please come in," Will Gaudium shouted from the rear of the house. "We have breakfast set up in the courtyard."

General Bowdin moved quickly through the richly adorned room to the courtyard. "Kind of a frilly place, Will."

"Tremendous food and service, Frank," Gaudium enthused. "Better than The French Laundry."

"Never ate in a laundry," the General said, seating himself under the outdoor heater.

"I flew in last night, but got here in time for a great dinner. I flew in to talk with you, Frank. There's so much going on, and I just thought we should compare notes. I have some questions," Gaudium began.

"There is a lot going on. And it's working, they think it's the Chinese. My guys in the Pentagon say they're working up options for a meeting with the President," the General asserted. "Pass the bacon there, Will. Thanks. What are your questions?"

"Well, Frank, we said we would avoid fatalities and yet people have died in the blackout out west, and others would have died if the truck bomb had made it to the Globegrid node at Moffett Field. Then there was the pancake house." Gaudium spoke haltingly, deferentially, to the man he employed.

"That wasn't us, Will. We didn't do the pancake house. Speaking of which, do they do pancakes at this place?" General Bowdin answered, chewing his bacon, looking at the food he had piled onto his plate.

Gaudium ignored the question. "But people *have* died in our operations, Frank."

Bowdin raised his eyes to look at the man opposite him. "I said I would *try* to avoid fatalities, and I have tried. But you can't go 'round blowing shit up without someone gettin' hurt. I told you that going into this. How else do you think we're gonna stop these godless perversions? Did you think that in the Final Days there wouldn't be a struggle, even before Armageddon? We don't know how long this struggle period will be. Could be generations." He reached across the table for the bowl of grits.

Gaudium sat, watching the General eat, then tried again: "I think we should back off now until the election. Things are getting too hot between America and China. It could get out of hand. And if Senator George can get elected, he'll stop all of these technological excesses, peacefully, with laws and executive orders, international treaties."

"Will, that ain't gonna happen and you know it," Bowdin said, putting down his knife and fork and looking straight at his employer. "George can get the nomination, but he's not going to unseat the incumbent. Even if he did, the Congress, the courts, the bureaucracy would set up hurdles, slow things down. Anyway, this stuff is going on offshore, overseas, more and more. And international treaties, Will? Like the ones against nuclear weapons? Did they stop Pakistan, India, North Korea, Iran?"

Gaudium did not answer, and the General continued. "Yes, Will, things are heating up with China, and it looks like this President of ours might actually do the right thing for once, go protect Taiwan and let it announce its independence. Taiwan is on our side. China persecutes Christians, like Rome did to Saint Peter and the early church. It's just like that over there now—secret bishops, underground churches. We have to stand up to them."

Gaudium stood and walked around the courtyard, his hands deep inside his pants pockets. He stared at the brick patio floor. General Bowdin got up from the table and walked over to him. "Will, look, you are doing the right thing and history will say that. You will be a national hero a generation from now. You have spent over two hundred million of your own money on this operation because the government wasn't doing its job."

Will Gaudium lifted his head and threw back his shoulders. Looking at his employee, he said in what he thought was a command voice, "General Bowdin, I want you to suspend the operation until after the election, until mid-November, when I will review my decision. No more operations, no more deaths. That's an order."

Francis X. Bowdin chuckled and walked toward the back gate of the courtyard. "Well now, Will, that may pose a problem. I got the FBI and Navy investigators pouring all over the ranch out in California. We may have to throw them a few guilty bodies. I got two pain-in-the-ass investigators from the Intelligence Analysis Center, a wiseass gray-hat hacker, and a fuckin' Harvard professor woman getting too close to figuring things out. They may all have to go. To say nothing of the devil children; they get their special formula delivered to them Monday. Besides, I may have to plant a few more fortune cookie crumbs leading back to the Reds on the Mainland."

Gaudium was stunned. He raised his hand, made a fist, then pointed his index finger at the General. "Frank, you're not listening. I gave you an order. You work for me!"

Bowdin walked slowly across the courtyard to Gaudium. "No, Will. No, actually I don't." He dropped a large hand down on Gaudium's shoulder. "Listen, why don't you come out to the hollow with me. You've never seen our training facility, and it's not far from here." As he spoke, he unrolled his hand and then, with a chopping motion, struck Will Gaudium sharply on the temple, between the forehead and ear. Gaudium slumped, instantly dead. "It's the Ides, Will. Beware the Ides."

Holding the body up with one arm, Bowdin spoke into the sleeve of his other arm. "Todd, there's a red house up the street behind the inn and across the street. See it? There's a parking lot out back of it. Pull the Hummer around there and drop the hatch open. We got something to take back to the hollow."

1028 EST

Intelligence Analysis Center

Navy Hill, Foggy Bottom

Washington, D.C.

"Mr. MacIntyre, have you heard from Susan?" Jimmy said as he and Soxster burst into the IAC Director's office.

Rusty eyed the NYPD detective and the long-haired young man with him. "Actually, I'm on the line with her now. Who the hell is this?"

"Oh, sir, this is Soxster," Jimmy explained. "He works with us."

"He does?" Rusty asked. "Is he cleared for Top Secret?"

"Well, ah, at this point, yes," Jimmy fumbled. "I'll explain it all later, but yes, yes, he is."

Rusty arched an eyebrow. "I'll put her on speaker."

"Susan, are you all right?" Jimmy asked anxiously. "I should never have let you do things alone."

"Yeah, I'm okay. I'm on a Coast Guard cutter. We just rounded up the last of the Dominion Commonwealth agents. They were making for Florida, but we chased them in the helo and vectored in the cutter." She paused a moment. "I do solo just fine, thanks."

"Susan, see if they can chopper you over to Lauderdale. I've got a chartered VLJ waiting to get you back here. I just finished reading Foley's report about Gaudium and General Bowdin. It convinces me, but we'll need to punch it up so that when Sol lands he can brief the Principals at tonight's White House meeting. Also, we need to find those two guys, Bowdin and Gaudium, and get them arrested," Rusty said both to Susan on speaker and Jimmy standing next to his desk.

The transmission from the cutter *Bertholf* was crystal clear on the speaker: "Sure, but, Rusty, we need to find a way to warn the parents of the children conceived with the help of that lab. They get the poisoned formula tomorrow and the director at the lab wouldn't give me the list of parents, didn't believe I was a U.S. federal government officer."

"I got your message on that, Susan, and I am about to give that clinic director a call. Then I'm calling FedEx to have them find and stop the packages. The last thing I want to do is have to go public with this and make the appeal through the media," Rusty said as he scanned Susan's e-mail on his screen. "There'd be a witch hunt in this country, people trying to track down the superkids, people trying to kill them. It would be like—"

Soxster interrupted. "We already know where Gaudium is, or was this morning. And where he probably is now." Russell MacIntyre shot him a look that said, *Who told you that you could speak?*

Jimmy came to his rescue. "We got Gaudium's credit-card number from the Mandalay in Vegas and then checked to see when he used it last, which was last night for dinner and overnight accommodations in Rappahannock County, Virgina." He did not bother to tell Rusty how Soxster had acquired either piece of information. "So I used a little professional courtesy and called the sheriff out there to see if Gaudium was still at this inn. Turns out he had a guest this morning that fits the description of General Bowdin to a tee. Then they both disappeared."

Rusty looked from Jimmy to Soxster and back to Jimmy. "Dominion Commonwealth. I know that name from somewhere. Another case. Anyway, so how does all that tell us where he probably is now?"

Soxster leaped in again. "Property records in the surrounding area. Dominion Commonwealth Services owns about two hundred acres backing up on the Shenandoah National Park. Must be his lair."

Rusty looked back at Jimmy. "Lair? I was just out in that park two weekends ago, climbing Old Rag Mountain. Little forest fires all over the park because of the drought. Got the park rangers' shorts all in a knot. What's he mean, lair?"

"It's probably another facility like the one out near Twentynine Palms, hackers, control room, shooters, barracks, warehouses," Jimmy explained. "Probably why Gaudium was in Virginia, to go there. The General picks him up this morning and takes him there to show him about the next attack or something."

"Google Earth," Soxster said.

"What did he just say?" Rusty asked Jimmy.

"We looked at it on satellite imagery. It's at the end of a place called Thornton Hollow. Easily defended. The staff are probably heavily armed and are likely to be ex–Special Forces like the General," Jimmy explained. "We counted nine major buildings, probably all prewired with explosives on the roofs in case the place gets raided. They probably plan to blow them up, like they did to me out at their ranch in the desert. We figure they also probably got a smart fence to detect intruders, land mines, maybe remotely operated machine guns."

"Lovely. So we'll need the Delta Force to go in and get him," Rusty suggested.

Soxster shook his head quickly, no. Jimmy spoke their hesitation. "Well, sir, maybe not them. See, Bowdin used to command them, and probably a bunch of his Dominion guys were in the SF."

"So what are you suggesting?" Rusty asked.

"Well, uh, I had an idea," Soxster said. "Didn't they, like, kill the head of the Pentagon's advanced gizmo office, DARPA? I got some ideas how they can help."

"Oh, good." Rusty sighed and looked again at Jimmy. "Who did you say he is?"

"Soxster," Soxster said. "Didn't this use to be Wild Bill Donovan's office in World War Two? The OSS?"

1835 EST

Basement Conference Room 3

The West Wing, the White House

"So we would begin by shooting down their satellites, since they shot down ours," Secretary of Defense William Chesterfield said, addressing the powerpoint slide on the screen.

"They didn't. They hacked ours, or somebody did," the Secretary of State corrected. "And that slide says you're going to use ground- and space-based lasers. Didn't Congress refuse to fund all that Star Wars laser stuff?"

Chesterfield shifted in his seat and looked at the National Security Advisor, who said nothing. Chesterfield sighed and then answered, "Brenda, this is obviously sensitive, but yes, the Congress did cut the laser weapons in space program. They did not cut the space-to-ground, ground-to-space laser communication program."

"You're going to attack them with a communications system?" Brenda Neyers asked.

"Well, they're tunable lasers. And the way we developed them . . ." The Secretary of Defense again looked to the National Security Advisor for help.

Finally, Wallace Reynolds came to the Secretary of Defense's assistance. "The communications lasers can be tuned up to the point that they could fry eggs on Mars, all the way from Arizona."

Chesterfield kept going. "Then, because they blew up the internet beachheads and cut the fiber-optic cables, we would sever all of the internet connections in and out of China. Our specially equipped submarines are standing by, the *Jimmy Carter* and the like. DIA has found a Russian colonel freezing his ass off out in Vladivostok who will stage a few accidents where the fiber-optic landlines run from China into Siberia."

"You're proposing to blow things up inside Russia?" Secretary Neyers demanded.

Chesterfield did not answer her. "Of course, China may respond, if they think it's us that did all this. They might attack Taiwan, in which case we just use Op-Plan 5010, the Seventh Fleet reinforced by land-based strategic and tactical air."

"If they think it's *us*, Bill?" Brenda Neyers challenged. "Who the hell else are they going to think it is? Botswana?"

And at just that moment, Sol Rubenstein opened the door. "Sorry, everybody. I have an excuse for my tardiness. I was in Hong Kong earlier today." He plunked his weary body down in the seat behind the nameplate that read "Director of National Intelligence."

Wallace Reynolds looked relieved. "And how was the dim sum, Sol?"

"Never got any," Rubenstein said, opening his folder. "Now listen, it hasn't been China that's been doing all of these attacks. They gave me proof." He raised his hand against the responses around the room. "And I just got a call on the way in from Rusty MacIntyre. My investigators have confirmed who *has* been doing the attacks—and it's actually been Americans. A group of religious fanatics, neo-Luddites, and a former U.S. Special Forces general, all banded together."

"That's absurd, Sol," Chesterfield exploded. "The U.S. Army has been attacking the U.S.? Nonsense! And who else—Lud something?"

Wallace Reynolds's pleasure at Rubenstein's arrival had quickly evaporated, but the former Princeton professor explained, "Ned

Ludd, leader of an anti-technology rebellion, England, 1811. His followers were called Luddites. The term's used now for anyone who opposes technological advance, especially through violence." The other three in the room looked briefly at him and then continued.

"Does the FBI agree with this crazy Chinese theory?" Chesterfield asked.

"First of all, I did not say the U.S. Army was doing anything, I said a former member of it. And no, I have not yet briefed the FBI. I just landed, for Christ's sake," Rubenstein replied.

"Good, when you can prove it and the Bureau concurs, let me know. Meanwhile, the President has asked me for options and I am giving them in the morning. I have also issued a Warning Order to the relevant units and they are standing by. Is there anything else, Wallace?" The Secretary of Defense stood, nodded, and left the room.

"Really, Sol," Secretary of State Neyers asked, "all the way there and not enough time for dim sum?"

"The PLA is scraping for a fight over Taiwan," Rubenstein replied. "Wallace, did you get that? They're gearing up, too."

"I heard you, Sol," the National Security Advisor said, staring at the presidential seal on the wall. "I was just wondering why I had ever left Princeton."

2303 EST

Dominion Commonwealth Services Training Facility

Thornton Hollow

Near Shenandoah National Park, Virginia

"The aircraft will be ready at Dulles at 0600, sir. We fly direct to Antigua, refuel while you gentlemen visit the bank, and then disappear," the ex-Major explained.

"All right. We'll leave here in five hours," Bowdin responded. "Any more word from the Bahamas?"

"No, sir, but I confirmed that FedEx has the packages and they will be delivered by ten tomorrow."

"Well, then I think most of what we set out to do is on track. . . . What's that noise? Sounds like an aircraft?" General Bowdin and his aide walked out of the log cabin–style house in time to see and hear an old Cessna prop plane sputter and then continue on a path into the woods on the steep slope above their camp. "It's going in!" Bowdin yelled.

A few seconds later, they heard an explosion up on a wall of the hollow and then saw a bright yellow flash. "Send some men up there. See if anyone survived, although I don't see how. And get that fire out," Bowdin ordered, and returned to his cabin. A few minutes later, as he packed a suitcase, Bowdin saw shadows and lights on the wall. Turning to look out the window, he saw a line of flames moving down the hill toward the camp.

"What the fuck, Major!" Bowdin yelled from the cabin's

porch. The hill above was engulfed in flames, trees spontaneously combusting.

"Sorry, sir, the men didn't get on it fast enough. Everything's been so dry that it just lit up. It's in the camp already, sir, and I don't think we can hold it. All the men are out back trying to . . ." As he spoke, the warehouse a thousand yards behind them erupted with a concussive boom, and then came a secondary explosion as the helicopter on the pad next to the warehouse went up.

"I didn't give the order to evacuate camp yet!" Bowdin screamed.

"No, sir."

"Then why did that destruct charge go off, Major?" Another loud eruption farther up the road answered him. They could see pieces of a building shooting up into the night sky. "We're leaving for Dulles now. Get everyone who's going into my Hummer now! Get on it!"

Within three minutes, the Hummer was rolling away from the cabin as the wall of flames moved closer. "No, Todd, not the front gate," Bowdin directed the driver. "I don't know what's going on here. Take the side gate, the dirt road through the park." Another loud explosion boomed behind them. Bowdin, sitting behind the driver, turned and reached back into the vehicle's third row. He lifted out a stubby Russian KBP light machine gun, the PP-2010. The man sitting next to the driver carried the same weapon. "Get ready. There's something more going on here," Bowdin barked.

The guard at the side gate lowered the V barrier as the Hummer roared toward it. The driver shifted, and the Hummer growled as the rough dirt road ramped up the hillside. Looking across the hollow, Bowdin glared at the fire that covered the other side of the steep valley. The road leveled off and turned sharply left at a granite boulder. The driver shifted again, and again. Then the headlights and dashboard faded to black and the Hummer slowed and stopped. Bowdin leaned forward, next to the driver. "Todd, what the shit's—"

The total darkness around the Hummer abruptly became a ubiquitous blue-white light. "General Bowdin, Francis X. Bowdin, step out of the vehicle," a voice boomed and echoed off the mountain walls. "You are under arrest. Do not resist—your position is totally covered."

Jimmy watched the screen in the step van. There were six triangles moving over the map. "Which ones are which, Sox?" he asked.

"The red ones are the laser shooters that lit the fires. The yellow ones have the halogen lights and the speaker systems. The black one shot the electromagnetic pulse at the Hummer. And they're all only ten feet long and can fly for four hours," Soxster explained. "Ain't technology grand?"

"Very grand," Jimmy said, blinking his right eye. "Now, don't get out of the van this time, Sox." Foley climbed out and unholstered his weapon.

"Stay in the vehicle," Bowdin instructed the three other men in the Hummer. "Get down."

The General slowly opened the door and carefully stepped down, carrying the KBP gun. He walked forward with the light machine gun across his chest. Jimmy noticed the General was wearing an odd military-style vest, but it was not a bulletproof protector.

"Put down the weapon, General, or the sniper will do disabling fire. We're not going to give you a suicide by police," the voice echoed from above. Bowdin looked up but could not see through the light. His walk slowed and then he stopped and dropped the weapon onto the dirt road. He stood still, his head bowed. Suddenly, he lurched forward, running like a cheetah toward the light. Three shots cracked and hit the dirt in front and to the right of the running man. He seemed to accelerate, a black covered ball topped by a crop of white hair, flying above the dirt. Then the State Police sniper shot out Bowdin's right kneecap, causing the General to fall backward. As he fell, the General pulled the rip cord attached to his vest.

The explosion was blinding. There was a ball of white light hanging above the middle of the road, then yellow flame falling onto the dirt. Most of General Francis X. Bowdin vaporized; some parts of him were thrown up into the trees and slowly drifted down. Jimmy Foley realized his ears were ringing and he could not make out what the trooper was saying to him. A few seconds later, Jimmy could hear the speaker booming again: "Step out of the vehicle without weapons. Walk in front of the Hummer and lie facedown on the ground!"

The three men left in the vehicle complied. "Can you dim the lights a little?" Foley asked. In a line with four uniformed Virginia State Police, he walked forward out of the dark. One of the troopers, a sergeant, carried a shotgun pointed at the prone men in the dirt. "Don't move your hands!" the sergeant yelled.

"I suggest we wait for a bomb squad before we check the Hummer, and that we get these guys behind our truck quick," Foley suggested. He used his new eye in infrared zoom mode, scanning the road behind the Hummer for any follow-on traffic.

"Hands off me," Foley heard one of the men scream. "I have diplomatic immunity!" That got Foley's attention, and he walked back to the front of the Hummer. As he approached the man, the trooper who had just cuffed him handed Foley an ID. It was a rich, red leather folder. Foley opened it and initially fixed on the Chinese characters, then the elaborate English script across the top: "Republic of China."

"Take these cuffs off me. I am Ambassador Lee Wang. Taiwan."

9 | *Thursday, March 19*

". . . but I was elected on an independence platform, Ambassador. I cannot do a volte-face," the Taiwanese President protested. "You could just say these were rogue elements."

"I am not here to negotiate, but to communicate the intent of the President of the United States," Sol Rubenstein recited from his talking points. "That said, I would suggest that you say the autonomy is independence."

"That will not work," the President responded, looking at his shoes.

"Let me repeat. If you do not issue a declaration today that Taiwan is a Special Autonomous Region of China and offer to enter into negotiation about a written agreement with Beijing, the President of the United States will do two things. First, have the

Attorney General charge Ambassador Wang with murder and release the details of the investigation. Second, the Secretary of State
is in Beijing now. He would instruct her to tell the PRC government that we do not interpret the Taiwan Relations Act to require
the use of force by the United States to defend Taiwan. She will add
that the United States has no plans or intentions to move military
assets to Taiwan or surrounding waters."

Rubenstein was aware of the sound of the heating system kicking in, blowing air through the vents. Both men sat silently.

"When would these negotiations with Beijing have to be completed?" the President asked.

Rubenstein locked eyes with the man sitting opposite him.
"China is over five thousand years old. The Chinese people have a
longer time horizon than we do in the West." Sol caught himself
saying what he had heard from Chinese people so many times over
the years. Then he played the card that he had persuaded the
American President to give him. "Taiwan has accomplished many
great things, including creating an Asian democracy. We do not
wish to see it independent because of what that would force Beijing
to do, but we also do not wish to see Taiwan's rule of law and civil
liberties crushed. My talking points require that you 'enter into negotiations about a written agreement.' They do not say how long
those negotiations might last."

There was another brief quiet.

"Mr. Ambassador, you will forgive me if I end this meeting," the

President said. "I have quite a speech to write and give on television tonight." Both men stood and bowed.

1835 EST

Summers Hall, Allston Campus

Harvard University, Boston

"I'm sure you're right that substantively everything you say in this paper is not only correct but insightful," Margaret Myers was telling a student in her office, "but if the reader is distracted by the writing style, they can't see that. English is supposed to have been your native language and you were supposed to have learned how to write it long before you came here. . . ."

Susan Connor did not feel badly about interrupting Myers's office hours; it sounded like both professor and student would probably welcome a way out of the conversation. "Next student," Susan announced as she knocked on the half-opened door. Jimmy Foley and Soxster followed her into the cluttered office.

"Well, well. This is an honor," Myers said as her student had quickly departed. "Shouldn't you three be writing your reports and doing debriefings? And such heroics, Susan—analysts are not trained for fieldwork of that kind. Far too dangerous."

"I've already had that reprimand from a number of 'senior Washington officials,' " Susan conceded.

"But they all then thanked her profusely," Jimmy added. "And Soxster," he said, draping an arm around the shorter man's shoulders, "who now actually has a consulting contract with us, back-dated, and with appropriate security clearance."

"We came to take you to dinner and to say thanks," Susan explained. "And ask for help again."

"Dinner I always accept, but we should all be thanking you. I didn't contribute, . . ." Margaret Myers protested.

"Facts, gaps, theory, analysis. We had some facts, but more gaps. We had theories, but they crumbled under analysis. The struggle between the Transhumanists and the Luddites was something Washington had entirely missed. And you told us to look for Layered Deniability. Then, of course, you told us about Soxster," Susan said while playfully punching Soxster in the side, "and Will— Will Gaudium."

The mention of Gaudium changed the mood from mutual appreciation of their success to a melancholy sense of regret. Myers broke the mood. "I think it was the right thing to keep his death at that camp quiet. The announcement from Jupiter Systems just said he passed unexpectedly on Sunday."

"He never really knew what the General was doing with his money. He really just wanted to call attention to these big choices that we are making implicitly, to bring them out in the open, slow things down, cause a debate, and then make some decisions as a civilization," Susan said. "He wasn't a murderer, and he put his faith in our electoral system."

Jimmy looked at Myers and flashed his trademark smile. "Just for the record, Professor, Susan and I really disagree about Gaudium and about these issues. Also Jessica and I are now planning a trip to the Bahamas, to Man-O-War. But Susan and I already had our disagreement out, and it's over. And Soxster here, he's on my side and then some." Soxster felt no need to go over his views of Gaudium again. Instead he just dropped into the reading chair by the window and began fishing inside his backpack.

"Gaudium really convinced you of some things, didn't he, Susan?" Myers asked, wondering how sensitive Susan was so soon after Gaudium's murder.

"I'm conflicted. He opened so many windows for me, showed me so much I didn't know was happening, caused me to think about questions that had never occurred to me," Susan mused. "Apparently his estate creates a foundation that will promote education, debate, and discussion on these issues of technology and society, on what it means to be human. We need that."

"And what about the help you wanted from me?" Myers asked.

"We need to understand more about the Transhumanists and the neo-Luddites," Jimmy noted. "We want to keep their debate peaceful."

On Storrow Drive, the cold rain had stopped and the rush-hour traffic was thinning out. The spotlit domes of the college house seemed bright across the darkened Charles. Soxster had quietly produced four stemless wineglasses and placed them on the desk. He poured the chardonnay and distributed the glasses. "Kistler 09," he announced, and then toasted, "To humanity's evolution, even if we do direct the next steps ourselves."

"And if we do," Margaret Myers added, "may we do so wisely."

"Well, then, let's eat!" Jimmy injected to lighten the mood. "Where's this place you made reservations, Sox? Hopefully not the Moskova."

Soxster smiled as he poured out the last drops of the wine. "It's Chinatown."

AUTHOR'S NOTE

In *The Scorpion's Gate,* I projected a world in 2010, with the United States and China competing politically and economically for a dwindling supply of increasingly expensive oil and gas. That competition naturally took them to the Persian Gulf, where the largest oil deposits remained. The Persian Gulf of 2010 was unstable, with the United States threatening Iran, and fundamentalist Islamic forces emerging in Saudi Arabia. Corruption and giant corporations made Washington a political battleground. While I noted at the time of publication that the work was not meant to be predictive, many of the trends in the novel have already developed and are dominating the news.

Breakpoint, set in 2012, *is* meant to be predictive, at least about technology. It may read to some like science fiction, but it is based on emerging technologies that are the subject of research today. Scientists and engineers differ in their views about when the research will result in deployed technology, but their differences are most often a discussion of "when," not "if."

This novel is intended to project you a few years ahead, to start readers thinking now about the political, social, and economic changes that technology is about to create. Those changes could be wrenching, creating tensions in our society. A woman's right to choose, the teaching of evolution, and stem-cell research have already created social and political discord in the United States. The coming technological events may make these current controversies seem like a practice round, a warm-up. For the next debate may be about "what is a human": Should humans change the species with human-machine interfaces and genetic alterations?

The opening rounds have already occurred. The Transhumanist movement is real and has regular meetings around the country. In 2002, the National Science Foundation issued a stunning report, "Converging Technologies for Improving Human Performance: Nanotechnology, Biotechnology, Information Technology and Cognitive Science." The report, which overall has an upbeat and optimistic tone, concludes that connections between the human brain and computers will transform the way humans work, other technologies will eliminate disabilities and diseases that have plagued the human condition for centuries, and human creativity will flourish due to both improved understanding of the human mind and enhancements to the brain. A year later, the President's Council on Bioethics issued its report. "Beyond Therapy: Biotechnology and the Pursuit of Happiness" which took a somewhat dimmer view of using technology to enhance human beings. Chaired by Leon Kass, a fellow at the American Enterprise Institute, the commission included conservative political figures such as Francis Fukuyama and Charles Krauthammer. They believe that genetic science should not be used to enhance human performance, only to fix mistakes that make some humans less healthy than the norm. In 2004, Californians voted on a referendum on stem-cell research and approved funding for research. Court fights have delayed the spending of state monies.

As to some of the specifics in *Breakpoint:*

- The concept of Globegrid arises from the fact that supercomputers in Japan, the United States, and Russia have already been linked through Internet 2, a high-speed network being developed by a consortium of 207 universities. U.S. and European labs are actually engaged in a project to reverse engineer the human brain.

- Living Software does not yet exist, but companies like Watchfire Fortify, Coverity, and others are already developing software to test software for human error.

- Very Light Jets (VLJs) have been approved by the U.S. Federal Aviation Administration and are in manufacture. They are four- to six-seat aircraft meant to operate like taxis. Eclipse Aviation's Eclipse 500 and Citation's CJ-1 are among the first deployed VLJs.

• Intelligent video surveillance, in which the software and cameras (not people) recognize aberrant behavior, are already being deployed by companies such as DVTel and Vidient in subways, airports, and other facilities.

• Exoskeleton suits are already in the prototype phase. The U.S. Army has teamed with the University of California at Berkeley to develop the prototype, which will allow soldiers to carry 180 pounds, while feeling as if they are lugging five. Plans on the drawing board at the Army's Natick Labs in Massachusetts show soldiers being able to run, jump, and throw the way they are described in the baseball game in *Breakpoint*. The other capabilities that make up the full suite of technologies in the exoskeleton suits (night vision, network connections, GPS, remote cameras, and vital-system monitoring) are all part of a program called the Objective Force Warrior Ensemble, set to be deployed by 2010.

• People in the United States will begin driving Chinese-manufactured cars like the Chery product line in 2007–08. Experimental cars powered by ethanol derived from switch grass exist today.

• Driven by the large number of U.S. casualties in Iraq, Marine and Army amputees are now receiving prosthetics far more advanced than what is available in the civilian community. Known as sea legs, these new prosthetics are driven by microprocessors at each joint. They use innovative new materials and techniques to respond to signals from the human brain to straighten a leg or flex a muscle. Servicemen and women who once would have been unable to lead normal civilian lives are now able to return to the battlefield.

• Human nerves have already connected artificial ears directly to the brain. Paralyzed patients are today using their thoughts to move computer mouse devices. Some patients suffering from severe depression and other disorders already do have miniature wires leading to parts of their brain and do have battery packs implanted behind their collarbones. Other human-machine interfaces (HMIs) are in development.

• Artificial retinas for people suffering from blindness caused by diseases such as retinitis pigmentosa or macular degeneration are in the development phase and have already seen some success in restoring limited vision in clinical trials. The devices work by implanting a small chip at the back of the eye that stimulates retinal neurons. They are powered by solar receptors fed by the light that enters the eye. Replacing the full eye with a silicon-based optical unit may be feasible, but it is also likely that the ability to regenerate an eye through stem cells may happen sooner and be more appealing.

• The state of cyber security described in the novel is, unfortunately, not fiction. Identities (name, date of birth, Social Security number, credit-card number, and so on) are bought and sold in cyberspace hacker chat rooms. Software coding errors are regularly used by hackers to enter networks and computers. Scientists at U.S. government national laboratories have demonstrated the possibility of taking down the power grid through hacking.

• The company iRobot has sold large numbers of robots to clean floors. Asimov, the robotic dog, could easily be a reality in the near term. Sony's Aibo already can mimic the actions of a "real" dog. Moving from Aibo to the fictional Asimov will require adding voice-recognition technology, a wireless web link, limited artificial-intelligence capabilities, and advanced motor devices to power its arms and legs. In some form or another, these technologies all exist today.

• Performance-enhancing pharmaceuticals (PEPs) is my own name, but the concept is not fiction. For memory enhancement, a compound known as CX717 has proven effective in boosting the brain chemical glutamate, the substance that is key in learning and memory. Studies have shown it effective in treating narcolepsy and ADD. It has also proven effective for otherwise healthy individuals who need to stay focused over longer periods without sleep. For sports, regulatory authorities are fighting an uphill battle, with gene doping and performance-enhancing pharmaceuticals becoming more sophisticated, more effective, and safer than steroids. The Pentagon is developing drugs that will allow soldiers to go for long periods without sleeping.

• Cellular regeneration of organs and other body parts is in its infancy but will likely yield real-world results by the end of this decade. Embryonic stem cells are thought to hold the most promise for treating a wide range of maladies, from cancer to spinal injuries. Human adult stem cells are already used to treat a variety of ailments. Fixing retinas, cloning hair for baldness, and regrowing teeth are all showing promise. Progress on stem-cell research has slowed due to the Bush administration's unwillingness to fund research on embryonic stem cells. This decision has slowed progress and shifted much work overseas, where governments have embraced the promise of this research. It is quite possible that the United States will be left behind in what will be the most pivotal medical advance since the decoding of the genome.

• Aircraft without onboard pilots are already in use. I fought a bureaucratic battle with CIA in 2000 to get them to use the unmanned Predator to hunt for terrorists and in 2001 to arm the Predator with missiles. When the Predator finally was used to attack terrorists in Afghanistan and Yemen, it was probably the first time a robot intentionally killed a human. The U.S. Air Force is now developing UCAVs, unmanned combat aerial vehicles, fighter planes whose pilots will sit safely on the ground hundreds or thousands of miles away from the aircraft. Lockheed has plans for an unmanned version of the F-35.

• The laser gun depicted in *Breakpoint* is a technology set to emerge sometime within the next decade, depending on the prioritization it receives in Pentagon budget negotiations. The Airborne Laser is being built by Boeing to be mounted on a 747 for use against ballistic missiles. When the Joint Strike Fighter (JSF) was first put on the drawing board in 2001, plans called for a solid-state laser as an offensive weapon. Although it has been delayed, the Lightweight Tactical Laser weapon may now be incorporated in the F-35 block 30.

• The initial mapping of the human genome was completed in 2000. Detailed mapping of the individual chromosomes is under way, with most of the existing human chromosomes already mapped. The first genetic therapy was approved to treat patients in 1990. Today, genetic therapy is used to fix flaws in some human coding, including sickle-cell anemia, Huntington's disease, cystic fibrosis, and hemophilia.

• Nanotechnology is already in use in cosmetics, tennis racquets, paints, and fabrics. The National Nanotechnology Initiative is the largest new federal science project in recent years. Researchers have successfully used gold nanoparticles to deliver DNA molecules safely into cancer cells as part of a program to defeat cancer.

• The field of Synthetic Biology is also real and has resulted in the creation of Bio Fab plants, named to sound like the plants (called Fabs) that made silicon-based computer chips. Synthetic Biology has created bacteria that seek and invade tumor cells, yeasts that produce the antimalarial drug precursor artemisinic acid, and biological sources of renewable energy.

Sometimes you can tell more truth through fiction.